BLOOD MOON

BLOOD MOON

Marilyn Todd

This first world edition published 2009
in Great Britain and in the USA by
SEVERN HOUSE PUBLISHERS LTD of
9–15 High Street, Sutton, Surrey, England, SM1 1DF.
Trade paperback edition published
in Great Britain and the USA 2009 by
SEVERN HOUSE PUBLISHERS LTD

British Library Cataloguing in Publication Data

Todd, Marilyn
  Blood moon
  1. Women priests - Greece - Sparta (Extinct city) - Fiction
  2. Murder - Investigation - Greece - Sparta (Extinct city)
  - Fiction 3. Secret service - Greece - Sparta (Extinct
  city) - Fiction 4. Serial murders - Greece - Sparta
  (Extinct city) - Fiction 5. Detective and mystery stories
  I. Title
    823.9'14[F]

ISBN-13: 978-0-7278-6729-2   (cased)
ISBN-13: 978-1-84751-110-2   (trade paper)

All Severn House titles are printed on acid-free paper.

Typeset by Palimpsest Book Production Ltd.,
Grangemouth, Stirlingshire, Scotland.
Printed and bound in Great Britain by
MPG Books Ltd., Bodmin, Cornwall.

To Cathy Fish,

for whom the swans sing

ONE

The man knelt, naked, on the rock, his arms outstretched in supplication. Overhead, the Milky Way snaked across a blackness set with a million twinkling stars, a celestial mirror image of the river at his feet. Graceful, unhurried and serene.

The man had no interest in the stars.

In his left hand he held a small, but tightly-stoppered phial, and in his right, a knife shaped like the crescent moon. Both were silver, a metal crammed with lunar magic, and in the moonlight the stallion engravings galloped and reared.

'Sweet Mistress of Enchantment, whose light rises from the grave of a thousand sunken suns,' he chanted. 'Hear me, your faithful servant.'

No cloud passed across the moon's waxy disc. He took this to be a sign.

'For the times when you rise thin and small to shine your beauty on the earth, I give you this white rose.'

He watched the petals bob away on the current.

'For the times when you contract and hide, I give you berries from the nightshade.'

Each landed with a soft plop in the water.

'But tonight, when your fullness transforms night into day and brings the promise of eternal life and youth, I give you this.'

White for purity, black for death, red for maturity and ripeness.

'Blood from the sacrifice.'

Consigning the sickle to the moon's reflection, the man rose and stretched the stiffness from his legs. His first scalp had been taken at the Wolf Moon, when the snow was deep and wolves howled in their hunger. Since then he had taken five more, six including tonight, though he still needed another two before his mission was complete. By then, the harvest would be gathered in and the heat of high summer also long past. Traditionally, this was always a time of letting go and clearing away, but for every ending there is a new beginning.

Come the Blood Moon – the first full moon of the new year, when the leaves would just be beginning to turn – the servant of the moon would embark on the next phase of his operation.

The phase in which Servant became Master.

Dressing, he tucked both phial and scalp into his belt, barely glancing at the mutilated remains that had, until a few hours ago, been a fresh-faced and carefree young woman. With a nudge from his foot, she rolled down the bank, like the rubbish she was, barely making a splash as she entered the water.

When he turned away, the Servant was whistling.

TWO

The agora was seething when Iliona approached the portico that ran around the plaza. Along the wall of the Council Chamber, honey producers lined up their terra-cotta jars like painted soldiers, fanning them with ostrich feathers to keep the murderous heat at bay. cheese sellers swatted blue-bottles with the one hand and cut wedges with the other. Lambs bleated on their tethers. Iliona wondered how the poor souls in the dungeons below must feel, knowing there was so much vitality buzzing about overhead. Or whether, after months of imprisonment and torture, they felt anything at all.

'I wonder why this boy wants to meet you here, and not the temple?' Beside her, Jocasta was forced to shout above the guinea fowl clucking in their crates.

'He's a man, not a boy,' Iliona said, sidestepping a pile of squirming octopus. 'Next month, he qualifies as a warrior.'

The portico was new. White marble and etched with the faces of a thousand routed Persians, it commemorated a victory not just for Sparta, but for all the hundreds of city states who'd put aside their blood feuds and power struggles to unite against the common enemy. Then found, to their surprise, that unification brought prosperity, as well as peace.

'How do you know?' Jocasta swerved to avoid a runaway piglet. 'I thought you'd never met him.'

'I haven't, but that was the message. *I am about to join the ranks, please meet with me.* And the colonnade is not where we arranged,' she said. 'I just like coming here.'

Not merely the pomegranates, apricots and plums that fanned out in rainbows across the cobbles. Iliona enjoyed touching the newness of the marble, feeling the freshness of the carvings, knowing that this portico provided something for everyone at some stage during the day, whether shade, companionship or simply a place to rest their aching bones.

'For me, it symbolizes everything that's happening in the Hellenic world today. Temples rising from the ashes, beauty swelling from decay—'

'Is this where you give me some it-makes-me-proud-to-be-a-Spartan speech? Because if so—'

'—reminding me that, for the first time in our history, tombs are filling with the bones of greybeards, not their grandsons in their prime.'

'You see, you are. You wrap it up in fancy sentiments—'

'And secondly,' Iliona continued levelly, 'if you're a strapping youth looking to make your mark on the world, you'd hardly want to be seen visiting a shrine where the poor, the enslaved and the sick flock to have their fortunes told in riddles and their runes cast by the Oracle.'

'So our hero wants his fortune told in riddles, except on neutral ground instead, and have the Oracle cast his wretched runes in private?'

One could never accuse Jocasta of being subtle, but her aim with the bull's eye was constant.

'Doubts are doubts, no matter who's afflicted by them,' Iliona said. 'We all worry about our future at some point in our lives, and since it's my policy never to turn anyone away who seeks my help—' She stopped.

'What's wrong?'

'Nothing.' In the sheet of silver at the far end of the portico, a woman with fair hair and the bluest eyes she'd ever seen was staring intently in her direction. It took her a few seconds to realize that the woman was herself. 'Stone in my sandal, that's all.'

The mirror reflected her companion, too. Hair as dark and glossy as a raven's wing, eyes flashing constantly with passion. Iliona ducked a string of black puddings dangling from a porter's pole and wished Jocasta would bloody smile occasionally. Physicians were supposed to project a genial bedside manner. Not scare diseases off.

'I see our visitors are getting yet another dose of princely treatment.' Jocasta nodded towards a group of pantalooned foreigners, being given a tour by the City Elders. 'Are they still the bane of your life?'

Iliona rolled her eyes. 'You have no idea.'

These Scythians had voyaged from the far side of the Black Sea, braving pirates, storms and shipwreck, to discuss the trading of furs, gold and timber in exchange for porphyry, pots and horses. A deal which, if successful, would enrich Sparta's economy even further and benefit everyone who lived here. Yet could people see it?

'Since they arrived,' – and it was two months ago now – 'I've been swamped with petitioners in search of charms, psalms and amulets to protect them against head-hunting monsters who use human skin to cover their quivers and reputedly drink nothing but horse blood.'

It would only be a matter of time before they were boiling babies for breakfast.

'The land of the Amazons, huh?' Jocasta wrinkled her nose. 'You don't suppose they're on a mission to reclaim the Golden Fleece?'

'If they are, it's not putting the City Elders off.'

Accommodation at the Palace? Banquets in their honour? The legislation was bending over backwards to win the Scythians' approval, and together they watched as the tour guides moved on to the Temple of Hera. For all their ferocious reputation, though, quite a crowd had gathered, as curious about their unusual weaponry as their beautifully stitched kaftans and high, red leather boots. Iliona was lucky. Her father had been a close friend of the previous king's, who, as a royal ambassador, had travelled all over the world, often taking his family with him. Indeed, her experience was one of the reasons the new king had appointed her to the post of High Priestess.

That, and the fact they were related.

'Beware grown men who find the need to curl their hair.' Jocasta sniffed. 'Especially when they plaster half a bucket of grease on their ringlets.'

'They use hot tongs to create those elaborate spirals. The oil puts back what the rods take away.'

Jocasta wasn't impressed. 'What do you know about the delegation?'

'It's headed by the man with the beard—'

'The one who looks like a hawk whose prey's just fallen through his talons?'

'Aeërtes.'

Who either took a very keen interest in Greek religious sculpture or was a truly remarkable actor. As the Elders pointed out the ancient pear tree that was sacred to the goddess, Aeërtes would nod and ask questions, murmuring comments to his colleagues as the significance of the various emblems was explained.

Except not everyone was entranced by tales of centaurs and nymphs.

He stood no taller than the rest, and yet it seemed so. The gold on his headband glinted when it caught the sun, as did the rings on his fingers, and diplomat my foot, Iliona decided. The way his eyes were constantly scanning the plaza while his hand rested oh-so-casually on the hilt of his dagger smacked of a bodyguard and she wondered who, or what, would make these men wary. Hardly Spartans, who outnumbered them hundreds of thousands to one, a danger the Scythians would have weighed up before they'd even set off. So what, then? As she turned away, his eyes locked with hers. They were as dark and hard as seasoned oak beams, and bored through to the back of her skull.

'Where have you arranged to meet?'

Iliona jumped. 'What?'

'This young recruit of yours. Where *are* you meeting him?'

When she looked round, the Scythian had gone. 'The Square of Democracy.'

'Exactly where I was headed myself,' Jocasta breezed, and suddenly it made sense. Her prickly mood. Her insistence on accompanying Iliona this morning. Not everybody wears their heart on their sleeve.

'I'd rather go alone, if you don't mind.'

This was a lie. By far the quickest route to the square was through the artisan quarter. A network of narrow, twisting passageways where anything could happen, and very often did. Robbery. Rape. And with every able-bodied man away on campaign, women were easy pickings. The difference was, an attacker would think twice before tangling with the High Priestess of the Temple of Eurotas. Whereas Jocasta was a *helot*, a slave, and a foreigner at that, considered by many to be the lowest of the low. Killing her would be like squashing an ant.

'Are you sure?'

'Absolutely.'

Such was the assurance in Iliona's voice that Jocasta saw no reason to doubt her. But then she'd learned a long time ago that confidence was paramount when predicting the future, transferring its conviction to the seekers and giving them the strength to carry on. In fact, it came as quite a shock to discover that the vagueness of her prophecies didn't matter one iota. People simply needed to talk out their problems and have a balm rubbed over their emotional wounds – and quite honestly, who could blame them? When your masters view you as nothing more than tools with a pulse, to feel valued by the gods is beyond measure.

'I usually meet up with friends at the Shrine of Poseidon,' Jocasta said. 'You're welcome to join us afterwards.'

This was her way of saying she'd wait.

'I'd like that.'

This was Iliona's way of saying thank you to someone who refused to be thanked, and whilst there were times when Jocasta bristled harder than a porcupine, perhaps that was no bad thing. Parting company, it crossed her mind that even Hades might think twice about arousing the young physician's wrath. Far easier to let her patients keep breathing.

Within no time, the ripe smells of the market gave way to the earthier scents of potters and wheelwrights. Day rolled back to night among the tightly packed buildings, and the heat from the fires of the blacksmiths and bronzesmiths stuck Iliona's robe to her skin.

At least, she hoped that was the reason for the sweat.

Spartan men were bred to be warriors, their women skilled in management and administration. And since both were full-time careers, it was left to the lower caste, the *perioikoi*, to craft, buy and sell – which they also managed, whilst also juggling the absence of their menfolk, who were conscripted as auxiliaries and scouts when the army was on campaign. Yet what did they receive in return? Hefty poll taxes for one thing, sales taxes for another, but without any political influence or voting rights, and Iliona glanced nervously round. Free men, who were anything but free yet formed the country's economic backbone, did not take kindly to citizens stomping over their territory. You only had to look at the faces of the flute-maker, the coppersmith, even the young bullet-maker's apprentice, to see the suspicion that her presence was arousing. Nor did it help that, for a stranger, it was all too easy to take a wrong turn. Once or twice, backtracking through the labyrinth, she had the impression of being followed, which was nonsense. Who'd follow her here? All the same, she was relieved to emerge into the Square to see him waiting exactly where he said he would, and what a magnificent specimen. Strong of shoulder, broad of back, pulsing with the characteristic arrogance of youth.

'You're prompt.' His voice was deep and resonant.

I have to be, she thought. With so many petitioners swamping the temple, her absence required rigid planning. 'I assumed you'd be needed back at the barracks,' she said instead.

The army didn't allow its recruits much time off under normal circumstances, and on the run-up to any passing-out ceremony, furlough was cancelled as a matter of course.

'The Prefect's given me two marks of the shadow clock.'

One quarter of which would already have passed getting here, she calculated swiftly. And even if he ran back – and he looked the type who would – that reduced the time left to half.

'Then we'd better get started.'

'Not here.' His lip curled at the crush of moneychangers weighing coins, artists touting for commissions and old men playing knucklebones for pebbles by the fountain, their tunics dark with sweat. 'They stink. The artisan quarter stinks. The whole place is a pigsty, I'm used to fresh air in my lungs. Let's take a stroll by the racecourse instead.'

They. He said, *they*. As though craftsmen and merchants

were a species apart, and the smell of hard work a reason for shame.

'Wherever you wish,' she replied wearily. The cocky glint in his eye was already beginning to annoy her.

Struggling to match his cracking pace across the square, she glanced towards the gentle rise that led to the acropolis, where temples soared majestic and serene. Athene, Aphrodite, and the Muses. For a brief moment, when the sticky breeze ruffled through the cypress grove, it seemed the Goddess of Victory flexed her gilt wings in the sun. Iliona made a mental note to see whether lanterns at her own shrine could achieve a similar effect. Several of her routines there were growing stale.

'You didn't ask which racecourse,' he said, snatching a sausage from the coals of a street corner vendor.

'Foot races,' she said, doubling back to pay the poor man.

'So it's true.' He wiped a dribble of grease from his beard with the back of his hand. 'You do count the grains of sand on the shore and measure the drops in the ocean.'

Iliona wanted to slap the grin off his face and say that it was hardly inner vision. The hippodrome lay on the far side of town, and any walk out there would not accommodate his tight timescale. 'What aspect of your future concerns you?' she asked levelly.

'Aren't you curious to know my name?'

He must be new to the business, if he imagined she knew the names of the thousands of people who passed through the temple gates every year.

'It's Myles,' he said.

'Very well, Myles. What is it you wish to know about your future?'

'Let's talk about my past for a moment.'

Passing beneath the Colossus of Democracy, Iliona told herself she mustn't judge. All right, he wore his soldier's kilt cut higher than most, and though long hair was a symbol of strength – and therefore the mark of a warrior – his was also longer than average. But if Myles was worried enough to consult a prophetess, it suggested the bravado was merely a mask.

'What's there to talk about?' she said. 'Every soldier's life is pre-ordained from the moment he sets foot in the barracks.'

'Let's talk about it anyway.'

Semi-circles of seats, rather like a theatre, afforded views over the oval track where young men competed several times a year. Iliona chose a spot in the shade of an ancient holm oak and fixed her eyes on the obelisk at the far end. The paving stones shimmered like pools in the heat.

'Very well,' she said. 'At the age of seven, you left your family to board full-time with the army—'

'D'you know we were never, not even once, allowed to just have fun and let ourselves go? Every game revolved round building stamina and self-control, even at that tender age.'

'Are you bitter?'

'About the army? Not a bit. Every aspect of our lives is geared towards creating the strongest of bonds between the men, something that is especially enforced when serving overseas.' He did not join her, but remained in the aisle, feet apart, with his thumbs looped into his vest straps. 'Brotherhood is the glue that binds our fighting force together.'

Was it, Iliona wondered. Peace was fragile, and the only thing that stopped a thousand city states from clawing each other's throats out again was the strength of Athens' navy and the threat of Sparta's army. Through discipline and training, they'd turned themselves into the finest fighting force the world had ever known, but peace commands a high price. The men might be strong, the women independent, but beneath the equipoise and teamwork, darker threads were holding this society together. Take *helots* like Jocasta. Natives of adjoining Messenia, they were enslaved by the State and forced to work the land, yet were bitterly despised because of it. Equally, the artisans, prisoners in their native land . . .

'What else?' Myles asked and, in the sunlight, the colour of his hair was a cross between ivory and overripe wheat.

'After another seven years, you passed into your training squad—'

'Lynx Troop, where for the whole of our first year, winter or summer, we were kept barefoot and hungry. D'you know what we used to do?'

What every boy did. 'Let me guess. You stole food from the farms?' It was a way of teaching them survival techniques, and no one said it was fair.

'Damn right, but by thunder, if we got caught, weren't we beaten without mercy.' His voice rang with the acid taste of experience. 'Anything else you might want to add to my chronicle?'

'Only that once you pass a series of initiation tests, you qualify as a warrior, and I'm assuming you've already passed most of them, or you wouldn't have sent a message asking to meet.'

'What about the fact that I'm not allowed to marry for another seven years?'

'Is love what troubles you?'

'No.' He shook his head, and turned his eyes on the stone wall that ran down the centre of the track. 'I won six races here, y'know.'

'Congratualations, now can we please—'

'I did it by starving myself for three days beforehand, and promising myself a meal if I won.'

'Self-denial is not a noble trait.'

'Nonsense. It bears testimony to a man's inner strength.' He smiled. 'I thought you'd be proud of such a quality.'

'Myles, I really don't have time to waste feeding your ego. Eurotas is overrun as it is, and it's going to get worse as the day progresses.'

'Oh, come on! Not that hocus-pocus in the hills tonight! The world's moved on, or hadn't you people noticed?'

'That hocus-pocus in the hills is designed to propitiate the Queen of Darkness, who unlocks the Gates of the Underworld one night every year,' she said evenly. 'People are frightened enough on this night at the best of times, but this year her powers coincide with the full moon.'

They had visions of Hecate unleashing the Hounds of Hell to wreak panic, death and destruction.

'Don't tell me you believe in that ghoulie-ghostie-witch-craft crap!' He snorted. 'I can just see the mathematicians who designed these temples having sleepless nights worrying about banshees, can't you?'

'What I, they, or even you believe is unimportant,' she said, running her fingers down the pleats of her robe. 'What matters is that the people who come to my temple do. Now, do you want your runes cast or not?'

The magnificent specimen pursed his magnificent lips.

'Were you aware that we drill through the night, as well as the day?'

'Sparta trains its warriors to fight without the need for vision,' she said, standing up. She really didn't have time for this. 'Then, if the dust that's kicked up in battle blinds their eyes, they still retain the advantage.'

'You have a reputation for being able to see through the eyes of the blind yourself, and speak with the voice of the voiceless. Is it true?'

'Let's find out.' She shook the little drawstring bag that contained the bones and invited him to reach inside. 'Or are you too much of a coward?'

That wiped the smirk off his face. He grabbed the sack. The first draw pulled out *Eta*, the second one *Tau*, the third bore the mark of *Omega*.

'What do they say?'

Iliona looked at the runes in her hand. '*Eta* symbolizes the sun—'

'How appropriate.'

'Excuse me?'

'Sun. Such a lovely word, don't you think? You should use it more often.'

'Myles—'

'No, really. Roll it around in your mouth for a moment.' He ran his own tongue under his top lip to demonstrate. 'Now tell me how it feels when you look me in the eye and say it. Sun.'

'Sorry, but I—'

'Can't do it, eh?' He shrugged. 'Not surprised. Eighteen years have gone by, since I dropped from the womb. Eighteen to the day, in fact . . . oh, I say, steady on there.'

It couldn't be. No. Impossible . . .

Iliona felt herself falling back into the seat. It was happening again. The same gut-wrenching sensation as the first time she knew the parasite was inside her. The first time she felt it kick. It was strong. It clung on. Resisting stonecrop, hedge-hyssop and all the other aborticides. It kicked, and it kicked, and it kicked, and it kicked.

Now the bastard was kicking again.

THREE

Jocasta did not meet with friends outside Poseidon's shrine for the simple reason that she had none. Being a physician, she was acquainted with hundreds of people, but in the same way a High Priestess remains apart from her enquirers, so a good doctor keeps his distance also.

Except in Jocasta's case, it went deeper than that.

A lot, lot deeper than that.

'Sorry to trouble you, ma'am, but I wonder.' The little blonde wreath seller patted her bump. 'Can you recommend something for the morning sickness? I've tried everything, honest I have. Handstands before bed, shaking castanets when I wake. I've drunk the blood of a lizard mixed with the ashes of a weasel, washed my feet in stale urine—'

'Yes, well, you might want to put a halt to those for a while.'

Bloody quacks. Judging by the hollows under her eyes and the yellow tone of her skin, the poor cow could hardly afford food, much less what those charlatans were charging.

'Drop by the temple tomorrow at noon. I'll have an infusion waiting that will ease, if not cure it, but while I'm here, I'll take a myrtle wreath, please.' She handed over a quarter-obol piece. 'On second thoughts, make it two.'

Once out of sight of the stall, Jocasta tossed both chaplets to a little beggar girl, who ran away whooping with joy. Where the north portico joined the east, half a dozen small boys kicked an inflated pig's bladder about while their mothers gossiped, and incense burned in bronze tripods outside the shrine of Apollo. It was a homely, reassuring, practical scene. At least, for the artisan class, who were at home, reassured, and able to practise their trades here. They might be looked down on, Jocasta thought bitterly, but they weren't reviled. When the Spartans conquered their land all those centuries ago, they hadn't displaced them. Or cast the poor sods into slavery.

Hard eyes fixed on the mountains to the west. Thirty

miles of rock and pines and oaks and meadows was all that separated *helots* from their homeland. Thirty bloody miles. Jocasta bit her lip. It would take what? Two, three days at most, to cross those coiling canyons and boiling snowmelts, and navigate its gorges, caves and chasms. Thirty miles. Three days. That's all that stood between slavery and freedom . . .

'Thank you for what you did for my grandfather, milady. He's looking a whole lot chipper these days.'

Jocasta turned to the salt seller's wife, whose worn and mended veil was bobbing up and down with gratitude. 'It was nothing.'

A tonic of caraway, celery, sage and angelica, mixed with wine to soften the taste, was all the old man had needed.

'Maybe not to you, ma'am, but he swears you saved his life with that elixir of yours.' The woman laughed. 'The old bugger'll probably outlive me now.'

Jocasta's lips parted in a reciprocal smile, which did not reach her eyes. And as she ambled round the Agora, enquiring after the sandal-maker's warts, the stonemason's baby, the cough that plagued Iris the courtesan's lungs, she wondered whether the Secret Police were watching her now.

Probably.

The *Krypteia* had spies in the most unlikely of places. The girl measuring out three fingers' worth of beeswax? The youth pouring spiced wine? The scribe washing the ink off his vellum sheets, so he could re-use them? Any one of them could be in the pay of the Secret Police, and even fellow *helots* weren't above suspicion. Blackmail and intimidation were as much weapons in the *Krypteia*'s armoury as daggers and garrottes. Jocasta never went to bed without a knife under her pillow.

'Very sorry, madam.' The young schoolmaster came trotting over to retrieve the book he'd thrown at a pupil but missed. 'Trust I didn't hurt you.'

'Words can wound, but they are unlikely to cause physical injury.'

'*Tonight,*' he whispered, bending down to retrieve the scroll. '*When the moon stands directly above the peak of Mount Parnon.*' Aloud, he said, 'Ah, but this is Aeschylus, madam. His latest work, "Seven Against Thebes".'

'A tragedy. Yes, I can see how that might wound the heart. *Where?*'

'*The Cenotaph of Leonidas at the Temple of Eurotas.*'

'*Have you taken leave of your senses? That's where I live! Where I practise!*'

'*Exactly.* I thoroughly recommend this play to you, madam. In my view, it's his finest so far. *The one place the Secret Police won't be expecting us to meet.*'

'*They could be hiding anywhere in that damned willow grove and we'd be none the wiser. At least, not until it's too late.* Thank you, but I prefer comedy myself. If I wished to be depressed, I would stay at home. *And what about the locals? They're constantly murmuring prayers over that bloody memorial, touching their hero for luck.*'

'*You worry too much. Everyone will be too busy propitiating Hecate tonight, and the beauty of it is, among such crowds, we won't be missed, either.*'

'*You're a fool.*'

'*And you are starting to sound like a coward.*' The schoolmaster bowed. 'My apologies if I have inconvenienced you, madam, or delayed you in your tasks. *Just be there,*' he hissed. '*Before we start questioning where your loyalties lie.*'

Moron. Jocasta watched the pompous little prat return to his pupils, and thought, he had no idea. His self-importance blinded him to the fact that there were young men out there – men like the one Iliona was meeting right now – desperate to prove themselves to their superior officers, and never more so than at the initiation test stage. Pushing through the crush of olive oil sellers and guard dogs for sale, she considered the extremes of hunger, thirst, heat and cold that recruits were required to endure. Such survival missions were literally life or death ventures, endurance being crucial to Sparta's success, since its regiments were conditioned to survive in conditions their enemies otherwise could not.

Except this process of physical toughening was only one half of the story. Warriors also needed to know how to kill.

Stabbing sandbags and slitting the throats of straw dolls wasn't enough. Before he went into battle, a soldier apparently had to experience the spurt of hot blood on his face, smell the guts of his disembowelled opponent. No matter how adept he might be at stalking animals, the Administration argued, taking human life at close quarters was different. These were fellow Greeks he'd be killing. Somebody's father, somebody's son, certainly someone too young to die. A recruit needed to be exposed to the terror he would see in his victims' eyes, and be immune to their agonized screams.

So how did they practise?

On *helots*.

Skirting the bath house, Jocasta's ears were assaulted by the echoing chatter from men working out, loud grunts as stiff muscles were pounded into submission, the slap of masseur's hand against flesh. She paused, as she always did, inhaling the hot steam and scented oils that mingled with the perfume of the prostitutes who touted the hallways. Here was a world where decadence and necessity walked together, hand in hand, and where the essentials rubbed shoulders with luxury. It was also a world she would never experience beyond these marble portals. Like libraries, treasuries and public assemblies, bath houses were out of bounds to *helots*. Lingering on the doorstep was the closest she would ever come.

Jocasta chewed her thumbnail.

With *helots* outnumbering citizens twenty to one, the threat of insurrection was constant. The *Krypteia* dared not rely on informants alone, and to gather intelligence from this widespread, tightknit, agricultural workforce, they resorted to wilier techniques. They despatched agents to live off the land and merge with the landscape, sometimes for months at a time. And though Jocasta had no time for jumped-up, petty dictators (that schoolmaster was risking the lives of dozens of individuals, dammit, not to mention the Cause) she also had to be careful. In the same way there was a fine line between dedication and fanaticism, so there was between vigilance and paranoia. Her nail cracked. As much as she despised that little prick's arrogance, the truth was, he was probably right.

The chances of a camouflaged soldier holed up in the willow grove, purely on the offchance of catching rebels in the act on this particular night, were slim in the extreme. All the same, she lived knowing that the eyes of the *Krypteia* might be at any window at any time, their ears pressed against any door. Or that a knife might slide between her ribs without warning, or a noose slip round her neck. If it advanced the day when her people were free, then it was worth the sacrifice . . .

. . . but to play fast and loose with someone else's life was a different matter entirely. Which was why, when Iliona returned, Jocasta was sitting on the Steps of Poseidon, friendless and alone.

While from behind one of the white, carved, marble pillars of the portico, the Servant watched her every movement.

Morning drifted into afternoon. The heat intensified. Labourers collapsed from heat stroke in the fields. In the guest quarters of the palace, cooled by high ceilings, running water and tightly bolted wooden shutters, Aeërtes scanned the faces of the four men he trusted most: tattooed Tzan, playful Barak, Karas, best described as vanity personified, and, of course, Sebastos, the clever one.

'You all know what to do?'

They nodded.

'And in which order, and when?'

They nodded again, this time more forcefully.

'Timing is crucial,' Aeërtes stressed, glancing at Sebastos, whose hand, even now, rested on his dagger. 'Tonight we will need to run faster than our own shadows, and make half as much noise.'

Karas grinned. 'That will not be a problem, my lord.' In the space of three heartbeats, he'd vaulted the couch then somersaulted soundlessly back to his original position.

'Three gold pieces say you won't be able to do that in a year's time,' Barak quipped.

'In a year's time, I shall be even faster.'

'And I say rich living will have softened those stomach muscles to mush. You'll probably need a slave to roll you out of bed.'

'Speak for yourself,' Karas retorted. 'But if you're serious, let's make the stakes worthwhile, eh? If I'm not every bit as lithe and firm by this time next year, I will pay you twenty – no, let's make it a hundred gold pieces. If I am, you eat that stupid red headband of yours. Deal?'

'It's my tribal band, you arsehole, and yes, of course it's a deal.' Barak smoothed the embroidered bandolier that he wore even in bed. 'No one makes the amount of money we're going to make without it changing them, right, Tzan?'

Tzan didn't answer directly, but turned to his leader. 'Are you sure we will end up as rich as you say? You've run through the figures and they all add up fine. I just don't see how the client is able to obtain the funds.'

'I can assure you, gentlemen, the client will pay.' Aeërtes' voice was firm. 'Croesus will be a pauper, compared to what we shall sail home with.'

He began to pace the room, hands clasped behind his back. Fragrant cedar beams. Shiny oakwood floors. Statues. Tapestries. Chalices of gold, silver and bronze, and bedlinens softer than a courtesan's breast. He pursed his lips. The luxury of the palace would surprise many people, if they didn't know that this image of an extremist lifestyle, devoid of laughter, songs and comfort was largely a myth. Propaganda promulgated by the Spartans themselves, to convince allies and enemies alike that their resolute determination went deeper than it actually did. What exceeded Aeërtes' comprehension, however, was their notion that human destiny was decided by a bunch of fickle, two-faced, promiscuous deities. This, when it was the sun that breathed life, the moon that sent rain, and the earth that provided man with everything he could ever need: food, shelter, fuel. Having said that, he smiled. Hellenic religion was proving an endless source of amusement.

'Any more questions, gentlemen?'

'No, sir.'

'Until tonight, then.' He dismissed them with a tilt of his head, but as they filed out, he laid a hand on Sebastos's shoulder. 'Do they suspect anything?' he murmured, closing the door.

'Why should they?' Eyes as dark and expressionless as seasoned oak beams returned Aeërtes's stare. 'We converse in a language the Greeks don't understand—'

'Not the Spartans.' The mirror reflected Aeërtes's long, barbered beard and hair that was neither red, nor brown, but some point in between. The colour of a kestrel's flight feathers. 'Our people.'

'It's a large delegation—'

'I meant the juggler, the poet and the athlete.'

'I see.' Sebastos pulled at his earring. 'Well ... Barak's mother's a moon priestess from Colchis. It was from her that he learned how to juggle knives, swallow swords and eat fire, but whether she taught him the intricacies of temple politics, who can say. Tzan? Tzan sings ballads that would make his tattooed griffins weep, all of them about death and betrayal, while Karas . . .' He shrugged. 'Karas has dedicated himself to the pursuit of perfection, whether it be his equestrian manoeuvres, his gymnastic displays or his bronzed and faultless physique.'

'So what are you saying?' Aeërtes asked, noting that Sebastos's physique was equally bronzed, his musculature no less flawless, and that he wasn't prone to trading in half measures, either.

'I'm saying, who knows,' Sebastos said levelly. 'But if you want my advice, trust no one, my lord.'

'No one?' Aeërtes was surprised. 'Not even yourself?'

Sebastos held the older man's gaze without blinking. 'The man who makes exceptions makes mistakes,' he said, and before Aeërtes could open his mouth, the bodyguard had turned on his heel and was gone.

In a cave in the hills, seven candles burned.

The Servant was not there to watch them flicker. It didn't matter. He had only recently come across this little refuge, but once he was sure that no one else came up here, he quickly claimed it as his own. And tonight, when the Thunder Moon was at its full, it would be time to light another.

From time immemorial, the moon had been served by nine priestesses. Only one more moon, then, before the first phase of his operation was complete. After which, the new order could be launched. He smiled.

Oh, the Blood Moon was so very aptly named . . .

FOUR

'You look tired, my lady.'

'Simply the heat, Lichas.' Iliona diffused the lie with a smile. 'It invariably affects me in the late afternoon.'

Eurotas was one of the few rivers in Greece to flow

right through the summer, so it was hardly surprising that the god who made it his home should be venerated for his constancy and strength. The trouble was, his High Priestess was also expected to demonstrate the same qualities. Even to her young scribe.

Even when her world was falling apart.

'I understand, my lady.' Lichas nodded in sympathy. 'An ass can shoulder a burden for only so long, before the hour comes when its back starts to break.'

She leaned back in her chair, inhaling the familiar scents of ink, vellum and parchment overlaid with the incense that permeated the whole temple complex. Outside, the Song of the Maidens carried up to the heavens. So harmonious, so gentle, so why did she want to burst into tears?

'Is that how you see me?' she asked. 'A donkey?'

'Oh, no, my lady! Certainly not! I didn't mean to—'

'I know, Lichas. I was only teasing.'

A pointless exercise, since he had little, if any, sense of humour.

'I would never knowingly offend you, my lady.' He bowed solemnly. 'I am indebted to you for giving me this post.'

'Don't be too grateful, Lichas. It's only until the Scythians set sail.'

Which was a pity, in many ways. His filing system was second to none and his attention to detail quite stunning. And with so many petitioners swamping the temple, she'd needed help keeping track of which riddle she'd set, whose dream she'd interpreted, and in which particular way. But as efficient as he was, the King would not sanction the scribe's full-time appointment. He might be an aristocrat (the King's nephew to boot), and he might be bright, conscientious and hardworking. But when Lichas was four, he fell under a wagon. His left leg and arm were both horribly crushed, to the point where they were now withered, distorted and feeble. Iliona rearranged the oil lamps on her desk and thought, in a society where deformed babies were thrown over a cliff, being forced to hide one's imperfections behind walls was misery enough. But when that society was also a warrior cult, cripples stood no chance.

Why couldn't the parasite have been crippled?

'To have purpose in one's life, no matter how temporary,

is extremely important, my lady. I'm happy to know my assistance is of value.'

'Good,' she said, forcing her mind back to business. 'Because right now I have the bone worker's apprentice down in the plane grove, expecting me to interpret the bronze chimes in the wind. The dyer's wife with her hands pressed to the trunk of a cypress, waiting for it to read her thoughts, while Callipedes' widow is hoping for answers down by the fountain.'

In other words, a typical day.

Oh, if only—

'Let me see. Bone worker's apprentice . . .' Lichas hobbled over to the niche in the south wall and plucked out the second scroll from the top, three rolls in. 'Is he still worried the Scythians are going to flay him alive?'

'He's convinced they favour pale skins.'

Even if it was true, the boy would have nothing to worry about, she thought. Lichas was white from rarely venturing beyond the palace. He was sure to be top of their list.

'To date, you've advised him to dig a pit in the earth and bury three sprigs of mint, invoke Apollo's protection on a night with no moon, and pour a libation of honey for Heracles, whose strength is eternal.'

'Then this time the Oracle will pronounce that he need take no further action, the gods have other plans for his future.' Iliona did not wait for Lichas to scratch the notes in the file. His memory was equally prodigious. 'As for the dyer's wife, she's terrified Hecate's going to summon vampyres from the Underworld to suck the soul from her newborn baby.'

New mothers were always desperate for reassurance, and with good cause, too. Mortality rates for infants were notoriously high, but as it happened, Iliona had spoken with the midwife only yesterday morning. The boy was as strong as a lion cub.

Weren't they all?

'Let the record show that the bark of the cypress has revealed that beneath a canopy of sorrow, she will discover a candle of joy. Light it, and all will be well.'

Canopy of sorrow meant the colonnade beside the Cenotaph of Leonidas, commemorating the men who died defending the Pass at Thermopylae. And if the dyer's wife didn't quite make the connection? Well, there were plenty of other clues for Iliona to drop.

'We need to get that candle placed quickly,' she added.

Young mothers hate to be parted from their babies, and already the poor girl would be fretting. *Was she the only one in the world who had not?*

'Callipedes' widow is worried about the same thing she worries about every year. That Hecate's going to release the souls of the dead at midnight, and her husband will come back and haunt her.'

The bastard beat her black and blue on a regular basis, while his master stood by, saying nothing. Not even when Callipedes broke three of her ribs, her wrist and her jawbone. Then one day she came to consult Jocasta about the burns he'd left on her back. Took home a tiny phial of drugs. The next day, her husband was found dead in his bed.

'Callipedes, Callipedes . . .' Lichas drew out a scroll from a different niche, and untied it with his good hand. 'Previously, you've advised her to strew yew at the crossroads, lay split pomegranates on her doorstep and bury garlic cloves deep in the woods.' His pale eyes looked up from where he'd been reading, one of the rare occasions he made visual contact. 'If these measures are so effective, why does she keep coming back?'

Because even though he's dead, she's still terrified of the bastard, and the fact that she killed him magnifies her fears ten times over.

'You're right, Lichas. It's time she understood that Callipedes cannot hurt her any more. Let the record show that the Oracle had a vision in which the petitioner was seen throwing a waxen image of a monster into the fire. As it melted, so did his power.'

There would need to be a lot of thrice-times-threeing and ritualistic chants to convince her that it was the river god speaking, not simply the priestess. But by the time Iliona had ploughed through the rites from beginning to end, the widow would believe she was finally free of his shadow, and normally this would make Iliona feel good. Normally, being the operative word.

'Will you be attending tonight's ceremony?' she asked.

Perhaps among the hordes? In the dark? With long robes
to hide his disfigurement . . .?

There was a pause while Lichas tidied the scrolls. 'It's a
long trek to the shrine, my lady. I'm not sure my leg's up to
those hills.'

Yes, of course. He was banned from attending, because his
shame was the King's shame and it was insurmountable. As
was Iliona's about wanting him gone.

'Before you leave, my lady.'

At least after tonight there would be no more nonsense
about the Dark Witch drawing down the moon and draining
its light from the sky.

'Lichas?'

From now on, it would only be a question of offsetting
whatever fiendish deeds the Scythians might be plotting. And
given there was a harvest to be brought in, ploughed fields
to be harrowed and stacks to be built, never mind the preparations for the vintage, she didn't see people having much
time on their hands to worry.

Iliona was the one with the problem.

'You made no mention of the young man with whom you
met this morning.' He held up a blank sheet of parchment
enquiringly. 'What shall I note in the file?'

Mocking blue eyes flashed before her, along with hair that
was midway between ivory and overripe wheat.

'Nothing,' she snapped, instantly regretting it. This wasn't
Lichas's fault. 'There's nothing to record,' she added, forcing
a smile. 'The boy failed to keep the appointment.'

At midnight, when the moon was high over the mountains,
three things happened at once.

First, two small boys at the back of the crowd got bored with
the proceedings. Being too short to see, and with all the best
perches taken, they couldn't see the altar, the statue, the choir,
much less the puppy that was about to be sacrificed.

They decided to go off and slay monsters instead.

The setting was perfect. Being the patron of wild woods
and forests, Hecate's shrine was set in a grove on the side
of the mountain, so she could watch over the world far below.
But it was also set off the same road that led to the Pyramid,

where horses were sacrificed to placate the winds. What better place to find hundred-headed, fire-breathing serpents than coiled round the stallion that rode for eternity?

With twigs for swords and imaginary bows, the boys set off up the track. Behind them, torches flickered and drum beats rolled. The scent of burning juniper oil pervaded the forest. The closer they climbed, though, the more the woods around had been cleared to afford a clear view of the peak. Now, the only sound was their own sandalled feet, crunching on the wide, stony path. Ahead of them, the monumental gateway loomed white and solemn, and in the hot, sultry silence they could almost hear the serpent's breath as it wound itself round the plinth of the statue.

'Ready?'

'You bet!'

Charging forward, they deflected the poisonous barbs of its spine, dodged its bone-crushing undulations and cut off its heads with a flourish. It was the smaller of the two, the bookseller's son, who first remarked on the rider. He'd stopped to catch his breath, having saved yet another maiden from a fate worse than death, and when he looked up, it was funny, but he didn't remember seeing a rider on the other times that he'd been up here. And, oddly enough, now he came to think of it, neither did the carpenter's boy.

Especially one that had been gutted, its belly stuffed with herbs and sewn back up again, then spitted from neck to coccyx to keep it upright.

Around the same time, Jocasta was pacing the Cenotaph of Leonidas. This was madness, she thought. Suppose the Secret Police were out there, doing what the bastards did best? Mastering the art of invisibility? Under the full moon, every conspirator's face would show clearer than lamplight, and she didn't need a diagram to tell her what would happen if they raided the place. It was why she carried extract of celandine. Heart failure was preferable to torture.

She reached the end of the colonnade, turned and marched back. All right, the odds were against the *Krypteia* being camped on the far bank. But suppose someone decided Sparta's great hero would give them better protection against the Powers of Darkness than a priest's prayer, a dead puppy and half a dozen hymns? The bronze was already worn from being touched for good luck. It only needed one person to mention what they'd seen here tonight, and the Cause would be set back a year.

She stopped. Listened. But all she could hear were the wind chimes jangling in the hot, clammy breeze and the tseep-tseep-tseep of tree frogs.

She should have put her foot down with that supercilious prick. What did he know about freedom? He'd never built a fence, ploughed a field or shorn a sheep in his life. Wouldn't last a day out there, reaping, sowing, or weeding. She continued to pace, her fists clenched into balls. Everything the schoolmaster had learned about Messenia's gentle coasts and rich fertile valleys was gleaned from books, so how dare he talk about reclaiming a land he'd never seen! But when she took him to task at their last rally, she was shouted down.

'You've never been there, either,' the schoolmaster had sneered.

'Damn right,' she snapped back. 'But I rub balm into my fellow *helots*' sun-burned skin, and while I treat their snake bites, bathe their infected cuts and soothe their ulcerated lungs, I listen to their stories.'

They came so Jocasta could minister to their jaundice, their rickets, their arthritis, their fevers and to rid them of parasites inside and out. But equally important to their physical wellbeing was their desire to talk about the old days. The days when their homeland belonged to them. The days when they were free . . .

'If you came to my healing room,' she told him, 'it would be for a blister on your arse from sitting under that awning all day long.'

People laughed, but they were missing the point. He was a Nobody who found that by inciting insurrection he could be Somebody, and because he was educated they clung to his every word. They loved the sound of *streets running red with rivers of blood* and rose to the challenge that *the time was coming for us to rise up*. Perhaps it was human nature to reject the notion that one's leader is weak and self-serving, when you're chained and despised yourself. Such words make you strong. They give you the illusion of power in a world where you have none. In their eyes, the schoolmaster could do no wrong.

Jocasta stared at the moon rising over the peak. Soon, people would start trickling in, ready to cite murder and rebellion with no thought to the consequences, and that little creep would be the first on the scene. Basking in the glory of crowds hanging on his every word and knowing the instant he stood up, he was a hero. She sighed. As much as she'd love to challenge his leadership, though, no self-respecting Messenian would back her. Only Spartan women enjoyed genuine equality, and whether you were a *helot* or not, the Hellenic world was a man's one.

Who ever thought she would envy her oppressors?

In the distance, an owl hooted, followed by the short bark of a deer. She could always walk away, of course. Leave the schoolmaster to face whatever might be waiting out there, but the trouble was, it wasn't just him. There were others to think of, every last one of them downtrodden and poor. Their very desperation blinding them to reality.

Jocasta bit into her lip. She had no choice but to tough it out tonight, but dammit, she'd at least check the environs again. As with every other Greek shrine, most of the staff, from lowly acolyte to exalted libation pourer, returned to their own home after work. Only a handful of personnel actually slept on the complex, and these were all where they were supposed to be. Standing guard against thieves, watching over the tripod in which the eternal flame burned, or averting witchcraft and magic up in the hills. The only risk came from casual visitors—

—and the dreaded Secret Police.

The moon rose, its light filtering through the leaves of the trees that lined the bank of the river: willows, alders and poplars. Close by, the sluggish waters of Eurotas gurgled and sloshed. Moths diced with death round the torches that burned for the dead.

One last patrol, Jocasta decided. One final check for the *Krypteia*. She picked up a rock and hurled it into the far bank. Birds flew out screaming, frogs plopped into the river, and Jocasta released the breath she'd been holding. No death squad could possibly hide from so many wild creatures, no matter how—

What in Tartarus—?

She squinted into the willow grove, blinking to make sure her eyes did not deceive her. But this . . . this was no trick of the moonlight. Grabbing the horn that hung from the Cenotaph, she blew as hard as she could. The guards were on the scene within seconds.

'What is it?' Their weapons were drawn, and she could see that the edges had been recently sharpened.

'I have no idea,' she answered truthfully. She hadn't got past gloating over the schoolmaster's discomfort, and the fact that his plans for tonight's meeting were scuppered. 'But if you want an educated guess, I'd say it was a corpse.'

Spread-eagled in the top of the trees.

While up on the Acropolis, Abas the kitchen slave was cursing his luck that it would be his turn, wouldn't it, to dump the waste on the middens?

'Mind Hecate's black dog doesn't get you.'

'Watch out for the ghosts.'

'Be careful her spells don't turn you into a tortoise!'

Oh, yeah, laugh, he thought. But who wasn't even brave enough to poke their nose outside when it was their turn earlier, eh? While here he was, struggling with four buckets instead of the usual two, and the jaws of hell yawning wide.

'Cowards.'

But his voice was a whisper, because he had no intention of advertising his presence to whatever evil spirits might be flitting around. In any case, his good, kind friends had already shut the door behind him and barred it.

'Miserable, sodding, bloody cowards.'

Abas muttered and cursed his way down a street in which the only thing that moved was his shadow. Below, between the cypresses and temples, he caught glimpses of the torches round the palace flickering with hospitality and welcome, making him feel smaller and even more isolated. The King wasn't home, of course. He was at Hecate's temple, along with the rest of the royal family, and Abas bet the slaves in the palace hadn't had to draw lots to see who was going to take the slops out tonight! In fact, he'd heard there were ten slaves to every task in the palace, and that they all lived like lords, sleeping in soft, feather beds and dining on meat every night. Meat! How long since he'd tasted—

'*Shit.*'

He'd forgotten the barbarians.

They didn't believe in the gods, like normal people, so they hadn't trekked to the hills, but remained in the palace. Abas wasn't surprised. There was nothing about them Scythians that was normal. Pantaloons? Boots? Men who wore ear-rings? Abas's eyes bulged, though he would have called it bewilderment, rather than fear. Because he knew for a fact that their tribes didn't marry and only reproduced through rape. That the steps of their temples were stained red with blood, and that they lured ships on to the rocks with false lanterns. He broke into a trot. Well, they weren't sticking *his* head on a pole over their chimneys, the bastards.

In his haste, he tripped. Cabbage stalks and fish guts flew over the cobbles, along with eggshells, date stones and curds.

'Yeah, well, stuff that.'

He wasn't hanging about, scooping all that back up, either. Not tonight. Not with witches and Scythians on the prowl. He kept moving. Not far to the middens, if he took the short cut. All right, slaves weren't supposed to cross temple grounds, but what the hell? There was no one around to tell him to shove off. Even the guards stayed indoors tonight.

For a moment, he didn't realize what it was, dumped over there by the fountain. Then he saw it was the body of a woman. She'd been stripped of her dignity, as she'd been stripped of her clothes, but what made him pull up short wasn't the hideous mutilations. He'd seen worse during his stint as an orderly in the Persian campaigns. Much worse, in fact. And more blood.

But Abas had never seen a head with the scalp ripped off before.

He dropped his buckets and ran like the wind.

FIVE

'No, Lichas, I will not make an exception.'

Iliona kicked off her sandals and massaged her pounding temples. This was the first time she'd sat down today, because when she stopped, her head filled with demons. Demons that came from the barracks, though. Not through the Gates of the Underworld.

'Her father has made several lavish donations to Eurotas's treasury,' the young scribe reminded her gently. 'Three gold tripods, a set of carved ivories, lustral bowls inlaid with mother-of-pearl—'

'I don't care if her father's Croesus, or Midas, or whether she's Hera incarnate.' Iliona strained wine from the jug and topped her drinking cup to the brim with a hand that wouldn't stop shaking. 'With two hundred pilgrims wailing and beating their breasts in the precinct, individual consultations are out of the question.'

'She only wants to know if her forthcoming marriage will be blessed by the river god, my lady.'

'There is no such word as "only", Lichas.'

This girl's family had money and, more importantly, influence, and for people like that, divination takes time. The supplicant would need to be bathed and anointed with sacred oils before being led into the special underground chamber. Herbs would need to be burned in the tripod. Musicians and singers would have to be gathered, their music filtered through pipes hollowed into the walls to create a sense of unearthly magic. For the rich, the Oracle's prophecies could not be rushed.

'Tell her it's all or nothing,' Iliona said. 'You can wrap it up in whatever diplomacy you like, but fundamentally the girl has a choice. Either she waits until the panic's died down—'

'That might take days!'

'—or she can join in one of the mass propitiation services that I shall be holding.'

Something flashed behind the scribe's pale eyes. Disappointment? Anger? Irritation? It passed too quickly to identify, but whatever it was, it took her by surprise. Lichas was a past master at hiding his emotions.

'If you say so, my lady.' The humility was back.

'I do say so, Lichas. In fact, until further notice, perhaps you would be kind enough to pass the word that there will be no preferential treatment for anyone, not even the King.'

His connections with the palace would ensure the news travelled fast. One-to-one consultations, at a time when Sparta was in panic, were simply unviable she would argue. Only she would know it was a lie.

'Very good, my lady.' His face was once again cast down to the floor. 'I will advise the bride of your decision at once.' As he limped past, his elbow knocked Iliona's arm, spilling wine down the front of her robe. 'I'm sorry, I'm sorry, so sorry, my lady!'

'Don't worry.'

'It's my leg. Some days it drags more heavily than others—'

He mopped at the stains, but she brushed him away. 'I've done worse and it bleaches out.'

'I'd be happy to replace your gown at my own expense.'

'Lichas, really. It's fine.' In fact, she hadn't done worse and it wouldn't bleach out, but his fawning grated her nerves. *And Lichas was dark, when Myles was fair. Where his limbs were weak, the soldier's were strong . . .*

Outside, her acolytes were about to bear the brunt of a night spent shaking and sobbing, pacing and vomiting, followed by a day spent trying to hide behind her job.

'I know it's chaos here today, but that's no excuse not to change the water in the lustral basins,' she barked. 'I've asked you at least twice to strew oregano for peace, and you know I won't tolerate dust on the steps of the temple.'

In their haste to snap to it, none of them noticed blood-less cheeks that had been stained pink with wine lees. Among the bustle, they missed the chalk that whitened the hollows beneath her eyes. All they saw was a fresh white linen robe, whose knife-sharp pleats radiated authority and whose gold edging brooked no disobedience.

'You need to lighten up the incense, as well.' The customary resins cloyed in this heat. 'And dot at least a dozen sprigs of blackthorn round the precinct.'

Pilgrims would find reassurance in this propitiation of the Goddess of Discord. Maybe, in time, Iliona would, too.

And the silly thing was, at the back of her mind prowled the suspicion that Lichas had nudged her elbow on purpose.

The sun set. The moon rose. And in a cave in the hills, shafts of silver shone down on eight candles flickering in their rocky niches. The Servant closed his eyes. Eight now. Eight exquisite moments to savour, when each whoring bitch knew that she was doomed to die and there was nothing she could do. *Not one bloody thing*.

He picked up the phial lying on a bed of downy Artemisia. In the moonlight, the engravings sprang to life. Stallions. Prancing, dancing, rearing, stomping. Riders of the wind and bringers of rain. Begetters of terror and screams.

Slowly, the Servant caressed the silver phial that contained his future. Then, reaching down, he caressed himself.

SIX

Within the confines of the inner courtyard, the wails and cries of traumatized pilgrims were muffled by tall, whitewashed walls, for which (may Eurotas forgive her) the High Priestess was exceedingly grateful. It wasn't the pilgrims' fault they were scared. Superstition was a child conceived out of poverty and raised out of ignorance. All they knew was that, on the night services were supposed to avert witchcraft and magic, all hell broke loose instead.

Iliona ran her hand over the thick green leaves of the fig that scrambled over the walls. Many blamed the priests for what happened. They should have lit more torches round Hecate's shrine, since the lights obviously weren't bright enough to blind the souls of the damned and prevent them from leaving the Underworld. Others maintained they were *too* bright, that's the trouble, which is how the fiends were able to see to go about their grisly business. But . . . She watched the flock of white doves pecking away at the caraway seeds that kept them coming back to the temple. The vast majority believed it was the fault of that little black puppy. Had the sacrifice gone ahead, as was planned, its death would have appeased Hecate's bloodlust. But no. The little bastard escaped, and being denied was the reason for the goddess's vengeance.

Iliona splashed her face in a fountain shaded by ancient, gnarled pomegranates. On top of everything else, she now had to convince them that the puppy slipped its leash *after* the boys raised the alarm, not before, and that the corpse in the willows was already cold. But memory, unfortunately, can be short and selective. Rather than incur Hecate's wrath by accusing the goddess herself (or even the priests who served her shrine), they'd decided to make the puppy the scapegoat.

Puppies don't answer back.

'*Seven are the messengers from bleak Tartarus.*' The Oracle should at least make some effort at drafting her speech. '*From house to house in darkness they creep.*'

Make that, *creep they*, it sounded more sinister, but what rhymed with Tartarus? Oh, for goodness sake, did it matter? The main thing was to convince people that the Queen of Ghosts could be placated, and seven sacrifices sounded about right. And if seven lambs and endless burning herbs didn't set their minds at rest, she'd think of something else to focus their attention. Until then, she had bigger issues to worry about. Issues with blond beard and blue eyes, who didn't want his future told, only his past . . .

Such a lovely word, you should use it more often.

At the very least, the High Priestess should be busy marking the votive offerings left for the river god, or overseeing the purification of the altars with hyssop—

Eighteen years have gone by, since I dropped from the womb. Eighteen to the day.

Duty be damned. She took herself down to the sacred plane grove, where Eurotas sucked and burbled his way to the delta, and the songs of the washerwomen drifted downwind. She slumped on a marble bench in the shade. Another day, and the trill of skylarks hovering above fields brimming with the spikes of ripe barley would have calmed her, and lifted her mood. Today, their music was shrill and the tree crickets shredded what was left of her nerves. What she wouldn't give to fly with the eagles soaring over the mountain tops. Fly, and never come back . . .

She closed her eyes. Memory rolled back like parchment. It was the Ceremony of the Toys. Iliona was fifteen and pretty, with the world at her feet. The sun had been shining, but there was none of the sweltering heat like today. Just blue skies, a warm breeze, family and friends gathered around as she consigned her toys, her spinning top, even her battered tambourine toys to the altar. How everyone cheered as Iliona marked the end of her childhood with this public transition to womanhood. Everyone, that is, except Iliona, who'd kept her smile in place as she handed the priest her rag dolls and skipping ropes, wondering what people would think if they knew that every morning she woke and ran her hands over her belly, before binding it tight with a bandage. Or that every night, when she unwound it, the beast had swelled just that little bit bigger, kicking and pushing in its bid to be free.

And now it was. Free to walk, to stalk, to taunt her again. *Free to return and reclaim its name.*

'I daresay you've heard the King's proposals for the temple?'

Iliona lifted her head from her hands.

'His plans to divert water from the river and channel it through the precinct?'

The trees were old, their trunks were broad, and they afforded many hiding places for a seasoned soldier. Except no man, not even the head of the *Krypteia*, could hide from his own shadow. She closed her eyes again. There was nothing here except the disembodied voice of an over-wrought imagination. A figment of her anxieties and fear.

'He thinks ringing the shrine would add a certain refine-ment, but I've told him you favour a square section, to retain the harmony.' The voice dropped from the branches, landing softly as a cat. 'The King was most impressed.'

For a second, Iliona stopped breathing. First Myles. Now him. What had she done to so displease the gods, that they should punish her in such a way?

'Lysander.' Manners dictated that she should declare this an unexpected pleasure. Convention decreed that she must offer the hospitality that was her sacred duty. 'What do you want?'

Weeks – correction, months – had passed since their last encounter, yet suddenly it was no time at all. His limbs were possibly a little more bronzed and maybe he carried a few more scars than in the spring, and were those grey flecks at the side of his temple? But the lines round his eyes still gave nothing away, and the past and the present, she realized wearily, were interwoven as tightly as the braids into which a warrior binds his hair before battle.

The Commander of the Secret Police had not braided his. But even so, battle had commenced.

'The King also has it in mind to add a portico, a gymnasium and a public library.'

'What he needs to mind is his own business,' she said evenly. 'This is my temple, and I alone decide what goes where.'

'That's a fine way to talk about your sovereign.' Grey eyes bored into hers, as measureless as the ocean itself. 'Especially since he's also your cousin.'

'Second cousin,' she corrected, and she'd forgotten just how much gravel he kept down his throat. 'We are hardly close.'

Lysander gave his full attention to a gatehopper butterfly probing the brambles. 'If you invested your profits into a second treasury, instead of distributing them among the poor, you might find the gap closer than you think.'

'Distance has its advantages, then.'

'Not when the King's philosophy is: the closer the better.' He cracked his knuckles. 'He would still very much prefer to see his sister wearing your robe.'

'Then he should not have appointed me to the post.'

'He assumed you would be compliant to his directives, but once again the Lady Iliona defies her King's wishes.'

A portico would be wonderful, a watercourse even better, both bringing supplicants closer still to their god. But the price was just too high to pay.

'Are you here to reverse my decision?'

'Regrettably, I appear to have left the thumbscrews behind.' One shoulder lifted. 'Still. I daresay it's more comfortable to write the letter with fingers that haven't been broken.'

'Eurotas has no need of further statuary or gold.' She wondered why she felt compelled to explain her stand on the matter. 'Not when food and medicine go much further.'

He fixed his gaze on his thumbnail. 'Medicine has a tendency to be rather dangerous around here.'

So that was it. Iliona felt her stomach unclench, and wondered what on earth made her think she had something to fear. 'Simply because my physician is a *helot* doesn't make her guilty of plotting rebellion.'

'Every *helot* plots rebellion, Iliona. It's only a question of how far they're prepared to take it.'

'What can you expect,' she shot back, 'when we officially declare war on them every year, which they take as an excuse for us to go round murdering their people?'

'Hm.' He scratched at his jaw. 'I prefer to think of it as neutralizing threats, but then that's only my opinion, and in any case, that's not what I meant.' When he smiled, it was colder than a midwinter frost. 'By the way, how is Callipedes' widow these days?'

'Who?'

A muscle twitched in the side of his cheek, but he made no reply. He leaned his weight against the soft, smooth bark and folded his arms over his chest. Iliona waited. He could not possibly know it was she who had approached Jocasta in the first place. That it was she who had suggested a permanent solution to the brutal rapes and vicious beatings.

The herb that heals is the herb that kills, the Oracle told Callipides' wife, when she came in once again covered with bite marks and burns. *When the heart is pure, it can do no harm.*

If there was a case to be made, it would have been made long before now. Lysander, she decided, was fishing. All the same, a trickle of sweat snaked down her backbone, and her palms seemed unnaturally clammy.

'There are some fine views to be had from these branches,' he said. 'Would you care to take a look?'

Was this another joke? 'High Priestesses don't climb trees.'

'Perhaps this particular High Priestess might make an exception?'

When the head of the *Krypteia* offers his hand, one would be ill-advised to decline.

'Why?' she asked, trying to ignore the absurdity of him hauling and her clambering her way up the trunk. 'Is this another of the King's policies?'

'A whisper from me and it could be,' he rasped. 'But now do you see what I mean?'

Iliona hoped he'd put her shallow breathing down to lack of fitness. 'If you've brought me up here to point out the three missing tiles on the depository roof, I am already aware of that fact.'

'The river, in particular, comes into its own from this height.'

'Yes, indeed. Very pretty. Now can we go down, please, I'm dizzy.'

She was wasting her breath and she knew it, and, as her eyes followed a pack of vultures above the far bank, she knew Lysander was also circling his prey. Her head throbbed. Did he know she was still helping deserters? A treasonable offence, punishable by being trussed and thrown in the river? No, of course not. After that last business, Iliona had learned to cover her tracks a lot better. Not even the Secret Police could catch her out there. So what then? She saw no obvious reason why he should drag her up here, but all the same, when she tried to swallow, she couldn't.

'Can we get to the point, please, only—' The words died on her tongue as the flight of vultures fell into place. '*Another corpse?*'

She would not have fallen, but his hand lashed round her wrist anyway.

'Well, that's the thing,' Lysander said, and his skin against hers smelled of leather and woodsmoke. 'Technically speaking, it isn't another corpse.' Grey eyes swivelled sideways. 'It's the same one.'

Was stress playing tricks with her memory? 'But I watched it being cut down and taken away.'

'Taken to the Shrine of the Snow Goddess, where it was packed in ice, that I might take a leisurely look at our leaf-loving visitor.' Snow lingered right through the year on the uppermost peaks, and it went without saying what this heat did to dead bodies. 'You can imagine my surprise when I went to make my inspection, and found that all that remained was a large pool of water.'

'I can imagine other people's reactions.'

'Assuming word got out,' he murmured. 'Which, so far, it hasn't.'

But it would, she reflected. It would. You can't keep it secret for ever that a naked corpse in the care of the Secret Police subsequently returned itself to the place of origin and tied itself back up again.

'What do you think's going on?' she asked, curious in spite of herself.

'Me?' His hand was still locked round her wrist and she could smell the mint which he chewed to freshen his breath. 'I think someone's trying to make the *Krypteia* look small, and I think they're this close to succeeding. But . . .' His mouth twisted sideways. 'It's not what I think that matters. The King, the Council, in fact the entire Administration, is convinced that all three deaths are the work of an Athenian agent.'

Yes, indeed. World peace might depend on the strength of Athens' navy balanced out by Sparta's immense military capability, but try telling that to Athens. Not content with half the power, they craved the bloody lot, which meant there was always an agent working undercover somewhere in Sparta.

'It's a better theory than demons rushing from the Underworld,' Lysander added. 'But only just.'

Nonsense. Expert organizers and first-rate planners, Athens produced some of the finest generals in the world. It made perfect sense that their counter-intelligence officers would exploit local superstition in a bid to undermine Sparta's authority, and, let's face it, three unidentified corpses found in bizarre circumstances on the very night witchcraft was supposed to be averted would certainly suggest the gods had turned against them. And then, once Sparta's allies began to tie in with Athens, the balance of power would quickly start to swing.

On the other hand, there were few advantages to be gained by telling the Head of the Secret Police that he'd lost his objectivity. Especially when one was twelve feet off the ground.

'What are you going to do?'

'About him?' Lysander glanced at the vultures, which were starting to settle. 'Nothing.'

One of the birds flapped off with something in its beak, and Iliona was beyond caring what it might be. 'You can't just leave him there.'

'Why not?'

She turned her head as they began to rip and tear. 'It's barbaric.'

'And it's your ability to hit the nail on the head with such accuracy that brings me out here this morning.' Lysander released her wrist as though he'd forgotten he'd been holding it, and with anyone else, that might have been true. 'You didn't say it was sacrilegious, or even irreverent, to leave our anonymous visitor spread-eagled high in the treetops. The word you used was barbaric. The act of a barbarian.'

'You think the Scythians are responsible?'

'Not think. Sure.' He carried her to the ground as though she was a child. 'All three deaths bear the trademarks of their culture, but to prove my theory I need an agent inside the palace, someone the delegation can trust.' He paused. 'An interpreter, if you like.'

'Then talk to the priest at the Shrine of Menelaus. He's crossed the Hellespont god knows how many times, and even speaks a few words of their language.'

'By interpreter, I mean someone who reads people and translates their behaviour.' Lysander brushed the dust from his kilt. 'The very qualities, in fact, that made you such an asset on our previous collaboration.'

After two sleepless nights, Iliona was in no mood to play politics. 'Collaboration, my arse. That was coercion, and you can go to hell.'

Grey eyes held hers. 'It's not often someone defies the King and the *Krypteia* in the same day.'

'It's not often someone is blackmailed into travelling to Sicily, forced to act as a spy, then framed as a traitor to her country.'

'I am interested in results, not sentiment. But if you can think of a better way to expose the Scythians, I'm open to suggestions.'

Given time, she could probably think of dozens. 'Lysander, even if I wanted to help you, I don't have the time.' No need to point out that her mind wouldn't be on the job. 'In case you hadn't noticed, the temple's under siege, and every one of these people is relying on my personal assurance that Hecate won't draw down the moon and steal the light from the sky, or unleash the thousand Red Hounds of Hell.'

'Hm.' He pursed his lips. 'The *Krypteia* tends to concern itself more with dogs of war than hounds of hell, but now you raise the issue, how is that little puppy?'

'Puppy?'

'The one that escaped the priest's knife the other night.' He scratched his neck. 'Strange business,' he rumbled. 'I wonder what the penalty would be, had someone, say, stolen it from the altar and was keeping it hidden until the furore died down. I don't suppose you'd know the answer, would you?'

Professionally, that person would be stripped from their post and vilified as a perverter of justice. Legally, they would be charged with sabotaging a religious rite, be exiled and have their lands taken from them. Morally, of course, they would be guilty of letting down the many thousands of people who had previously looked up to them.

'No,' she said crisply. 'I wouldn't.'

'Oh, well. Just a thought. Only, the thing is, I couldn't help noticing a black pup in your bedroom an hour ago. Chewing your blue sandal to shreds, as it happened.'

It came as no surprise that he had horses saddled and waiting.

Aeërtes leaned back in his chair, stroking his beard, staring across at the mountains.

A mistake had been made.

Not necessarily a disaster.

But a mistake nevertheless.

SEVEN

Taygetus was named after the nymph who escaped Zeus's advances by being turned into a doe. Dense forests certainly provided ample food and shelter for her, but they also gave rise to numerous legends. Unsurprisingly, the peak shaped like a pyramid engendered the most. Eerie and shadowy, this was the place where the Winds called to one another in low, haunting tongues, and no tree dare spread its roots.

And since the Winds thundered in on celestial hooves, it was only fitting they be placated with a stallion each spring. Now, whether Iliona's horse could smell the blood of a thousand slaughtered ancestors or simply sensed a porcupine, she couldn't decide. But the instant it approached the monumental arch, her horse began to snicker and pull.

'Two slight detours before the palace,' Lysander had said.

Wiping the sweat from her brow as she dismounted, she wondered what constituted a large one.

'Don't write off our corpse in the willows as the most unusual thing you've ever seen,' he was saying, tethering both sets of reins to a pine. 'Not until you've seen this.'

Iliona followed, but at a more leisurely pace, taking careful stock of her surroundings. Not that she wasn't familiar with the site. But today she was seeing it through different eyes.

Eyes that belonged to a killer.

The moon was full the night the boys came here, and many of the surrounding trees had been thinned out, to render the precinct more conspicuous and therefore much grander. By its light, they would have seen the engravings on the pillars every bit as clearly as she saw them today: the North Wind, the West Wind, the Whirlwind, scrunching her old woman's face into a scowl. Which means that if another person had been up here at the same time, the boys would have noticed. Wouldn't they . . .?

She passed through the gateway. Unlike Eurotas, this was an open space designed purely for the conducting of sacrificial rites. It was too far, and too difficult, to expect people to climb to the top of the Pyramid, and only those who could afford horses, and more importantly the time, attended the ceremony proper. But with its altars decked with ribbons, and shrines to Apollo and Zeus, an air of unravelled mysteries and unspoken secrets pervaded this site. Not least the stallion that rode for eternity.

'He's not what I was expecting.' She lifted her eyes to the rider sitting astride it.

He'd be what? Forty? The same age as Lysander at a guess, but with a neatly curled beard and thick head of hair, and

the most sumptuous kaftan she'd ever laid eyes on. She
reached up to touch it. Red felt, stuffed with probably horsehair and covered with appliquéd ibex and stags, the kaftan
was a work of art in itself.

'Who is he?'

'No idea.' Lysander paced the ground, searching for traces
he might have missed. 'The entire delegation is accounted
for, and yet . . .' He spread his hands wide. 'Despite the King's
theory that he's nothing more than a drifter dressed up by
the Athenians, I'm convinced our horseman is Scythian.'

Iliona agreed. Never mind the fancy clothes, the Athenians
wouldn't have taken the trouble to sew a false beard on to
his skin, or glue his eyelids together. She bet that was a wig,
that had been sewn on, as well. Beneath rider and mount, a
thick, yellow substance had pooled on the plinth.

'Wax?' she queried, kneeling beside it.

'Forgetting there was a full moon in a clear sky, it is the
King's view that the Athenians needed candles to work by.'

Iliona had only met her cousin a handful of times and had
always found him a stubborn little prick. 'What explanation
does he put forward for the elaborate embalming?'

'He is awaiting reports of a stolen corpse any minute.'
Lysander's lip curled, and it could have been humour, but
then again it could have been contempt. 'If not, it will only
be because whichever unfortunate foreigner it belongs to has
set sail before their people noticed it missing.'

Oh, for heaven's sake. Who on earth disembowels
someone, stuffs the belly cavity with herbs, sews him back
up again, then dresses him in the finest of clothes – only to
forget all about him? But the King was too close to his politics to see beyond sabotage, she supposed. Because whoever
this man was, he meant something to someone. Dead, if not
alive.

'Which herbs were used?' She'd noticed a patch where the
corpse had been cut open and samples removed. No one could
accuse the *Krypteia* of not being thorough.

'According to the mortician, it's a mixture of frankincense,
parsley seed, anise and something called galingale, which is
a new one on me. Have you heard of it?'

'I came across it during the time my father was posted to
Babylon.' If she remembered correctly, it was a rhizome,

imported from even further east. 'Its juice is reputed to enhance male sexual performance.'

Lysander paused from scouring the ground. 'Hardly the erection our friend here would have wanted.'

Iliona was more concerned with how he died.

'No obvious injuries.' The *Krypteia* returned to his inspection. 'We'll probably know more once he's unskewered, but for the moment that's another corpse I'm leaving in place.'

'Of course.' She nodded. 'The wax.'

Whoever spitted him had sadly misjudged the Peloppenese summers. They'd covered the skin with a thick layer of wax to preserve him, but Helius's rays were proving too strong. Sooner or later, they would realize their mistake. Lysander's men would be ready and waiting.

'And the second detour?' she asked.

'Now there we *can* rule out suicide, natural causes, accident and misfortune.' He took one last, lingering look through the gateway, pursing his lips at the lack of evidence. 'I've kept her body preserved in ice, but again we have no idea who she is.'

Three strangers, three deaths, Iliona reflected.

The Winds sighed at the sadness of life.

In the olive groves that stretched across the plain beyond the palace, a young man with slightly Oriental features and wide-set eyes sat cross-legged, fletching his arrows. The feathers were eagle, and came from birds he'd brought down himself. He was watched by another young man whose skin was covered in tattoos, who had positioned himself some distance off and was tuning his *komuz* with a plectrum. Satisfied that each of the three strings was chord-perfect, Tzan set aside the instrument, then picked up his horsehair fiddle. Painstakingly, he began to polish the wood. From behind, he heard a jangling of bangles, bracelets, anklets and chains growing louder. He continued to rub, even when the clinking was almost behind him, and accompanied by the soft fragrance of the scented orchids that grew wild in her homeland.

'If you buff any harder, you'll start a fire,' Liasa said.

Tzan lifted his gaze from the fiddle, following the curve of her knee, the swell of her breasts, the coins tied into her tumble of dark curls. Eventually he found himself looking into a pair of hazel-green eyes. Eyes which did not meet his in return, but watched the young man bent over his fletching jig. If Karas was aware of her, he did not glance up.

'It's too hot a day for a spark to ignite,' Tzan said, but she wasn't interested in his reply and had already started to speak.

'A man who puts so much effort into his work would make a wonderful lover, don't you think?'

'Some men are too interested in themselves to want to dilute the attention.'

'Karas isn't like that,' she retorted. 'Don't forget he is Gurdju and I am from Colchis. Perhaps he's only interested in marrying within his own tribe?'

'The Scythian nation comprises many people,' he agreed. 'Some intermarry, some don't.' Let her find out for herself that Karas's father had taken a Krk wife. Tzan resumed his polishing.

'You're right,' Liasa said at last. 'This heat would kill any spark dead.'

So she had heard. 'At least it's a dry heat,' he said. 'Not like the humidity we have to put up with at home, and thank Txa, we're spared the stink from the swamps.'

'I don't care, I hate this place.'

'Then why did you come?' Stupid question. The answer sat cross-legged a little way off, gluing eagle feathers to his shafts.

'See those peaks?' Liasa pointed to the east. 'Don't they just grimace at you like badly worn teeth? And the other range.'

'Taygetus.'

'The mountains look like they're running with blood in the sunrise.' She threw up her hands. 'And see those white tracks that zigzag up to the passes? They stand out like bloodless veins, and I tell you, Tzan, this country gives me the creeps.'

He waved his arm in a leisurely are. 'The valley's been tamed.'

'What wants tamed?' she flashed back, fixing on Karas again. 'Who in their right mind wants to work this rusty, red dust, when they can mould our heavy black Colchian soil in their hands? Can you smell the perfume of lilies on the breeze here? Can you, Tzan? Can you hear the waves of the Euxine sucking and spitting back pebbles?'

'I can hear the clucking of the pheasants Aeërtes brought for the King. Who is even more delighted with his gift, incidentally, now he knows he can eat them.'

Hazel eyes remained on Karas. 'The gorges of the Caucasus are lush and green. It never gets too hot up there, either.'

One minute she wanted humus-rich pastures. The next she wants snows eight months a year. 'Karas is a butterfly,' Tzan said slowly. 'He left the Caucasus years ago, Liasa, and never stays in one place for very long.'

'If he found the right woman, he might.'

Tzan picked up his komuz.

A noble young villager, honest and brave,
Owned a house, a herd, all things other men craved.
Everything, except the woman he loved.

'Stop it.'

He shrugged. 'I was just making a point.'

'Yes, well, it's not unrequited love.' When Liasa tossed her wild, gypsy curls, the coins in them chinked in defiance. 'Karas simply doesn't know me, that's all.'

'If you say so.' Tzan returned to his fiddle, and as he worked, the jaws of the panther on his forearm widened and closed.

'What happened to the tabby cat that followed you home from the city, all mangy and covered with bites?' She was reaching out to be friends again.

'It had tumours.' Tzan didn't want friends.

'Yes, but what happened to it?'

He tried to ignore her, but there were times when Liasa was like a dog with a bone. She just wouldn't let go.

'It was hanging around you for ages,' she said. 'Looking a whole lot sleeker for the scraps that you fetched it, then suddenly, after the full moon, it was gone.'

'So?'

'So I'm curious to know where it went.'

'Didn't anyone ever tell you, Liasa?' Tzan collected his instruments and stood up. 'Curiosity killed the cat.'

He turned and slowly walked back to the palace. Karas didn't look up from his arrows.

EIGHT

The Snow Goddess ruled from autumn to spring on the bleak peaks of Mount Taygetus. Child of the icy winds of the mountains, she smothered the landscape with her white, fleecy cloak, while her mother howled and her sisters wailed, and her brothers, the wolves, hunted in packs. But in summer, she slept. And while she dreamed inside her little sanctuary of pine, hares watched for hawks in the lush upland meadows, salamanders scuttled across the tracks in the woods, and jackdaws pecked at the stones of the dry river beds to flush out creepy-crawlies and worms.

'Sir.'

The uniformed soldier saluted. Clearly, the *Krypteia* were taking no chances this time around. He'd stationed a guard on the corpse.

'Sergeant.'

Lysander acknowledged the salute and pulled aside an oiled hide that had been hung across a cave in the rock. Iliona shivered. Sanctity had suffused every inch of the precinct where the horses laid down their lives for the Winds. Up here, despite the stunning views, menace seeped through the jagged rock. Crows cawed their hostility from the crags.

'She was found on the Acropolis exactly as you see her now.' Lysander brushed away the sarcophagus of loose ice with his hands. 'Naked and slashed almost to ribbons.'

'Such anger,' Iliona whispered to the girl on the floor. Sunlight had flooded the cave, showing that she could not have been more than twenty years old. 'Who could hate you so much?'

'Now there's the thing.' Lysander dropped to his knees beside her. 'In many societies, the spoils of war are divided according the number of enemy killed. For some, like the Egyptians, this means cutting off the left ear or perhaps the right hand, while the Gauls have a penchant for chopping off their opponents' heads. But the Scythians . . .'

He cleared the snow from around the victim's hair, revealing a torn, bloody patch over the forehead.

'The Scythians take scalps as proof of kill, but there's something else you need to know.'

Something balled in her throat. 'He's done it before.'

'So help me, I'll have those blabbermouth guards up on charges. I specifically told them not to breathe a word—'

'No one talked.'

'Then how—?'

Based on the number of bite marks and stabs, this was the work of a confident hand. 'I count the grains of sand on the shore, remember.'

'Which are probably fewer in number than these wounds.' He traced a few with his finger, and she saw they were curved. 'You see what I mean about the Scythian connection? The very word comes from their invention, a certain agricultural implement.'

Of course. The scythe. A large sickle, that cuts through grass and grain from a standing position, rather than having to bend. And which also meant that curved blades were sacred to them.

'I've seen similar wounds before,' he added, 'only much larger. They were made with a bill-hook.'

'Suggesting her killer used a miniature sickle,' she said perring closely. 'The small type used in religious rites, usually gold, though occasionally silver.'

'Hm.' A muscle twitched at the side of his cheek, which might have been cramp from straightening up. 'A sadistic but also a ritualistic murder. Is that not a contradiction in terms?'

'Unfortunately not.' She looked at the girl lying in her melting sarcophagus. 'How many before this one?'

'Did you know that when a body goes into the water, it very quickly sinks to the bottom? While it's down there, and apart from providing a feast for the fishes, it gradually bloats up with air, until three days later it's so buoyant, it bobs to the surface.'

'What does that have to do with the number of previous victims?'

'Because so far we've found two, and on both occasions, they surfaced three days after the full moon.'

And the delegation arrived three full moons back . . .

'What I don't understand,' he mused, 'is why this one wasn't thrown in the river.'

Good question. Most killers followed a pattern. 'Perhaps Abas disturbed him, forcing him to leave in a hurry – no, no.' She found the flaw in the argument straight away. 'Even the most confident murderer wouldn't be raping and slashing in so public a place, especially beneath a full moon.'

'Maybe he no longer feels compelled to hide the evidence.'

'But to deliberately dump a corpse in plain sight?'

'He might be throwing down a challenge. Catch me if you can.'

'Or it's his way of saying he's too clever to be caught.'

Something rumbled deep in his throat. 'He wouldn't be the first to make that mistake.'

No indeed, Iliona thought. The *Krypteia* was notorious for its patience and stealth, and though years might pass in which a killer believed he'd got away with it, sooner or later Nemesis caught up with him. And the first he'd know of it was the brush of cold metal slicing his windpipe, or a dagger ripping into his heart.

'If his previous victims didn't get the public exposure he wanted,' she said slowly, 'then leaving a mutilated corpse in full view is a pretty reliable way of getting talked about.'

'I didn't want panic when the first victim was found, and I certainly don't want it spreading now.' He ran his hands through his long warrior's hair. 'If it's publicity this bastard is after, he's in for a disappointment, because I've already passed word that she threw herself under a chariot, and that the kitchen slave was mistaken about what he saw.'

Poor Abas. Branded a liar, a neurotic, a drunk, take your pick. His character shredded for political ends.

Lysander stepped out into the sunlight. Iliona lingered at the girl's side, committing her features to memory. Dark, springy hair, a slightly hooked nose, full lips that would never break into a smile again.

'Were the other victims plump?' She blinked, as her eyes adjusted to the glare of the fierce summer sun. Although she couldn't see them, snow grouse clucked to one another in the scrub and the scent of broom wafted up on the breeze, overridden by leather and woodsmoke.

'Far from it. In fact the only thing the three have in common

are soft hands that are clearly not used to work,' he replied.
'Otherwise, the first had long, straight, dark hair, tiny waist,
and was probably in her thirty-fifth summer. The second was
two, maybe three years older, but taller than average, with
blonde hair verging almost on white—'

'Ah.'

'Ah?'

'I think I know why the bodies weren't claimed.'

Even these days, Cretans of both sexes would sometimes
bind their waists with copper girdles to keep them wasplike
(and no wonder their digestions suffered). Nordic peoples at
the top of the Amber Route tended to be handsome, blond
giants, while the girl in the cave bore Arabic features.

'The girls are foreign,' she said. 'Now maybe their ships
sailed without them, like the King suggested with the stuffed
rider, or else they could be prostitutes he picked up from the
docks.'

Brothels were state-owned and state-run to regulate the
brisk trade that was inevitable with a busy port and thousands of unmarried soldiers stationed in barracks. But, as
with any vibrant economy, there's always room for free enter-
prise. Freelance prostitutes were by no means uncommon.

Lysander leaned his shoulder against the rock face, folding
his arms over his chest. 'Now you see why I need you inside
the palace.'

'To interrogate suspects, search their rooms for gold sickles,
and sell out my temple while I'm about it?'

'I was going to say report back on them for me, but then
you're the interpreter.' His smile was like the ice that clung
to the peaks. 'You're bound to phrase these things so much
better.'

On a wide meander where the Eurotas ran sluggish, Doris
the laundry maid closed her eys, drew a deep breath and
made the sign of the horns with her index and little fingers.
Common sense said she ought to clump her feet and sing or
shout, anything to scare away the snakes that might be basking
down here on the stones. But when you're minding your own
business, pounding tunics against the rocks like you do every
day, and suddenly a bloated, grey corpse pops up under your
nose, common sense flies out the window. All right, that was

over a month ago now. But you don't forget something like that in a hurry! Doris approached with trepidation. Poor cow, she thought. The river had really made a mess of her, too. Inching closer, she peered nervously into the waters. Nothing monstrous bobbed up from the depths. She heaved a sigh of relief. But fancy no one claiming the body. How depressing was that? Must've fell in upstream, the other laundresses said, but Doris had her own theory on that. Suicide. That's what it was. Suicide.

'If I was so lonely that nobody'd miss me when I'd gone, I'd want to drown myself too,' she told a tortoise grumbling its way over the pebbles. 'Give me nightmares for ages, it did.'

Mainly because she'd thought it was the water demon coming to get her, but that was beside the point.

'Oh, well. Onwards and upwards.'

Satisfied the river held no more unpleasant surprises, she kept her fingers pointed nevertheless, to ward off the evil eye. You couldn't take chances, not with the Scythians. And since the head laundress broke her leg and Doris had been appointed to wash their shirts in her place, she'd hardly let her fingers relax. Mind, it was quality stuff, she'd give them foreigners that, she thought, plucking the shirts off the thorn bushes where she'd hung them to dry. And pretty enough, too, if you're the sort who likes garish. In the swirling Eurotas, fish dodged the reflection of a heron passing over. Butterflies danced round the wild mint. Wonder their womenfolk didn't go blind from all that close stitching—

'Damn.' Doris scowled at the last shirt she'd picked off. 'Still there, are you?' She'd tried salt, she'd tried *everything* to get them stains off. Would they budge? Would they heck, and that was the trouble with blood, wasn't it. Always a bugger to wash out.

'What am I supposed to do now?' she tutted to a frog plopping into the water. 'Tell the gaffer this fancy chemise thing's spoiled for good?'

Sod that for a lark, Doris thought, because she knew what'd happen if she owned up to something like that. She'd end up washing loincloths for the rest of her life, because they'd say she wasn't up to the job. Well, she was. She worked hard, and she was a lot more conscientious than most of the other palace laundresses, which is why she'd been assigned these fancy, fringed shirts in the first place!

'And if anyone thinks I'm giving that up in a hurry, then they're daft.'

After all. She rolled up the shirt, and tucked it under her arm. It wasn't like her life depended on it. Did it?

NINE

The palace had changed little in the three and a half years since Iliona walked in, the daughter of a respected aristocrat, and walked out a High Priestess. Fountains still splashed with deceit and distrust in courtyards of marble and bronze. Frescoes of battles, legends, heroes and gods concealed the same patchwork of intrigue and lies, while the rich, woven tapestries only muffled the whispers.

Due to something called 'urgent government assembly', the King was unable to meet with his esteemed and noble cousin for the moment. Instead he sent a flunkey to convey his heartfelt appreciation that Iliona had accepted his invitation to approve the enhancements to Eurotas, along with his deep regret at any inconvenience the current political crisis may be causing her.

'Tell him his cousin understands perfectly.'

Understands the political crisis was of his own making, accusing Athens when the problem was under his nose. Understands that two hundred pilgrims were dreading the moment when the sun dipped below the horizon, without their priestess on hand to reassure them. Understands the King was deliberately making her kick her heels, either to penalize her for previous infractions or to draw up a new campaign to oust her from her post, quite likely a combination of both—

'This way, my lady.'

The flunkey led her through a labyrinth of antechambers and stairwells lit by flambeaux and sconces, past exotic birds chatting in aviaries and monkeys screeching in cages, to a small room furnished with tables of exotic wood. The wood,

she noticed, was inlaid with mother-of-pearl, but it was the
plans and proposals that had been spread out and anchored with
an assortment of polished pebbles that drew the attention.

'If you need anything, there is a servant within earshot.'
The flunkey snapped his fingers and platters of bread, cheese
and olives appeared out of nowhere. Jugs of wine glided in
on silent feet. 'The King would be most offended if you were
not comfortable during the adjournment.'

Comfortable? In this bejewelled prison, seething with spies
and suspicion, how could she possibly be comfortable? But
her father. Oh, her father would have been right at home.

And the fragrant oils that burned in the braziers only masked
the stench of corruption . . .

Once the flunkey had gone, she took the runes from the
folds of her robes. The first she laid on the drawing of the
new watercourse that would pass behind the temple. *Eta*.
The sun who sees everything, but who also watches, which
is not the same thing. Not at all. *Tau*, the rune of separation, she placed on the steps that were designed to bridge
the river and the precinct. Finally, she set *Omega* between
the architect's neatly drawn treasuries. *Omega*, for difficulty,
but also completion.

She poured herself a mug of wine and stared into the cup.
It all boiled down to the same thing, didn't it? Finality.
Inevitablity. Death—

How old was she? Ten? when she first suspected her father
to be a cold-blooded killer? That, day by day, drip by drip,
he was poisoning the King and there was nothing she could
do to stop it? To run to the King would have meant her entire
family put to death, but the worst part wasn't bearing such
a burden on shoulders so young. Hell, it wasn't even when
the poison drove him to slash himself to ribbons. It was
knowing the King went to his grave still believing her father
to be the best friend he'd ever had . . .

She stared beyond the dark, red, swirling liquor. Her
father believed he was acting in Sparta's best interests. That
his country would be stronger, richer, more powerful with
the present incumbent on the throne, and the irony of it
was, he was right. But deceit is an acid that erodes confidence and trust, and who knows how many other monsters
had slipped poison into a best friend's food, an uncle's

wine, had plotted their own brother's downfall with a smile?
Now she, too, was sucked into the web of intrigue and
deception.

Socrates once said, *If you had no memory, you could not
remember that you ever enjoyed pleasure in the past, and no
recollection of present pleasure would remain with you.*

Ah, but Socrates was never ten years old and forced to
watch a tragedy unfold, because he'd been powerless to stop
it. Nor had Socrates ever been pregnant with a monster that
had swelled and kicked inside his belly, or he, too, would
have pushed such memories into the deep, dark recesses of
his brain and prayed, not for recollection, but that they never
saw the light of day again.

Except Iliona's prayers had gone unanswered, and once
more impotence held her in its grip . . .

In order to unmask a killer, she was obliged to turn her
temple from a humble – all right, not so humble, but at least
authentic – place of worship into a showcase for politicians'
wealth, driving out the very people who depended on it and
who needed Eurotas the most.

All on account of one tiny little puppy.

Was it worth it?

When it turned its big, brown eyes on her, would she
have still snatched it from the sacrificial altar? Too late
now to re-write history, and to be honest, she wasn't sure
what made her do it at the time. Goats, bulls, sheep (even,
once, her favourite horse) had laid down their lives for the
gods, and she'd never batted an eyelid. But that night, when
she met the terror in its eyes, saw it quivering amid the
shouting, stomping, and blaring of horns and trumpets,
something snapped. And when the boys came yammering
down the path, screaming at the top of their lungs, it seemed
the natural thing to do. Grab the puppy, stuff it in her
saddlebag, then hide it in her chambers until the fuss died
down.

Iliona did not drink the wine. Instead, she gathered up the
runes and folded them inside her fist. *Eta, Tau* and *Omega*.
Watching. Parting. Death.

Perhaps the Queen of Darkness had the last laugh, after
all.

*   *   *

'I'm so pleased my husband was called away to Thebes.' The King's sister, a striking woman in her early forties, slid off a couch fragranced with sandalwood, leaving her exhausted lover sprawled over the damask. 'There are always such pleasurable compensations.'

Her quarters on the upper storey afforded stunning views across the palace compound, and even though Sparta prided itself on being a city without walls, sharp eyes kept sentry from strategically placed watchtowers, while guards in red kilts and bronze breastplates patrolled with clockwork regularity. With every city state a potential enemy and every *helot* a prospective assassin, taking chances was out of the question.

'With him away, I'll be able to see much more of you,' Ariadne added, peering over the gallery to where the sun was setting on one of the many splendid courtyards.

'I didn't think there was much more of me to see.'

'Oh, you'd be surprised,' she purred. 'Wait until I – *shit.*'

'What's wrong?'

'I'd have put money on that bitch defying my brother's wishes.'

'Now which particular bitch would that be, my sweet?'

He padded over to see who had caused Ariadne's features to twist into a snarl this time. Looking down, he saw peacocks strutting, women chatting at their looms and small boys galloping round the pool on hobby-horses, while a harpist rippled soft chords in the corner. A gentle enough scene, until he followed the focus of her anger where crisp, white, pleated robes contrasted with the soft and colourful folds of the other women's garments, and whose fair hair gleamed from the light of sconces set high in the walls.

'Ah. The lovely Iliona.' Strong arms slipped round Ariadne's waist from behind. 'Didn't you expect the High Priestess to obey the wishes of her sovereign king?'

'No, I bloody didn't,' she hissed back. 'In fact, I was banking on her opposition, if you must know.'

'Maybe she's come to reject his proposals face to face.'

'Maybe pigs'll fly.'

On previous occasions, Iliona had returned the King's orders in shreds, in ashes, or, on one notable incident, tied to a dead carrier pigeon. Compliance wasn't among the High Priestess's virtues, nor subtlety one of her strengths.

'Eurotas should be mine.' Ariadne twisted a strand of hair round her finger, conscious of the bleach that had coarsened it and robbed it of its shine. 'He promised it to me three and a half years ago, and I don't know what that conniving little bitch said or did to change his mind, but at the last minute he appointed her in my place. However . . .' She wagged a short, but perfectly manicured finger. 'He's had it up to here with her, I've heard him say so many times, and believe me, when I take over, the temple wouldn't be overrun with the vermin it is now.'

'I'm sure it won't. Come back to bed.'

He threw himself back on the couch and closed his eyes.

'I'll have treasuries and depositories lined up from here to the coast, if that's what my brother wants,' she said, remaining at the gallery. 'A solid walkway of marble, gold and statuary, if he so desires, with enough fountains to make the river god run dry.'

'Ah, but would you have thought to turn it into an oracular shrine?'

'Pff.' Ariadne's sneer showed what she thought of that. 'Smoke and mirrors! For pity's sake, what does she think this is, bloody Delphi?' She watched until Iliona disappeared back inside the building then returned to her lover, tossing her hair over her shoulder as she straddled him. 'That bitch can no more predict the future than my dog.'

A hand cupped her breast. 'The future is what we make it,' he said, his mouth closing over her nipple.

Ariadne pulled away sharply. 'Just who the hell's side are you on?'

'It's not a question of sides,' Lysander said, flipping her over and anchoring her wrists with his hands. 'As always, my dear Ariadne, it's a question of who ends up on top.'

Her laugh was deep and husky. 'You are a wicked, wicked man,' she said, abandoning herself to pleasure.

'You have no idea,' he whispered to the pillow. No idea at all.

TEN

The house of the Arabian frankincense merchant sat halfway up a hill overlooking the harbour. It was a small house made of mud bricks covered with stucco, and was quite unassuming, since the merchant's permanent residence lay across the ocean, fronting a very different gulf. And the merchant missed it. He missed the hawk-billed turtles, that made such a delicious stew. He missed the mangroves, and the eerie sounds that emanated from them, even the yellow-bellied sea snakes, and the houses built of reeds perched high on stilts. Unfortunately, this was nothing compared to the pain of separation felt by his wife. Being young, and a woman, it was only natural, he supposed, that she should pine for her mother and her father, as well as her seven brothers and two sisters, though perhaps if her womb had been blessed with a child, the ache might have eased.

He ran the thin scarf through his fingers. It smelled of chamomile.

How many times had he promised Ay-Mari that he would pack up the business here and return home? Somehow, though, deals always cropped up, but this was a good thing, he told his wife. So much custom will make us rich, and if we invest in a little myrrh, a little cinnamon, a little cassia, it will make us richer still. Which, of course, it had. Many times Lokman had looked inside his treasure chests and found the levels rising, and all because the Greeks had found that with peace came luxury. And few things were more luxurious than frankincense resin.

He pressed the stole to his face and buried his nose in its softness.

They burned it in their temples, they burned it in their houses, they handed it over as gifts and as bribes. Lokman's was particularly expensive, because he refused to take short cuts, a quality that stood him in good stead with the pernickety Spartans. They appreciated attention to detail.

As did his newest client.

Lokman pinched the bridge of his nose to ease the pounding in his head. He must admit, he was surprised when the Scythian first made contact with him. He would have expected them to undertake their own negotiations, not employ the services of a middleman. However, once the client had outlined the delicacy of the situation (not to mention the risks both parties would be running), Lokman understood the need for a middleman. It was just unfortunate that he had not been able to confide fully in his bride.

Sorry, my darling, but for the next few weeks I will be working even longer hours. One can't rush double-crossing the Spartans, y'know.

No, no, no, of course he couldn't tell Ay-Mari. He'd just said that, good news, he'd secured a contract for certain imports that would not only mean retirement for him and a life of comfort for her, but which also meant he would be booking their passage home very soon.

'Do you mean it?' Her face had filled with joy. 'We will return home before the seas close again this year?'

The seas closed after the autumn equinox. Lokman would need to be gone long before then. He'd kissed Ay-Mari's forehead.

'I swear it,' he'd said.

This was the first time he'd been in a position to give his oath. Seeing the happiness in her eyes, and feeling the strength of her arms as she hugged him, he'd experienced a surge of affection that he'd never felt before. A surge that, at the time, he believed had gone both ways.

'You wished to speak with me, my lord?'

'Yes, yes, come in.' He laid the scarf across his knees and beckoned his wife's handmaid into the windowless chamber that served as his office. 'I will come straight to the point, Nori.' He clasped his hands across his belly. 'My wife has not returned home for several days now—'

'Oh, I wouldn't say that, sir.'

'Do not take me for a fool, woman. I may be a busy man, but I am not blind to the fact that this is not the first time Ay-Mari has failed to come home.' Only her longest absence so far. 'Does she stay with her lover?'

The old woman's face reddened. 'No, no, my lord, she is faithful to you—'

'My bride has been unfaithful from the first month of our marriage,' he barked. 'Now tell me the truth, else I will have your nose and your lip slit for lying.'

The maid started to tremble. 'She may have been seeing a young man,' she stammered. 'But—'

'Is he one of us?'

Nori was too frightened to shake her head, but he could see the truth in her eyes. 'Enough,' he said. 'Go.'

'Please, sir, you—'

'Do you hear me? I said, go.'

For several minutes, maybe even an hour, Lokman remained at his desk with his hands clasped in front of him. On the left sat a pile of letters and reports that had been prepared by his scribe. On the right, a stack of notes that he had scribbled himself. A dish of frankincense resin burned in the middle between them. He sighed.

After his people consummated the marriage act, it was their custom to sit over incense to purify themselves, and they were forbidden to touch food or even utensils until they had washed every inch of their bodies with water. But Ay-Mari was young. She would be swayed, indeed attracted, by non-Arab ways, and it wasn't difficult to picture her lying naked in the foreigner's arms, drinking wine and eating sweetmeats, her sacred rituals abandoned in the name of lust.

Lokman picked up the scarf. Rippled the fringe through his fingers.

It had been a mistake, he realized now, to bring his bride to a far country. At the time, he'd hoped that the very Greekness of it would stimulate her mind and her senses, compensating for the hours he'd be spent locked away with his clients, especially with the promise of riches at the end. The merchant was not stupid. He only had to look in the mirror to see that Ay-Mari hadn't married him for his looks or his youth, which was merely a memory these days. On the other hand – he inhaled the chamomile scent of it – he had been able to bring luxury and status that she could not otherwise have known, and although he had hoped for fidelity in return, he was not surprised when she strayed after so short a time. His only condition was that her lovers be Arab.

Now this foreigner had turned her into a whore.

And the sad thing was, Lokman would have done anything in the world for Ay-Mari.

He swallowed back the pain and stood up. Attention to detail, that was the key. Attention to detail at all times. For instance, he would not even contemplate buying frankincense that had been taken from trees in which the Phoenician gum, storax, had not been burned. This was not out of concern for the workers' safety, where the smoke drove off the flying snakes which made their home in the branches. He needed to ensure no impure creatures were present when the resin was collected. Attention to detail, you see?

'Kem!' At the call, his manservant came running. 'Shave me.'

'But sir, I shaved you only—'

'I am well aware of the timescale. You will do it again, please.'

'Very good, sir.'

In true Arab style, Kem took the razor round his master's head in a circle from the temples down. When he was finished, he rubbed sandalwood balm into the scalp.

'Now fetch my green leather slippers and my finest turban.'

When he was dressed, Lokman put on his signet ring, tidied a desk which was already immaculate, folded his wife's stole into four and draped it over the back of his chair. Only when the preparations had been completed to his complete satisfaction did Lokman invoke his gods, then slash the arteries in both his thighs.

ELEVEN

'I had a horse like that once.'

Aeërtes looked up from where he was stroking one of the sleek, white stallions in His Majesty's paddocks. Across the way, the white stone stable block shimmered in the throbbing heat. Too hot to run the horses round the inner ring or train them in the harness. Instead, the horses clustered in small groups beneath the shade pines, swishing the flies away with their tails and occasionally snickering to one another across the flower-filled meadows.

'You were privileged,' Aeërtes said. 'He's a magnificent beast.'

Weren't they all, Iliona thought, and didn't mean the horses.

'I am flattered that the High Priestess of Eurotas takes the trouble to make my acquaintance.' The envoy performed a one-two-three gesture with his hand against his body. 'The King speaks very warmly of his esteemed cousin.'

Civility, charm and hardly a trace of an accent, the signs of a true diplomat. Or a spy.

'Who in turn speaks highly of you,' she replied, even though, for all she knew, he might have called them liars, cheats and thieves, since a week had passed without her summons to the royal presence. Time that she had at least put to good use, she supposed, given that it had enabled her to study the thirty-seven men and four women in the delegation.

Representatives from the different clans that comprised this young and ambitious nation, some had flat faces and high cheekbones, showing they hailed from the Caucasus, and beyond. Others were brawnier, with red hair and stocky frames that denoted the Danube connection. But whether listening to a bard, betting on cock fights or simply nibbling sweet-meats beside the fountain, the majority of the delegation had an air of visitors enjoying the diversions, but who'd far rather be home among the bosom of their family. Several compensated for the loss by stuffing themselves to excess, others drank until they threw up and many, if not most, were spectacularly unfaithful. But five showed no such inclinations.

The first time Iliona had noticed this little sub-group was from horseback, when she'd been heading for yet another fruitless visit to the palace. They'd retained their red boots and pantaloons, she noticed, but, in an effort to keep cool, had discarded their kaftans in favour of brightly coloured, loose linen shirts. Three of them had been sitting with their backs to an apple tree heavy with ripening fruit. Aeërtes and the bodyguard had remained standing, with their feet planted squarely apart. At first, she was struck only by the parallel: five men, five corpses. Silly really, and whether it was Aeërtes's beard that made the connection in her mind, it seemed to her that the two standing corresponded with the two male corpses, the others with the women who had been so sadistically abused. In fact, had it not been for that rather foolish little vignette (and perhaps the cold eyes of the bodyguard), she wouldn't have given them a second glance. A handful of Scythians shooting the breeze was hardly noteworthy material.

Until the men on the ground stood up, and all five strolled across the orchard in a manner that sent prickles down Iliona's spine.

Sparta bred warriors. Harmony of movement was key to the discipline and here, without doubt, was a band that trained together, worked together, fought together and who now, having just concluded one important summit, were set to embark on another. She'd stooped, ostensibly to let her horse munch on the orchard's lush grass. While a theory congealed in her stomach . . .

'The King tells me you count the grains of sand on the shore and measure the drops in the ocean,' Aeërtes was saying.

They, too, were standing in the shade of an old stone pine, where the scent of its needles filled the sultry air and tree crickets rasped like blunted saws. Iliona smiled. 'Surely you, of all people, Aeërtes, understand the difference between rumour and fact.'

'Only too well,' he acknowledged. 'To most people, we are the sons of Amazon whores, who happily chop off their own breasts that they may better draw back their bows.'

'You use the skulls of your enemies to drink victory toasts.'

'We flay men alive and use their skin for vellum.'

'Don't forget you bathe in virgins' blood and howl at the moon.'

'What can I say?' He spread his arms wide. 'We are savages.'

She laughed back. 'We all are, Aeërtes. Children more often than most.'

'Mine certainly. Four boys. Imagine the noise in our house! You?'

Did he notice her falter? 'Unfortunately, the gods did not see fit to bless my marriage with children.' Hardly surprising, given the contraception techniques she'd employed. 'Perhaps if they had, my husband and I would not have divorced.'

Another lie. The bastard slept with her sister, wasn't that grounds enough, and in any case, birthing one ogre was enough for anyone's lifetime. 'Though on balance,' she continued, making light of the subject, 'I would have preferred girls. They are much more amenable creatures.'

'Is that so.' In the blink of an eye, the laughter turned sour and the change of subject was swift. 'This horse,' he said coldly. 'I am thinking of buying it for my oldest son, to celebrate his twelfth summer.'

'He's a fine stallion,' she agreed, remembering what she knew about Aeërtes. That his position was neither elected nor hereditary, but came from seizing control in a military coup, backed by the powerful Amazon priestesses of Colchis. She wondered whether it was because he could not have achieved his position without them, or just women in general, that made him so bitter. 'But the King breeds his horses for chariot racing,' she continued. 'Before deciding, you would be wise to put this one through its paces.'

How had Jocasta described Aeërtes? A hawk, whose prey had just fallen through his talons? Physicians by their very profession were perceptive, so why had she offered no plausible explanation for being at the Cenotaph, instead of Hecate's shrine, when the corpse in the willows was discovered? Free or enslaved, all Greeks shared the same religious beliefs.

'An excellent suggestion,' Aeërtes was saying, as though the idea of a trial hadn't crossed his mind. 'Gentlemen?'

At his signal, the other four strode across from where they'd been leaning against the gate.

Nearby, a grey-haired groom was languidly baling stale water out of the drinking trough to replenish it with fresh, and what irony, she thought, watching him work. For one thing, a bucketful over his own body wouldn't hurt, he must stink to high heaven, and for another, where long hair for warriors was a symbol of strength, for *helots* it had become the mark of defiance. *You can dress us in rough clothing and bend our backs till they break*, was the message, *but you cannot make us cut our hair*. An admirable sentiment. In theory. Because when had peace ever come about, when one side was continually taunting the other?

'Karas.' Aeërtes beckoned forward a young man with

wide-set eyes that had a tendency to slant into slits. His dark curls were beaded at the tips, to give them weight, and his skin glistened with the same scented oils. 'Would you be so kind as to give this fine fellow a trial?'

Karas flashed a grin that encompassed Iliona, Aeërtes and seemingly half of Sparta, stretching his mouth to its limits, yet revealing neither warmth nor emotion. Just lots of even, and extremely white, teeth.

'With pleasure, my lord.'

Bounding across the paddock, and seemingly heedless of the heat that beat down on the land, he pulled off his shirt and tied it round the trunk of another pine. Grabbing a thick, red felt saddle from the fence, he threw it over the stallion's back, tossed a quiver full of arrows over his own, and though it would probably come as a disappointment to many people, the arrow sack was fashioned from soft yellow leather, rather than lily-white human skin. He kicked the horse into a gallop, and Iliona noticed the groom had used the performances as an excuse to stop work, watching arrow after arrow pumped into the shirt. Twenty in less than a minute. And the amazing thing was, that grin never faltered.

'I would appreciate the Lady Iliona's opinion,' Aeërtes said, while Karas tweaked the arrowheads out of the bark.

'What can I say? That has to be the most impressive performance I've ever seen.'

'No, no, no.' Aeërtes tutted in irritation. 'He took far too long to get started. Should have found his rhythm earlier and took too wide a loop on the turn. I will have a word with him later. We cannot afford errors when we stage our display for the New Year celebrations.'

Considering that was nearly three weeks off, Iliona wondered what refinements were needed, because to her mind his performance was faultless.

'I was referring to the mount,' he said, 'not the rider. Should I buy him?'

She studied the stallion, its flanks gleaming with sweat from its exertions. The groom shambled over with a bucket for it to drink from.

'Like I said, Aeërtes, the King breeds his horses for speed. If you want your son to break his neck, then this would be the perfect choice.'

The Scythian chuckled. 'You may or may not count the drops in the ocean, but you certainly have the measure of me. You're quite right, though. I was thinking of myself, not the boy.' He brushed a speck of dust off his pantaloons. 'Equally, though, I do not wish to take him home a donkey.'

'Then why don't you choose a horse from my personal herd? My gift, one spiritual leader to another.'

'My lady!' He laid his hand across his breast. 'I am not sure which stuns me the most. Your generosity, the fact that you consider me an instructor of minds, or that Greek women own land in their own right.'

'Only Spartan women,' she corrected, and oh, he was an instructor of minds, all right. Aeërtes was a natural-born leader. 'Unfortunately, the rest do not share the same freedom.'

On the contrary. As respectable wives and daughters, they weren't even allowed out of the house unless it was to attend religious ceremonies.

'Then you are to be congratulated,' he said. 'Not only for your independence, but also the opportunity to work with such wonderful creatures.' He smiled. 'In many ways, Scythia is similar to Greece, in that we, too, are a composite nation. The difference is, where you share the same language and religion, our bond is our mutual love of horses.'

'Nearly all our city states are remote and isolated lands,' she replied. It was why they spent so much time at war with one another. Fertile territory was a prize worth the winning. 'Many of the peasants won't even have seen a horse that isn't a statue, but whether Scythian, Greek, Egyptian or Arab, there are far more basic elements that bind people together than language, religion and horseflesh.'

'Humour?'

'Not necessarily.' Tell a joke to an Abyssinian and he'll laugh till his sides split. Tell the same joke to a Gaul, and he'll stare at you as though you had two heads. 'I was thinking more of dancing, music and games.'

'Then let us bind our cultures together right now! Tzan!'

At his prompt, a young man with suspiciously black hair and whose body was covered with tattoos picked up an instrument, the likes of which Iliona had never seen. Long-necked and with only three strings, he plucked a few chords, cleared his throat, then launched into a rich and haunting ballad.

It didn't matter that she didn't understand a word. As his voice stretched the notes so that they actually hung in the still, summer air, it seemed to her that Tzan encapsulated the love and pain of all mankind. Goosepimples crawled up her arms, and it wasn't purely the song. As he strummed, Tzan's whole body became one with his instrument, causing stags to leap and wolves to snarl through the open drawstring of his shirt.

'Now Barak.'

Aeërtes snapped his fingers before the last note had died, and the youngest of the group, the one with the red band round his forehead, rolled open the large leather pouch round his waist, exposing six broad-bladed knives. He had a long, pointed nose that matched his sharp, aristocratic features, and Iliona thought that his was probably the only head of hair that was naturally curly. Drawing out two of the knives, Barak began to juggle them in the air, and then, as he got into his rhythm, added a third, then a fourth, then a fifth, until finally he was juggling all six razor-sharp blades. She didn't dare take her eyes off him, until thud-thud-thud, they whizzed into a fence post, to form an almost perfect vertical line.

'But now, if you will excuse me,' Aeërtes said, bowing. 'I must rejoin the delegation. There are a number of important points in the draft agreement that need thrashing out before we meet with the Council again in the morning.'

Four turned as one. Only the bodyguard remained, as though carved of stone.

She turned to him with a smile. 'And what trick does Sebastos have lined up for me?'

Eyes as dark and as hard as seasoned oak beams bored into the back of her skull. 'Sebastos is not a performing bear,' he growled, heaving the red felt saddle over his shoulder. 'He leaves the conjuring to sorcerers, showmen and—' he paused '—priests.'

Here is a man who trusts no one, she thought, watching him stride back to the palace. But, by the same token, the man who doesn't trust is not to be trusted.

Across the way, stable boys were mucking out, cleaning the reins and polishing the bronzework on the harnesses. Engineers serviced the chariots in the sheds, greasing the axles and testing the balance. Others applied paint and varnish where it had flaked off.

'Does Aeërtes strike you as the type to need four second opinions on a horse?' the groom drawled through a mouthful of gravel.

Iliona jumped. *'Lysander?'*

'Invariably the best place to hide is in plain sight. It never fails.' He washed the flour out of his hair, and, as he untied it, the mark of defiance turned back into a symbol of pride.

'They came here for privacy,' she said.

'A conference of war?'

'Who knows.' How many times had the *Krypteia* been prowling round Eurotas, disguised as a merchant, a *helot*, a cripple, she wondered? 'I'm more concerned with why Aeërtes was so keen to impress me.'

'Why shouldn't he? You are a High Priestess, whose King speaks exceedingly highly of her.'

As she said. A man who doesn't trust is not to be trusted.

'Incidentally,' he murmured, 'that was a very generous gesture of yours.' The charcoal hollows under his eyes drained with the rest of the grime into the meadow. 'Offering Aeërtes one of your own horses.'

'I can afford to be generous,' she said. 'When I'm sending the *Krypteia* my bill.'

Something twitched at the side of his mouth. She wouldn't like to swear it was a sign of endorsement.

'So then.' He shook himself dry, like a dog. Or rather, the wolf that ran in sheep's clothing. 'What did you make of your first close encounter with our Scythian friends?'

Iliona turned her eyes to the hills, where provisions such as oil, wine and cheeses were stored in caves in the summer to prevent them from turning rancid. She listened to the cry of the eagles soaring over the peaks, to the skylarks hovering above the fields of ripe barley, to the crickets rasping in the long grass. And through the wispy branches of the shade pine, the rays of the sun burned her face.

'I know why you left the corpse in the willows,' she said.

In many ways, Scythia is similar to Greece, in that we, too, are a composite nation.

Aeërtes was right. Instead of city states, tribes from the Danube right round to the Caucasus had banded together for the sake of prosperity and peace. As a consequence, they had grown powerful enough to invade countries as far afield as

Mesopotamia and Syria, and, at one point, had even threatened Palestine and Judah. But whilst every Scythian
worshipped the sun and the moon, there were vast differences in the way they dealt with death.

'The one thing they all believe, though, is that fire is the
sun's holy gift and therefore must never be defiled with flesh
of any kind.'

That was one of the first things that had struck her. The delegation ate their meat boiled, braised, even raw, but would not
touch it if it had been cooked on a spit. A girl with coins in
her hair called Liasa had explained this, and it was from talking
to her that Iliona also discovered that certain Western tribes
laid their dead, naked, on ox-hides that hadn't been tanned,
knowing the stench would quickly attract vultures. These hides
were subsequently mounted on poles in sacred burial grounds,
and then, once the bones had been picked clean, they were puri-
fied in fire and buried.

'You're waiting for the bones to fall through the branches,'
Iliona told Lysander. 'To see who comes to collect them.'

'And you say you can't see through the eyes of the blind.'

She was in no mood for facetiousness. 'The clans of the
Krymean Peninsular inter their dead in corbelled stone vaults,'
she said, 'while others lay theirs to rest in square pits in the
earth, their possessions buried alongside them.'

He leaned his hip against the tree, folding his arms over
his chest. 'So?'

'So on the night of the festival, three bodies were found
in three different locations. Each was the recipient of ritualistic treatment, but in three contrasting ways.'

Lysander continued to let the pine take his weight, but it
seemed to her that his posture had stiffened. 'Are you
suggesting there are three different killers?'

Iliona had had a week in which to strengthen her theory.

'One man acting alone couldn't have mounted that rider,
any more than one man could have tied a corpse to the top
of the willows, so no, I don't think there are three different
killers.' She stared across at the snow trapped on the high
peaks, where, squinting, she could just about make out the
tiny shrine with its garland of cornel. Then she turned to the
man with eyes like the Snow Goddess's brother, the wolf. 'I
think it's more sinister than that.' She paused, checking her

theory over and over again, and finding the pieces fitted only too well. 'It's my belief these Scythians hunt in a pack, and that the pack is made up of the men you saw here: Aeërtes, Tzan, Barak, Karas and Sebastos.'

Would he laugh? Snort? Applaud her intellect? She waited. 'But?'

As always, it was the response she least expected.

'But . . .' And this was the hard bit. 'The girl is different,' she said. 'There was no reverence with her body.' In fact, quite the reverse. She'd been hacked and bitten, raped and abused, then dumped like one would throw waste on the middens. 'The attack was savage and angry, but the crucial point is, the killer took her scalp. Not for practical purposes, proof of his share of the victory spoils. He took this as a souvenir. A trophy, if you like. Something he can take out and look at whenever he wants, his way to re-live the moment.'

Lysander said nothing, and she wondered how she, an aristocrat, an educated and enlightened one at that, imagined the *Krypteia* would be camouflaged in the undergrowth or hiding behind rocks, while they spied on traitors and rebels. Eventually he prised himself away from the trunk.

'I wondered how long it would take for you to come round to my way of thinking,' he said. 'Now for goodness sake, don't keep the King hanging around any longer. It's making His Majesty grumpy.'

TWELVE

Jocasta unlocked the door to her *pharmakion*, savouring the emptiness and silence. Any second now and the first of the toothaches, ear-aches or boils would come trickling through the door, and suddenly the day would be over before she knew it. Then the evening would be swallowed up mixing salves and rolling pastilles, crushing bean meal for poultices and blending egg whites with astringents for sore eyes, checking potions in their cauldrons while infusions drip-drip-dripped slowly into bowls. But for one rare, precious moment, the room was quiet.

Dust motes, dancing through the sunbeams, made themselves at home on shelves lined with bottles, jars and boxes, each neatly labelled with papyrus and ink. Bronze instruments gleamed from hooks on the walls – scalpels, probes, cauteries, clamps – bunches of herbs hung from hooks in the beams. Something else Jocasta had to fit in to her schedule. Gathering plants from the river banks, the valleys, the woods and the hills, and she cast a professional eye over the bouquets in their various stages of desiccation. Purple sage, coltsfoot, horehound and hyssop. Lavender, violet and thyme. Without herbs, she thought, there could be no healing.

Without healing, what would she be?

The question scared and comforted her in equal measures. Scared, because without her skills, she would be just another *helot* breaking her back in the fields. Perversely, the very reason that brought so much comfort. And every day, she thanked Apollo for giving her mother, her grandmother, and her mother before that, the wisdom that allowed her to repair her people's bodies, minds and spirits. Life for *helots* was a tough grind with precious little reward, but at least, at Eurotas, she was in a position to make things easier for them. But for how much longer?

'Dear me, what have we got here?' She bent down and gently prised open the hand of a four-year-old girl, whose face was crumpled with pain. 'Looks like someone tried to cuddle a bee.'

'I only wanted to be friends,' the girl sniffed. 'But it bit me.'

'That's because bees aren't like your ginger pussycat, darling.' Jocasta tweaked the child's nose to distract her while she extracted the sting with her bronze tweezers. 'They don't like being cuddled or stroked, so whenever you see one, you give him a big wave. Bees *love* being waved at.'

She dried the girl's tears, kissed her swollen palm better and handed her a stem of candied angelica for being brave. Next, she treated a face burn with a salve she'd prepared from the mucilage of lilies, set the fractured arm of a field hand with palm-fibre splints, then tied a leather tourniquet round the wheelwright's thigh while she stitched the gash together.

'Next time you trip over a ploughshare,' she told her next

patient, peeling off the filthy bandage and cleansing his swollen ankle with an infusion of sorrel, 'don't wait until the wound is infected before coming to see me.'

'Well, there's the thing.' The ploughman chuckled, as she slapped on a poultice of yarrow and plantain. 'I wasn't planning to trip over it again.'

This would be gone in the blink of an eye, this badinage, this banter, this healing. The minute that architect walked in last week, setting his team of surveyors to measure, pace and peg things out, Jocasta knew her days at Eurotas were numbered. A new treasury here, a water course there, there was even talk of building embassies for other city states to move in and do business, and she wasn't stupid. As things stood now, the King was barely tolerating his cousin as High Priestess. When the improvements were finished, he certainly wouldn't sanction a *helot* in the role of temple physician.

She sorted out a nappy rash and treated yet another weeping sore, and thought, with her gone, who'd massage cypress, pine and rosemary oils into the joints of the labourers who worked the King's precious land? For *helots*, the river was both a blessing and a curse. It irrigated the valley, making it fertile and rich, yet at the same time the dampness took a dreadful toll. How many hours had Jocasta spent, mixing gargles for their sore throats, brewing syrups of horseradish, and infusing the flowering tops of hyssop for their chesty coughs? All that would disappear with his new developments – and then who could the poor bastards turn to for help?

Bathing a particularly nasty case of ringworm, it was the hypocrisy she couldn't abide. For the sake of clinging to her job, Iliona had sold out the very folk who depended on her, and they were all the same, these Spartans, underneath. When push came to shove, the High Priestess turned out to be no different from the rest of them. A self-centred, heartless bitch.

'My, my, this is a cosy little arrangement you have here.' The schoolmaster strolled into the treatment room, a hair's breadth away from a swagger.

Well, well, well. 'So you finally got that blister on your arse, from sitting under your awning for too long?'

Needless to say, that thin mouth didn't crack. 'This is for you.' He laid a loaf on her consulting couch, and it looked as stale and unappetizing as he did.

'Is this the bread of life to share, or have you just come down here for a loaf?'

Humour went the same way as irony. 'Do you know what this is?' he asked, drawing a piece of folded papyrus from his tunic.

Inside, was a small wad of pale brown resin. 'The aroma is too herbal for frankincense.' Jocasta sniffed again, this time slowly and more deeply. 'Hemp?'

'Correct.' He sounded surprised, as though he didn't expect her to know the answer, and was disappointed that he couldn't demonstrate his superiority. 'Burned in a hot tripod, it releases an intoxicating odour, in much the same way as the seeds of the hemp do.'

She squeezed the lump between her thumb and forefinger. It was solid, and also rather sticky. 'Are you proposing we char this together and ride the clouds on its fumes, as a prelude to a night of romance and passion?'

'Sarcasm does you no credit, and if you were my wife, I would whip you for your insolence.'

'Believe me, if I was your wife, I'd whip myself.'

His lips pinched white, but he did not pursue it. 'These are your instructions. On the very last night of the year, when our masters and overlords are engaged in feast and revelry, you will break this up and burn the pieces in tripods dotted throughout the temple complex.'

According to the calendar nailed to the wall of her treatment room, the New Year was eighteen days away. It would be cause for extra special celebrations, too, since this year it coincided with the Harvest Moon. And since when had *helots* taken to making citizens feel better about themselves, she wondered?

'Define tripods plural,' she said aloud. 'There's not enough here to intoxicate a mouse.'

'When you examine the bread, you will see it has been hollowed out to conceal a large block of the resin.' The school-master leaned closer and lowered his voice. 'Such blocks are being distributed to sympathizers all over the city, and immediately the bonfire is lit on the top of Mount Parnon, that is the signal to burn the hemp.' His lip curled. 'Fucking idiots won't notice. When their spirits rise, they'll write it off to drink and jollity, but the point is, the fumes will also put the bastards into a deep torpor.'

'Won't it put me into one, as well?'

'Not if you lock yourself away, and then, when the time comes that you need to enter the contaminated area, hold a damp cloth over your mouth and nose.'

When what time comes . . .? 'And exactly what might be the point of Spartans having so much fun, while we *helots* huddle away in sober little corners?'

'Bandage my hand or my arm or something, so people can see I came to you for treatment.'

'You didn't answer me.'

'I am the head of Vixen Squadron,' he snapped. 'I will explain as and when I see fit, and in my own time. Now hop to it.'

In the name of authenticity, Jocasta dug out the foulest smelling poultice she could find. Strange, but slugs under salt didn't recoil half as fast as schoolmasters with a stench beneath their nose.

'The opportunity will never be better,' he said, turning his head as far away as possible. 'With the army on campaign, the state is vulnerable but vigilant. New Year's Eve is the one night when that vigilance slackens, since we *helots* also like to let our hair down and celebrate.' He paused. 'This year, though, we shall celebrate with victory over our oppressors.'

Jocasta continued to bind the supposedly broken arm. 'It can't work,' she said. 'We may outnumber citizens by twenty to one, but you won't find the artisan classes standing idly by while women and children are slaughtered in their thousands.'

The lower classes might lack rights, but they didn't lack freedom, and many of them made a lot of money from the current system. Imagine them, sitting back and watching their livelihoods go up in flames!

'The barracks are full of warriors in the making,' she pointed out, 'and even if, by some miracle, we did manage to overpower all these landowners and politicians, there's still the matter of getting out of here.' The trek across the mountains was long and arduous. 'We'd be cut down before we even reached sight of Messenia. Which, I might add, is under Spartan occupation anyway.'

'For heaven's sake, do you think I'm stupid?'

'I trust that's not a question.'

She wasn't sure whether the sneer was due to her insult or the poultice. 'In order to reclaim our homeland,' he said, 'we need to negotiate safe passage for our people, then agree a deal for self-rule once we're there. But in order to negotiate, we need hostages.'

'Hostages?'

'People have been primed. To eliminate as much opposition to the revolution, they have instructions to kill their masters in their sleep. But we need *helots* like you, in a position of trust and authority, to take certain key hostages.'

When the time comes that you need to enter the contaminated area . . .

No need to ask who he expected her to take. Eurotas was Sparta's lifeblood. One of the few rivers in Greece that did not dry up in summer, it fed its people with enough left over to export, it provided transport links to the harbour on the coast, and its pastures nourished the finest horseflesh in the world. Offend the river god by holding his High Priestess to ransom and who knows what catastrophe might befall the State?

'The King, of course, the City Elders.' The schoolmaster ticked the rest off on his fingers. 'All the prime religious leaders will be our prisoners, and it goes without saying that hostage-takers must be prepared to kill their captives, if necessary.' He checked the strapping on his arm and seemed to find it satisfactory. 'I presume I make myself clear on that point?'

'Perfectly.'

'Have I your oath of honour that you're with us in this venture?'

Jocasta rinsed away the traces of the smelly poultice in the basin. Sparta wasn't the only city state that operated on some form of elitist principle. Slavery was practised throughout the whole of Greece, to the point where the island of Delos had become the central slave market for the Aegean. Indeed many colonies only existed because of raids on the interior. The difference was, *helots* were not displaced persons shipped in

from Illyria, Dacia or Thrace. They were an indigenous popu-
lation who had been conquered by their neighbours then
enslaved to the State, rather than individuals. Which meant
they could not be bought or sold on the open market, and
being State-owned dehumanized them in a way other slaves
could not imagine. For instance, there was no way for them
to buy their freedom, or even marry into it. For eight generations they'd been trapped in this living, working hell, and
while plots and rebellions had never been far from their
thoughts, little was ever done about it.

Until the Persian Wars.

Instinctively, and without any thought to the consequences,
helots threw in with their Spartan overlords, even standing
shoulder to shoulder with them at Thermopylae. As a reward
for their heroism, the Assembly advocated giving *helots* their
freedom, and though the proposal was vetoed in the end, the
debate proved more dangerous than if it had not been aired
at all. Seeing liberty dangled in front of their eyes, only to
have it snatched away at the eleventh hour, sharpened the
desire for freedom in a way that had never been seen before.
This time Jocasta knew there would be no stopping the rebels.

'Where did you get the resin from?' she asked. If it was
to be burned in every villa, assembly hall and temple, vast
quantities must have been smuggled in from somewhere. 'And
where on earth did the money come from, to buy it?'

Such stuff would not come cheap.

'Organization is not your affair,' he said. 'Now answer my
question, because this isn't the first time I've needed to question your loyalty of late.' His smile was pure evil. 'And I'm
sure you know the penalty for disobedience.'

'Oh yes, Great Head of Vixen Squadron, I'm well aware
of the consequences, and yes, you also have my oath.' Her
smile was equally vicious. 'Whether you have my respect,
though, is a matter for conjecture.'

The schoolmaster stood up. 'Be sure I will not forget your
insolence.'

She opened the door. 'Be sure I will not let you.'

Outside, Iliona was kneeling beside the little girl with the
bee sting, showing her how to feed the sacred doves. They
both stopped to smile and wave at the schoolmaster as he
passed. The schoolmaster smiled and returned their greeting.

Jocasta's eyes flicked from one to the other and back again. Then she beckoned the next patient forward, and gave his dislocated shoulder her undivided attention.

Iliona looked up from the sacred doves, and thought, that was all she needed. Another of Jocasta's bloody moods.

'Like this?' The girl tossed a fistful of birdseed in the air, most of which landed on her head.

'Just perfect, darling. But if you throw it forward a teensy bit.' Her hand closed over the child's for at least the fifteenth time. 'See? Now the doves can peck at it so much better.'

She sighed. The poor trusted in the temple physician to treat their wounds and superficial injuries, but, believing sickness to be a burden imposed upon them by the gods, it was to Eurotas that they prayed for a cure. Consequently, Iliona would seat them in the sacred grounds, listen to their problems, and then, while they were counting out the wind chimes or watching birds for the Oracle to interpret, she would be consulting with Jocasta. Jocasta would then prescribe the relevant medication, after which the Oracle would set the patients riddles.

Beneath the storm, beneath the surge,
In cup quite warm, is found the purge.

Zeta was the symbol for storm, and hold on a minute, wasn't there a giant letter Z nailed to the cypress two hundred paces down the road? Praise be to Eurotas, the remedy was waiting for them, when they went to look.

Where tree becomes snake, but the leaf does not shake,
Where the bough is calm, doth lie the balm.

The statue of the god of healing stood just outside the gateway, the snake of prophecy was wrapped round his walking stick – and look! The linctus they needed was lying behind it. Eurotas hears the prayers of the sick!

It was important the riddles were kept simple. You couldn't have people wasting time on complicated puzzles. For one thing, they worked so hard in the fields that their spare time was precious, and secondly they'd only come here because they were ill. But the riddles bought enough time for Iliona's acolytes to flit round, placing the remedies wherever the Oracle predicted.

Today, though, the Oracle took one look at Jocasta's

scowling face and decided people could damn well wait for the moment of midnight, the second crow of the cockerel, the first star of the evening, whatever. She'd done enough of stroking egos at the palace.

She blamed herself, for trusting the *Krypteia*, even in that, but it never occurred to her that he would trick her into believing the King was making her wait for an audience, not the other way round. The delay had antagonized him even further, of course, and it was no coincidence that his sister had sat in on the meeting. And if anyone ever wore the expression of a hyena who'd just picked up the scent of blood, it was Ariadne.

'Issat better?'

'Yes, darling.' Iliona brushed the latest layer of birdseed from the child's hair. 'Much better.'

Still, Ariadne hadn't been handed the ceremonial robes *just* yet, and in the meantime there was a temple to run. Obviously, Iliona could push the issue with Jocasta. She was in charge, after all, and her word was law. But quite often medicines needed several hours to infuse, and today, as with most days, none of the ailments on Iliona's list suggested an immediate threat to life. More the usual seeking reassurance that the river god was listening to his people's petitions and that, to him, if not their masters, they were important. She stared at the door of the *pharmakion*, showed the child one more time how to throw the birdseed, then went back to work.

With no idea how costly her decision would prove.

THIRTEEN

In a cavern in the hills, in what used to be a wine store, the Servant stropped his knife. Since the passing of the Thunder Moon, when he'd left that Arab whore in the gutter where she belonged, he covered the rock face with pale blue paint. Now, day or night, even when there was no moon in the sky, the cave would be bathed in perpetual moonlight, and he'd hung various emblems on the walls, as well: horseshoes, pruning knives, reaping hooks, gelding knives.

In fact, anything that was shaped like the crescent moon, in homage to his mistress. Even cat claws.

In the quiet of the night, Spartans slept and owls hunted down their prey on silent wings. The ferocious heat of summer was almost past, but the Servant saw no need for clothing as he rasped his cutting edge against the stone.

'Soon, Sweet Queen of Dreams. Soon, your horns will emerge from the blackness and start to swell again.'

Fourteen days from tonight. Fourteen days, before the Harvest Moon rose rounded, white and full. Before the Old Year ended, and the New Year began.

Before he could kill again.

He broke off from his stropping to open the door of a shrine he'd fashioned out of cedar wood in which eight scalps hung suspended from white ribbons. One by one, he laid them upon the downy altar, arranging them in colour from the palest to the darkest, and noting once again how the textures ranged from silky fine, to thick and strong, to wiry and frizzy.

'Look,' he told the moon. 'Behold the eight priestesses I have found to serve you.'

They would be humble and obedient in their service to the moon, he'd made damn sure of that. Beating the bitches into obedience and slashing them in to humility, then sowing his seed inside them to teach them the value of chastity.

'Whores that I personally saved from corruption,' he added.

In repentance for their sinfulness, they would serve a mistress who was the epitome of purity. For as the moon passed through the three phases of new to full to waning, so women passed from virgins to wives and then, once they had reached their fullness by bearing children (children born of fidelity in marriage, mind!) so they, too, waned with their inability to conceive.

'Increase, replete, decrease, it is the very cycle upon which life turns,' he chanted.

Unlike the sun, whose power peaked once a year on the summer solstice, the moon's power never dimmed.

'There will be no more fornicating with men who were not their husbands for these dirty, filthy slags. I have put paid to their dirt and wickedness.'

Base-born louts planting their sons in the bellies of noble-women could only result in catastrophe. In place of pedigree stallions, mules would be birthed, leaving the purity of their bloodline tarnished and disgraced. Well, he had saved these women that. And as he re-hung the scalps in their appointed order – Wolf Moon, Snow Moon, Flower Moon, and so on – he knew the priestesses understood that he had done this for their own good.

Just as he knew that they were grateful to be chosen.

FOURTEEN

'You haven't forgotten that you are scheduled to solemnise the treaty of the new waterway, have you, my lady?'

'No, no, Lichas. I'm on my way to do it now.'

All the same, Iliona remained on the steps of the shrine, watching the construction workers, their skin browner than bulrushes, dig out the channel and wheel away the excavated soil. Every now and then, one stopped to wipe the sweat from his face or take a swig of water. Others winched in the foundation stones. From the south, a hot wind rustled the reeds, bringing the Reaping Hymn to the temple, its rhythm setting the beat for scythes to swish and grain to be gathered in armfuls.

Thanks to all those wasted days spent at the palace, it was a struggle to keep up at Eurotas, with too many ceremonies being rushed. Worse, any hopes that people would be too busy to worry about demons, death and destruction had also been dashed. With the old year coming to a close and the new about to unfold, people found themselves riding on the cusp of uncertainty as never before – and where was the god's mouthpiece when they needed her most? Discussing treasury dimensions and the placing of bloody statues!

'The architect is waiting,' Lichas reminded her gently.

'Then I must delay further, that he may fully appreciate the virtue of patience,' she countered, but as ever, the young scribe did not see the joke.

If he wasn't careful, she thought, watching him shuffle away,

he would end up lonely and friendless, his heart crippled
with bitterness the way his body was now. Yet still she made
no move to pour the libation. In twenty-one days, the autumn
equinox would be celebrated with prayers to Apollo, asking
for balance and stability in life. In sixteen days, the New
Year would be ushered in with music and dance. And in ten
days, the Harvest Moon would light up the night sky, the
cue for a monster to again satiate his lust for power through
blood . . .

'I call upon Eurotas, son of the Great Mother Earth, whose
rich, black soil suffuses this plain, to bless the new watercourse that runs through the precinct of his holy shrine.'

According to which part of the ritual she was undertaking,
Iliona alternated between professional gravity and professional smile. But the music of the flutes went over her head,
the songs of the choir passed her by. An acolyte stepped up
to lay purifying hyssop on the altar. Two more carried the
scared *rhyton* from which the libation would be poured and
set it on a tripod by her side.

'As this canal brings your waters closer to the people, may
your guidance and support be closer also.'

The *rhyton* was beautiful. One of the loveliest objects that
Iliona employed in her rites, and heaven knows, there were
hundreds to choose from. Pale amber in colour, with crystal
beads forming the handle and a crystal bead necklace draped
round the collar, it was her favourite ceremonial object. Today,
it could have been a clay drinking pot.

'Let the bridge that crosses the watercourse act as a bridge
between divine and mortal,' she intoned absently. 'May the
reflection people see in your waters reflect the obedience
they owe to the gods.'

Through the swirling grey incense and the twirling white
robes, she could see nothing but dark, springy hair, a slightly
hooked nose and full lips that would never break into a smile
again . . .

No woman deserved to die in such terror, yet after all her
time hanging round at the palace, Iliona was no closer to
'interpreting' the five Scythians as Lysander had hoped.
Keeping themselves to themselves in the men's quarters, they
rarely ventured outdoors, and Iliona's only real contact in the
delegation was Liasa, and even that was tentative.

But one thing was sure. Unless she exposed the bastard responsible for these killings, it would be her fault that another girl died.

The ceremony finally ground to a close. The architect made obeisance to Eurotas, the choir and the music drifted away, and Iliona returned to her quarters to change.

The last thing she expected, or wanted, was to find Myles sitting cross-legged on the floor, that same insolent grin on his face. Beside him on the tiles, exhausted from play, the black puppy lay curled up in sleep.

'Don't pretend you didn't expect to see me again.' You could almost see the chip on his shoulder.

'I don't suppose there's any point asking how you managed to slip past the guards,' she said levelly. Breaching not only the inner courtyard, but her own private quarters would be child's play for a youth trained to sneak up on *helots* and kill them. 'Or how long you've been here.'

'Did you miss me? Did you presume I'd have called in on you before now? Yes, I can see on your face that you're surprised it took me so long, and I would have come sooner, I really wanted to, y'know. Unfortunately, it's not easy getting time off.'

'Then I'm sorry you've had to waste it today.'

'Are you cross with me?'

The rich cadence of his voice reflected the importance the army paid to singing. Music, of course, being the lynchpin of its choreographed fighting techniques, as well as its foundation for marching. None of it made her like him any better.

'Of course not,' she lied. 'But I'm running behind schedule, so if you'll excuse me, I need to change out of my ceremonial robes.'

'We never did get round to reading my future.' He held out the runes in the palm of his hand. *Eta, Tau* and *Omega*. 'Though you kept them by your bedside as a reminder, I see.'

'I haven't had time to put them back.' More lies, getting bigger every time. 'In case you hadn't noticed, the temple's under siege from anxious pilgrims, there's major construction work underway and tomorrow we celebrate the Festival of the Heroines, which means even more preparation.'

'I'll bet you a *chalkoi* to an obol you read the runes, though.'

'Then you'd lose.'

Blue eyes stared her out for a count of perhaps ten. She'd forgotten that they were bluer than the sky. 'Tell you what,' he said. 'Why don't we see what they say now?'

'Make an appointment, Myles.'

'There you go. Changing the rules.' A playful finger wagged as he rose to his feet. The puppy twitched and suckled away in its sleep. 'Down by the racecourse, you were willing to read the stones on the spot. Suddenly, I have to come to the temple and make an appointment.'

'If you'd come in through the main gate, you'd know the rules.'

'Well, that's where it gets so confusing, you see. All this business of rules.' He stroked his beard, as though thinking things through. 'There are hoplite rules. All that man-to-man, thinking-as-one, shoulder-to-shoulder routine. Then there are social rules. Spartans-aren't-allowed-to-trade, merchants-can't-own-land, artistans-can't-enter-the-cavalry kind of stuff. And then—' He pulled at his lower lip. 'Then there are the rules of the Secret Police, which . . .' He clucked his tongue. 'Means no rules at all.'

'I wasn't aware that wanting one's fortune told fell under the category of survival missions, but if your thirst for knowledge can only be quenched by breaking and entering, let me see.' She snatched the first stone out of his hand. '*Eta* is the rune of Bright Apollo, who rides his fiery chariot across the sky and watches everything that happens below. And given that he is also the enforcer of promises and oaths, then I would say that whatever you swear in honesty and truth will turn out well for you, Myles.'

And the reason why pledges were sworn to Apollo was because he can see the deceit inside a person's heart. And right now, he was looking in hers.

'*Tau* stands for parting, in your case leaving the other recruits behind as you progress into warriorhood.'

He leaned down to tickle the pup's little fat tummy. 'But it can also mean forced separation, presumably?' He did not look up. 'For instance, a baby snatched from its mother's breast and handed, screaming, to a stranger would also be symbolized by *Tau*, would it not?'

I never held you at my breast, she wanted to shout. *And it was me who was screaming, not you.*

'*Omega* is the sign of completion,' she said instead. 'So my interpretation of these runes is that you have reached a critical point in your life, but if you call upon Apollo the Far-shooter to help you, there is no reason why you should not go forward with confidence to follow your destiny.'

'In other words, I will meet all my goals, will have good luck in future ventures, and no doubt prosper in my financial transactions and love.'

'I did not pick the runes. You did.'

'And the women who come to you will all meet tall, dark, handsome strangers?'

Pretty much, yes. Iliona did not believe in the jangle of runes any more than the throw of a dice, so if people were superstitious enough to need such crutches for validation, there was no point in shattering what little confidence they had in themselves. The only difference was, she usually wrapped it up in obscure language. With Myles, she felt no need to play games.

He ruffled the pup's ears, making it squeak in its sleep. 'I came here for answers.'

'And I have given them to you.'

'Actually, you've given me nothing but platitudes. But since you have never denied that I am your son, even to the point of treating me like a child, I guess that gives me the right to call you Mother from now on.'

'I've checked up on your background, and your mother is a—'

'Barren Spartan woman of good, though not, I might add, aristocratic standing, who told me long ago that I was adopted. It was only quite recently, however, that she admitted who my real mother was.'

'She's mistaken.'

He strolled across to the mirror propped on the table and examined his blue eyes and blond hair in great detail. 'Mistaken, you say?'

'Get out.'

'That's not a very nice thing to say to your—'

'Get out before I scream and tell the temple guards you broke in and tried to rape me.'

'How very Oedipus.'

Iliona reached for the emergency horn.

'All right, all right, I'm going, but I warn you.' He tapped the door frame twice with his knuckles. 'I'll be back.' He winked. 'We have unfinished business, you and I.'

With all the agility of his training, he'd gone. Bounding across the courtyard, shinning over the wall. To cap it all, the puppy woke, and pined for his playmate.

I'll be back, Myles had said. *We have unfinished business, you and I*, but Myles was wrong.

Her business with him ended the day he was born.

All the same, darkness had fallen before Iliona finally stopped shaking.

FIFTEEN

Survival missions were tough. The first time Nicodemos was sent on one, it was winter and he'd been given no warning. The Prefect of his training squad simply came up to him one morning during breakfast and marched him into the mountains. Here, he was given a knife, a sling and some bullets, and told that if he showed his face in the barracks even one hour before sunset, two moons from thence, he would be sent back for another two weeks.

Oh, and the Prefect would also be taking his cloak, if he didn't mind.

And did he mention that he'd be sending men to search for him and that, if caught, Nicodemos would be whipped on the acropolis in full view of the public?

There was no time to complain at the injustice of it. Survival started that very instant, it was live or die from that moment on. Except the army didn't raise recruits, only to have them freeze to death. The Prefect led him close to a bear's den, and Nicodemos's first task had been to kill the hibernating beast, where its skin then served as cloak and blanket.

After that, he found that all those endless cross-country courses, round the plains and over the slopes of Mount Taygetus, had stood him in good stead. The snow preserved the bear meat, and he took care to light fires only inside the deepest of caves, because being tied to the whipping post and jeered at was not for Nicodemos. Blizzards swept in and days passed when he could not venture outside and, to avoid the trackers, he was forced to keep on the move. At first, being alone after living in what was effectively a male tribe had been strange. No one to talk to, no one to wrestle with, no one to share his experiences with, and he'd had to gouge notches in a stick to keep track of time, since one day ran into another. But to his surprise, Nicodemos found he actually enjoyed the challenge of survival.

His father would have been proud of him, too. Though he'd died of a poisoned arrowhead four years before – on Nicodemos's twelfth birthday, as the gods willed it – he never doubted his son would avoid the whipping post.

'A boy can redeem himself by withstanding the birch until he falls unconscious,' he'd said. 'There's no dishonour in that.'

But he'd drummed it into Nicodemos that wiliness was preferable to endurance any day, pointing out that no recruit who had been brought back in shame had ever served in the King's bodyguard.

'If you need a role model, son, follow Lysander's,' he'd told him. 'He rose through the ranks, pushed his body to limits that many Spartan warriors couldn't even endure, and is craftier than a family of foxes. Learn from him, and when your time comes to serve in the *Krypteia*, Nicodemos, be sure to acquit yourself well.'

Nicodemos hadn't been conscripted into the Secret Police yet, although several recruits he knew had. Like the survival missions, you never knew when, or for how long, each stint might be. Only that between moving up to the training squad at fourteen and retiring as a veteran, you would have served a total of two years in the *Krypteia*, though whether in one stretch or several assignments was pretty much arbitrary.

And now Nicodemos was returning home after his second survival mission. Squinting, he could just about make out his mother's cottage nestling in the foothills. So much to tell her – and was it bragging to admit that it was his ambition to serve in the King's 1st regiment? To be part of the elite body-guard, like Lysander had been? Because where the winter mission had pitted man against elements, this had proved an altogether different kind of trail – and *still* he had triumphed!

'No snows to cover your tracks this time, lad,' the Prefect had laughed, and instead of taking his cloak, which of course he didn't need in high summer, he'd left him naked and shoeless.

Nor had he abandoned him in the wilds of Mount Parnon. This time it was deep inside occupied territory, where the burden of *helotry* was even more keenly felt by those enslaved, since this had been their land from the dawn of time.

So there he was. A youth, a foreigner, a soldier, naked and barefoot, surrounded by an enemy who would gladly slit his throat, and with seasoned trackers on his trail.

If you need a role model, son, you'd do worse than follow Lysander.

Nicodemos needed no further incentive. He remembered one poor sod hanging on the whipping post. A lad two years older than himself being taught the drawbacks of complacency at the wrong end of the birch. What a price for being discovered one day before the mission finished.

And so, deep in Messenian territory, Nicodemos had done what Lysander would have done. First priority, steal clothes. Second, come up with a good story. Third, use your long warrior's hair to advantage. Fourth, hide in plain sight . . .

He grinned as he loped on down the mountain track. Stretching out before him was the plain of Sparta, tawny-ripe and peppered with ant-people scything barley and winnowing the sacred yield. For twelve weeks Nicodemos had lived among the *helots* as one of them, in the one place the search party wouldn't think to look, and now there was nothing he couldn't tell you about sheep! He knew how to clip 'em, how to dip 'em, how to round 'em up and watch for wolves.

'That's me, eh, Ma?' His mother wouldn't half laugh when he told her. 'A wolf in shepherd's clothing.'

Aye, she'd be right proud that he'd listened to his father all those years ago. There were so many other things she'd want to hear about, as well, because he'd learned so much. And that was really what these missions were about, he realized now.

Self-discovery.

Finding his own food, water and shelter was only one part of the goal, and yes, the bodies and minds of recruits became hardened against pain, hardship, even death, on such missions.

But there were worse things than death and dishonour was one, but even there, it wasn't the thought of being tracked down that spurred him on. It was pride. Man's desire to succeed, rather than man's fear of failure, and there were other lessons, too.

Nicodemos paused to pick flowers to take to his elegant, beautiful, tall, clever, strong-minded, blonde-haired mother. She loved flowers. Whole rainbows of them. And whilst boarding in barracks from the age of seven taught a boy independence, it wasn't at the expense of affection. Home visits were limited, but the time spent there was valued and precious, and after nearly three months, Nicodemos was as excited as a child about his home-coming. It was tough for his mother, being widowed at such a young age, and although she was strong, he knew how desperately she still missed his father, and how lonely she'd been since he died.

But Nicodemos was here now! He had four full days before he had to report back for duty – plenty of time to mend the fences, chop wood for winter, dig out new middens, and bury the old. After all, he laughed, he'd been taught these tasks by the *helots* – which was something else he'd learned on his voyage of discovery. Enslaved to the State, *helots* could not be bought or sold, and worked the land under the supervision of Spartans, receiving in return half the produce of the citizen whose land it was. In what way was that life so different to his own? Spartan men were raised to be warriors, to train from sun-up to sunset, and their bodies were not their own, either. They, too, belonged to the State, just as they belonged to those who had lived before them, and those who were still to be born. Nicodemos had always understood that he was merely one tiny link in the chain. But he was damned sure his wouldn't be the one to break it!

He was still whistling when he approached the narrow path leading to the cottage. Through the trees, he'd glimpsed its clay tiled roof, pictured his mother sitting at her loom, preparing dinner maybe, the house spick and span for his homecoming, and how excited she would be. Together they'd lay flowers on his father's grave, and then, over a jug of wine, catch up on family gossip and political change, swap jokes and sing songs like they used to. She was a beautiful dancer, his ma. Something to do with her height, he supposed, but she was as graceful as willow and with her blonde, almost white hair, she reminded him of thistledown waving in the wind. Light and lissom and fluid.

'Ma?'

Out the back, he supposed. Picking vegetables or hanging out laundry.

'Ma, it's me. Nico. I'm home.'

She wouldn't be out, because she'd been expecting him today. He called louder, cupping his hands to his mouth.

In fact, Nicodemos had been so deeply entrenched in his joy that he hadn't noticed, until he was almost upon it, that the terracotta wellhead at the side of the house lay smashed in smithereens. Not even the wily *helots* could put that back together, he thought. But he was surprised, now he looked, at the weeds that had grown up around the shards. Odd, because they weren't poor. They could easily afford to replace the wellhead.

'Get out of bed, you lazy baggage,' he joked. 'It's your boy home from the wars.'

She was waiting for him behind the door, wasn't she? Ready to spring out and make him jump? Carefully he pushed it open, and gasped. Was it the smell of rotting food? The blowflies? The mustiness? He couldn't say. But looking at the thick layer of dust and the cobwebs hanging off the spinning wheel, at the smashed wellhead and weeds, Nicodemos discovered one more thing that he'd never experienced before.

The cold, cold grip of fear.

'Holy Txa, Liasa!' Barak spun round, stuffing something under the pillow too fast for her to see what it was. His face was almost as red as the band round his forehead. 'What are you doing in the men's quarters?'

'Other women come down here, I've seen them.'

'Not respectable women.'

'Prostitutes?' She was shocked.

'The official term, I believe, is companions.'

'Oh.' Now whose face was scarlet? 'Next time, then, I'll knock.'

'For the sake of your reputation, there shouldn't be a next time. What did you want, anyway?'

'Karas.' She gave her dark curls a nonchalant toss. 'I thought I saw him.'

Apart from Aeërtes, who, as head of the delegation, had his own private quarters, the other four shared a room, and Liasa had her story planned. *Oh, Karas, I found this belt in the courtyard and thought it might be yours.* It wasn't, of course. But the boys hadn't been around for a few days, and the sand in her timer was running out. If she didn't find a way to make him notice her soon . . .

'Then again . . .' Barak pulled a comical face. 'Maybe he's here, after all.' He dropped to his knees and peered under the beds. 'Come out, come out, wherever you are. You can't hide from us for ever, you know.' He lifted the lid of a clothes chest, checked behind a wall hanging, inspected the inside of a wine jug. 'How about under the counterpane?'

His clowning made her laugh, but all the time she was thinking, *I know he came down here, I saw him.*

'You haven't looked under the pillow,' she quipped.

His mood changed in a heartbeat. 'There's nothing under the pillow.'

He must have called in somewhere on the way. He'll be here in a minute.

Meanwhile, Barak was staring at her intently, and whereas she'd forgotten what he'd been doing when she barged in the room, curiosity stuck in her mind.

And the silence between them twisted and turned.

'You're very pally with that priestess these days,' he said, once it was obvious that Liasa had no intention of leaving.

'What of it?'

'I wondered what you talk about, that's all.' He examined his nails. 'Like . . . maybe she's been asking questions?'

'Some.' Liasa looked at the frescoes on the walls. Bloody battle scenes, lustful fauns, and a rather witty little mouse hiding from a cat in the corner. 'She's very interested in our customs.'

'Any in particular?'

Moon magic, mostly, Liasa thought. Such was their reverence for the wryneck bird, which laid pure white eggs, hissed like a serpent and built its nest in willow trees, all of which made it sacred to the moon. 'Why do you ask?' she said.

Barak shrugged. 'Just making conversation.'

She tapped her foot. What on earth was keeping Karas? Could she have got it wrong, perhaps? That he'd been going to call in on Aeërtes, rather than his own bedroom?

'How do you turn coins into acorns?' Barak said suddenly.

'What?'

'How do you turn coins into acorns?'

'I don't know.'

'Like this.' He leapt forward, waving his hand over the coins in her hair and spinning an acorn out of her ear. 'Look, now it's a raisin. And now dates.'

'Barak!'

She tried to brush him away, but he was conjuring a quartz seal-stone out of her ear.

'Idiot,' she said, but you couldn't help but laugh. He was such a joker, was Barak.

'Oh, and what's this, a quill?'

'What do you take me for, a goose?' she retorted.

'Not a goose,' he said, hunkering down. 'Duck!'

'I'll give you duck,' she laughed, lunging at the feather in his hand, but in overreaching, she tripped over the hem of her gown, grabbing the first thing that came to hand, which just happened to be Barak's shirt.

'Steady,' he said, but it was too late. Momentum sent him sprawling backwards on to the bed, where, with a shriek, Liasa landed on top of him.

Just as Karas walked in.

'Whoops.' He beat a rapid retreat. 'Didn't realize you were entertaining, Barak.'

He's not, she wanted to scream, but with her skirts awry and her fist ripping Barak's chest bare, Liasa knew what it looked like.

And the pain in her heart was heavier than any anvil.

SIXTEEN

The odeon was a large wooden structure with a pyramidal roof, but to really make the most of its acoustics, it was also set way out of town. Surely no perfumer's unguent could match the fragrance of the sun-sodden herbs that grew roundabouts, yet what passed for beauty before was colourless to Iliona. What had previously been bountiful in the harvest had become barren.

'Now it's the turn of Eurotas to sing the praises of the Heroines,' blared the announcer, once the applause had died down. 'As you know, in previous years they've come perilously close to winning this contest. Who knows, perhaps this year they'll succeed?'

No chance, she thought, though her smile suggested nothing but confidence as the twelve men of the choir stepped on to the dais. In the past, they'd trained for weeks, if not months, beforehand, only to be pipped at the post by the Aphrodite contingent. This year, the hours Iliona would normally have spent supervising their performance had been frittered away at the palace, with nothing to show for her visits except some beautifully drawn diagrams of libraries, porticoes and gymnasia.

And only nine days before the full moon . . .

At her signal, the men picked up their lyres and flutes, and the dancers skipped on to the boards. In loose-flowing white gowns, they swayed like the clouds over the peaks of the mountains, lighter than gossamer, more graceful than cats. For from music came dance, and from the dance came the poetry, and from poetry came balance and light. But today the girls' serpentine movements lacked synchronization, and as the music died away to a soft rattle of castanets, Iliona knew the bronze tripod would not be theirs to take home.

Ariadne had just taken another step closer to stealing her job.

'I'm not convinced your heart is in this paying-tribute-to-heroines business.'

She turned to meet eyes that were as grey as any mountain wolf's pelt, as measureless as the ocean in winter.

'To honour the memory of Heracles' mother is admirable,'
she replied. 'To worship her only because her son was a hero
denigrates every other woman who has ever given birth, and
as for these so-called martyrs . . .' She rolled her eyes. 'If
you ask Zeus to reveal himself in his true form, only an idiot
would not expect to die from his shining godhead.'

Lysander watched the Choir of Aphrodite take up their
positions. 'What about those women who sacrificed their lives
for the greater good of the masses?'

'Perhaps if they'd gone willingly, it would be different. In
which case, we would have a different kind of celebration,
one which would not be reduced to some silly music competition, but which honoured their courage and their strength.
But here we're honouring a king who sacrificed his own
daughters to avert a plague. Which descended anyway.'

'He was Athenian, what else do you expect?'

Iliona turned her back on the word-perfect, step-perfect,
note-perfect choir. 'Talking of Athens,' she said, 'I presume
my cousin has moved away from the idea of their agents
staging dead bodies to trigger unrest and fear?'

'Hm.' He cracked his knuckles. 'When I left him this
morning, he was talking about sinking their merchant ships
in retaliation. Disguised as piracy, of course.'

'Oh, for heaven's sake! The elaborate embalming. The theft
of the corpse to tie him back in the willows. The scalping.
The evidence speaks for itself.'

'Apparently not loudly enough.'

'But that's ridi—' Then she realized. 'You haven't told
him, have you?'

'Like you say, the evidence is plain for all to see.'

'No, it's there to be pointed out, and unless something's
wrong with your index finger, that person is you, and it'll be
on your conscience, if another girl dies Lysander, not mine.
Or doesn't it matter to you that women are being hacked to
pieces like butchered meat, dying in insufferable agony and
humiliation?'

She only stopped because she'd run out of breath. Needless
to say, the Choir of Aphrodite was lifting the trophy.

'Iliona, it's not your fault, and it's not mine, that women

are being killed.' He led her away from the odeon towards
a small shelter, where those who could afford to make the
journey on horseback had tethered their mounts. It said something for the support for the winners that no one noticed
them slip away. 'The blame lies with the sadistic bastard
who's targeting them,' he rumbled. 'Let's not lose sight of
that.'

'Those five are sitting there,' she hissed. 'Right at the front,
clapping, whistling and stamping their feet with the rest of
the delegation. And you tell me to remain objective, when
our own King values a trade contract over a cold-blooded
butcher!'

'What would you have him do? Clap the entire commission
in irons?'

'If needs be, yes! No. No, of course not,' she said, 'but
you should at least warn him—'

'Of what? That the murder weapon *might* be a ceremonial
sickle—?'

'Is *probably* a ceremonial sickle,' she corrected, 'and
whether silver or gold, both metals are fundamental to
Scythian religion.' One being sacred to the moon, the other
to the sun. 'He only has to look at these people, for gods'
sake. The rings on their fingers, their earrings, their buckles,
their belts—'

'Precisely why the Assembly is so keen to trade with the
Scythians. The Caucasus is riddled with gold. It even gets
washed down in the snowmelts, and they collect it by laying
fleeces across the river mouth, where the weight of the metal
causes it to sink in slow-moving water.'

'I know, I know.' Jason's quest for the golden fleece was
no idle legend. More a trading trip that had turned sour. 'But
the Argonauts sailed to Colchis, that's my point. Where the
Amazons still serve the moon as warrior priestesses, and their
devotion to silver verges on the obsessive.'

Liasa had told her, and Liasa should know. She hailed from
Colchis herself.

'I suppose Greek priests don't use sickles in their religious
rites?' Lysander muttered through a mouthful of gravel. 'Or
revere the gods with silver and gold?'

'It's not just the weapon,' she snapped. 'Galingale is expensive, it's rare, and it's not the sort of stuff you pack in your

trunk in case an embalming emergency should suddenly crop up.'

'I doubt the King will be appraising its mummification properties.' He stroked the head of a strawberry mare. 'More its value in enhancing sexual performance, which must command quite a fair price on the black market.' He paused. 'So you think I have a conscience?'

'What?'

'You said it would be on my conscience, not yours, if another girl dies. I'm flattered you think me capable of remorse.'

'I don't.' Above the smell of horse sweat and hay, she caught the unmistakeable scent of woodsmoke and leather. 'It was a throwaway line, because I know you, remember? You kill for a living.'

'I fight. People die. There's a difference.'

Iliona snorted. 'A couple of years ago Democritos discovered indivisible units that he called atoms. I suppose it's inevitable that someone would want to slice one in half, because no matter how you put it, you use people and when you're finished, you discard them like rubbish. Hell, you even considered your own sister expendable when it came to your precious cause.'

'Careful,' he warned. 'That cause is your country, and seditious talk is a capital crime.'

'You don't scare me, Lysander. What scares me is that the moon is approaching its third quarter, while a monster stalks another victim, and I know damn well that's what he's doing: watching, following, noting their every movement.'

You can't kill three women, probably more, and not have someone report them missing, if you're simply choosing at random. The bastard was targeting girls whose absence wouldn't be noticed. Suggesting stealth, cunning – and a voracious appetite for the chase.

Beside him, the mare snickered in pleasure. 'What else can you tell me about him?'

Iliona lifted her eyes to the hills, shimmering in the heat. Across the meadows, a hawk dropped like a stone, carrying a goldfinch away in its talons, while behind them, in the odeon, the audience was being treated to a poetry recital. Ironically, the bard sang of Andromeda chained to the rock by her father, as a sacrifice for the monster of the sea.

'The killer is vain.'

The mountain wolf stared impassively back. 'Go on.'

'He is emotionless, compassionless but also intelligent. In fact, he probably considers himself more intelligent than everyone else, for the simple reason that he's never been caught. But most importantly, there is only one person who matters to him, and that's the killer himself.'

The mare nibbled oats and barely from Lysander's hand. 'From my own experience of such men,' he said, 'he'll undoubtedly have started his career by torturing animals as a child, and, since he only kills on the full moon, it's safe to say he's highly disciplined.'

'A perfectionist,' Iliona agreed, picturing the bastard going over and over it in his head, anticipating events so he could forestall them, making sure he wouldn't make errors. 'But also a loner, who's either learned to conceal his inadequacies under good social skills' – or accomplishments, such as music, target practice, juggling, leadership qualities – 'or is just too damned arrogant to bother.'

Sebastos is not a performing bear. He leaves the conjuring to sorcerers, showmen and priests.

'The trouble is,' she added with a sigh, 'for all our analysis, we're still no closer to identifying which of the five is responsible.'

'Assuming he is one of the five.' Lysander's smile was as cold as the Styx. 'Which is why it would be foolish to jeopardize the trade mission until we have proof.'

'I disagree.'

'Then you would be wrong, and you'll just have to trust me on this.'

'I would rather put my trust in a nestful of cobras, and in any case, you don't intend to give the King proof.'

A riding accident, perhaps. A fall from the cliffs. The Krypteia, she saw now, intended to dispense its own brand of justice.

'I was hoping you'd confine your skills to interpreting the Scythians, rather than me, but I mustn't grumble, I suppose. In fact, I should be thanking you for diffusing a potentially explosive situation for me. Namely, the phenomenon of the vanishing corpse.'

'I didn't do it for you.'

What was given to Eurotas has gone back to Eurotas, the Oracle had pronounced, to explain the puddle of water in the Shrine of the Snow Goddess where a corpse had been previously laid. And she could only be grateful that whoever had tied him back up in the willows had chosen a stand out of sight of the main temple complex.

'I did it for all those people who believe Hecate's wrath has not been appeased, and that dark forces from the Underworld still walk among us.'

Which they did. But not in the way people thought.

'Which is another thing,' she said. 'Aeërtes hasn't taken me up on my offer of a horse for his son.'

Did they know the *Krypteia* was on to them? Was that why the five had hidden themselves away? To escape spies inside the palace?

'Then force the issue,' Lysander said. 'A prettily worded invitation is hard to resist, and I'm sure you know how to spin out the time so that day turns into a banquet to finish.'

'Do I interview you for the position of waiter, or will you simply appoint yourself?'

'It obviously didn't occur to you to invite the Commander of the *Krypteia* as an honoured guest, but we'll skip over that. In the meantime, you might like to know the blonde victim has been identified, and that you were right about her parentage. She was indeed of Nordic stock, which explains the fair, almost white hair, as well as her height.'

Being right did not make Iliona feel better.

'Her name was Sirona,' he continued levelly. 'She was widowed four years ago, and the reason her son, indeed her only child, didn't report her missing is because he's only just returned from a mission demanding several weeks' absence.'

The bastard raped her, he tortured her, he humiliated her, and then he took her scalp as a trophy. 'No husband,' she said. 'Family living on the other side of the world, and her only child away in the army.'

'Young, lonely and vulnerable. Exactly. The killer chose his victim with care.'

'*Is* choosing them,' Iliona corrected.

She turned to the horses, munching on bundles of hay under the awning, swishing flies with their tails. Behind, in the odeon, the audience applauded tales of female heroism, and the meadows still smelled of the sun-sodden herbs, while the thrushes still warbled and butterflies still fed on the thistles. The last thing Sirona saw before she died was a monster gloating over his handiwork. And unless Iliona whittled five suspects down to one before the next full moon, another girl would go to her grave with that sickening image imprinted on her retina.

In the west, the sun started to sink.

The sun started to sink and the first stars of the evening appeared. Dust, sprinkled over the heavens.

But the stars were nothing more than servants of the moon. And soon servants would become masters . . .

SEVENTEEN

Once the first haze of dawn showed over the mountains, Jocasta packed her satchel, locked her *pharmakion* and set off down the road. The croft was small, even by *helot* standards. A single chamber, thin thatched roof – it was a miracle that it withstood the winter storms – and its only light came from the open door. Inside, the darkness smelled of tallow, ash and oregano, but though the chestnut furniture was old and poorly made, it was clean and free of worm. A basket brimming with patched-up tunics sat on a chest carved with duck motifs, and horsetails for polishing the pans hung in bunches from the ceilings. None of this concerned Jocasta as she knelt beside her patient.

His legs had swollen to twice their normal size and his breathing was laboured. Also, whilst his skin was burning hot, it was drier than parchment. She thrust his bedsheet to the wife, who had been wringing her hands in the doorway, and told her to soak it in the river.

'B-but—'

'The quickest way to cool the fever is with water,' Jocasta snapped. 'Please hurry.'

The patient on the straw pallet thrashed and groaned. She took his chin in her hand and pulled open his mouth. His lips

were blue, and unsurprisingly so was his tongue. When she
pressed her finger into his leg, it left a deep imprint.

'What d'you reckon, ma'am?'

'Help me wrap him in the wet sheet.'

'He'll be all right, though, won't he?'

'You'll need to keep drenching him.' The sheet was already
warm. 'And fan him, if you can manage.'

'His breathing's gone funny.'

'That's because his lungs have filled with fluid.' The same
fluid that was making his legs swell. 'I'm leaving you this.'
Jocasta laid a small package on a table blackened by smoke,
and gave the woman instructions how to use it. 'You also
need to put a pinch of this powder on his tongue three times
a day, starting now.' Beside the little cube, she placed a maple
leaf tied up with string. 'If you mix it with honey, it will
lessen the bitterness.'

'He thinks I'm Aphrodite.'

'Then let him.' Jocasta patted the woman's bony shoulder.
'Delusions go hand in hand with the fever.'

'But what if Aphrodite gets to hear I'm posing as her divine
self? They watch everything, you know. On Olympus.'

Aphrodite. Goddess of love, beauty and sensual pleasure,
the most beautiful goddess of all. Was Our Lady of the
Fluttering Eyelids really going to throw a tantrum because
this worn-out, weather-beaten creature was impersonating her?

'I shouldn't worry about it.'

'Oh, but I do worry about it! Suppose she puts a curse on
me, or turns me into a tortoise? That's what happened to old
Labda, you know. Cursed I mean. Not turned into a tortoise.
But I daren't leave him to go and consult the Oracle, not
with him in this state—'

'Old Labda drinks, that's her only curse,' Jocasta said
briskly. 'But if you like, I could have a word with the High
Priestess. Ask her to intervene on your behalf.'

'Would you?' The woman dropped to her knees in gratitude, tears coursing down her cheeks. 'And he will be all
right, won't he? He's not going to die or nothing?'

Jocasta unhooked the woman's fists from her gown. 'You
need to give him the first dose of the powder as quickly as
possible. And you remember the instructions about that other
substance?'

'Yes, ma'am. Thank you, ma'am. Thank you so very much.'

Jocasta left her fumbling with the string round the maple leaf and did not look back. Outside, sixty-five miles of rugged peaks and pitiless crags rose abruptly from the plain on the one side. On the other, the mountain range that led to her homeland, Messenia, and for the first time in her life, Jocasta felt dwarfed by the scale. Not by the landscape. By her vocation.

Gradually, people's fear of Hecate was being replaced by faith in Dionysus, who protected the forthcoming New Year. God of comedy and ecstasy, as well as wine, it was to him that they were now saying prayers and leaving offerings of grapes, ivy and honey. For evil lived in darkness, and if the Gates of the Underworld were only opened once a year, then the light into which demons and spites had been thrust would surely cause them to shrivel and die. And since the Hounds of Hell hadn't ravaged the harvest and ghosts hadn't overturned tombstones, what further proof was needed?

Making her way back to Eurotas, Jocasta watched ox-carts piled high with grain bumping and grinding along the road. Dust from the threshing floors drifted on the wind, and the bleating of goats mingled with the songs of the reapers. Snaking through it all, of course, flowed the lifeblood of Sparta, whose banks gave shade to cattle, shelter to birds, and a living to basket-weavers, tanners and dyers.

What would it look like in a year's time, she wondered? Once the schoolmaster's hemp resin had drugged the rich into sleep, and hostages exchanged for the *helots'* return to their homeland?

What would the landscape look like, with no one to tend it?

'Is it true?'

Tzan burst into the room where Aeërtes and Sebastos stood, heads almost touching, in whispered conversation. Behind him, Barak and Karas wore the same anxious expressions.

'Is Lokman really dead?'

'Come in, gentlemen.' Aeërtes beckoned them forward, while Sebastos checked the corridor before closing the door. 'Sit down.'

He poured them all wine, then took a seat behind his desk.

'Yes, it's true.' He fixed his gaze on each of the three in turn. 'Two weeks ago, in point of fact.'

'*What?*'

'Lokman killed himself by cutting his arteries, and two days ago his entire household was arrested as they prepared to board a ship back to Arabia.'

'Holy Txa, why didn't you tell us?' Tzan demanded.

Aeërtes leaned back in the chair and steepled his fingers. 'Because, gentlemen, it makes no difference to our plans or, more importantly, to the means by which we get our money.'

'Bollocks,' Barak snapped. 'It makes all the difference in the world.'

'What's the matter, Aeërtes?' Karas's eyes disappeared to slits when he scowled. 'Don't you trust us?'

'Maybe I should ask you the same question, because it's obvious that you doubt my ability to carry this project through to completion and make you richer than you've ever dreamed of.'

Karas stopped bristling. Barak ceased to frown.

'You should still have told us,' Tzan said. 'We have a right to know what might affect us.'

'Absolutely, gentlemen, but like I say, Lokman's suicide makes no difference. Had it happened three, two, even one month before, then it would undoubtedly have thrown our plans into confusion. But the point is, it didn't.'

'You said his staff were arrested?'

'For stealing, that's all. The Arab was well-known in Sparta, and when his household steal out in the dead of night armed with his treasure chests, people notice.'

Tzan spread his hands wide. 'Suppose one of his staff talks?'

'And says what? That their master had dealings with two men who are now dead?'

'The authorities must realize by now that the corpse in the willows and the rider are both Scythian,' Barak pointed out.

'What of it?' Sebastos's broad shoulders shrugged. 'They were not members of the trade delegation.'

'None of the commission had ever clapped eyes on these men. We made sure of that when we hired them,' Aeërtes added. 'And that's why we left their corpses in prominent display. True, it honoured their individual beliefs, but the point is, so unusual were the circumstances surrounding these bodies, that the authorities will be running round in circles for months after we're gone, still trying to link two dead Scythians to this trade delegation, where no link ever existed.'

'And while they're scratching their heads about them, they won't be nosing around anywhere else,' Sebastos rumbled.

'In fact, gentlemen . . .' Aeërtes smiled. 'I think you'll find Lokman has done us a favour.'

'You know, by Txa, I think he has!' Tzan slapped his thigh in delight. 'His death has severed the last remaining connection to us.'

'Precisely.'

'Then the gods are truly with us on this venture,' Karas murmured, twirling one of the beads in his hair.

'We still need to remain vigilant.' Aeërtes leaned forward over his desk. 'Liasa was telling Barak that the High Priestess has taken a keen interest in our burial customs. Now it may be that she is simply curious about the poor fellow we tied in her willows. But today I received an invitation to visit her stud farm and choose a horse for my son, after which a banquet would be laid on in my honour. An invitation, I might add, that is extended to all five of us.'

Ripples of suspicion ran round the room.

'When?' Barak asked.

'*The last quarter of the moon*, were her words.'

There was silence. 'What are you going to do?' Tzan asked eventually.

'Accept, of course.' Aeërtes leaned back again and began to stroke his beard. 'Together, we will choose a horse for my boy. We will sing, swallow swords, eat fire and ride bareback for the lady, and what's more, gentlemen . . .' His smile broadened. 'We will probably have a bloody good time.'

Down on the training ground, west of the barracks, the phalanxes drilled in full body armour. On a dais, pipers played battle commands on their double pipes, setting the rhythm and pace for the fight. The sun's glare, reflecting off the burnished bronze, made the soldiers' eyes stream, and beneath their leather-lined greaves and two-inch-thick linen cuirasses, sweat coursed down their bodies like water.

It was said that it was not the Spartans that won the battle, but fear. Rebuffing the traditional battle hymns sung by all other armies, they marched forward in silence, the only sound that of hobnail boots echoing as they advanced. Silence was a weapon in itself.

When the practice was over, Lynx Troop having breached Panther's flanks and delivered several punishing bruises with their blunted spears and wooden swords, Myles pulled off his helmet and mopped his forehead with his cawl. It had been a good drill. Panther had been routed for the third time in succession, and it was good to see them scampering away, their black and red crests bobbing in disarray. They'd be on rations of blood sausage and bread for a week.

But in real war . . .

In a real war, the cavalry would take up the pursuit. The phalanx delivered the necessary strength and stamina to break the enemy's lines, but it was the cavalry who were the army's elite. Sons of aristocrats, they wore lighter helmets, thinner cuirasses, and carried long, curved slashing swords. Myles had watched them. Galloping over the plains, curling their swords back over their shoulders for a powerful, downward swing. Swish, went the straw-filled sacks that were the enemy running. Hack, went the wax opposition.

Myles untied his greaves and loosened his cuirass.

For all the Spartan warrior's fearsome reputation, it was the cavalry, with their dashing performance and debonair conduct, who remained the envy of every other nation. He waited for the other recruits to drift away, then picked up his dagger and swung it back over his head, exactly as the cavalry-men did.

Exactly as he'd done every day as a child, when he'd galloped into battle on his fallen log of a horse, cutting down all those who threatened stability and peace with just one flick of the wrist.

But only the sons of aristocrats qualified for this elite.

While across the plain, in pastures lush with grass, the horses of the High Priestess of Eurotas, second cousin to the King, chomped contentedly.

'You self-centred, insensitive, arrogant bitch!'

Iliona looked up from the receipts she was cataloguing. 'Lovely to see you, too, Jocasta.'

'Nine days ago Tibios the thresher comes to you for help, and what do you do? You send him away.'

'If you would calm down a minute and tell me—'

'You don't remember him, do you?'

Iliona shrugged apologetically. 'Thousands of people come through these gates. Unless they're regular—'

'Symptoms: vomiting, headaches, not sleeping, fatigue.'

Yes, that really narrowed the list. To anyone who'd ever suffered a hangover.

'Dizziness, confusion, muscle cramps,' Jocasta continued. 'Sound familiar?'

'Please make your point.'

'My point is that, thanks to you, Tibios is dying.'

'Me?' But all the same, her stomach flipped. Nine days? What happened nine days ago? Think, for goodness sake, think—

Beneath the storm, beneath the surge,
In cup quite warm, is found the purge . . .

Holy mother of Zeus. She folded her hands to stop them shaking. Nine days ago she'd been showing a little girl with a bee sting how to feed doves. Nine days ago, the Oracle had been furious. With Lysander, for one, for tricking her at the palace. With the King, for another, for his hostility towards her. With Ariadne, for practically licking her lips. But most of all, the Oracle was angry at herself for walking into the trap, and as a result the Oracle had taken one look at Jocasta's scowl and decided the medicines could wait until morning.

'Tell me,' she said.

'All right, but don't say you weren't warned.' Jocasta's eyes were flashing as she paced the room. 'Because if you'd come to me straight away, I could have told you that Tibios was suffering from heat stroke. I would also have told you that he'd had them before, in fact many times in the past. I would've told you that he's no longer in his prime, is overweight, and takes the laxatives I prescribe for persistent constipation and diuretics for his swollen legs. Tch.' She threw up her hands. 'The man eats like a pig and pays the price, but that is not the issue here.'

No. It was not.

And pique had signed the death warrant of a man Iliona didn't even remember.

'The issue is that you neglected to tell me what troubled him until the following morning, by which time it was too bloody late. The dry fever had taken hold, and a combination of the other medicaments and ongoing problems meant his heart had congested. By the time I realized something was seriously amiss, a whole week had passed, giving his lungs ample time to fill up with fluid. Oh, and his kidneys are failing too, if you're interested.'

'Jocasta, I am so, so sorry.'

'Not half as sorry as Tibios, who, you might care to note, will not be taking the speediest ferry across the Styx. Thanks to you, he's looking at weeks of prolonged agony.'

Iliona tried to swallow, but couldn't. 'Is . . . there nothing you can do?'

'I've speeded up the ferryman's oars, if that's what you mean, but I'm a physician, for Croesus' sake. I'm supposed to save lives, not take them.'

A serpent of ice coiled round Iliona and slowly began to squeeze. Of all the things that had happened of late . . .

'Can I do something, perhaps, for his' – she almost said widow – 'wife?'

'I'm sure the river god can compensate in financial terms, but what price do you put on being a woman, a *helot*, surviving in a land of heroes and soldiers? What price would you put on loneliness, Iliona?'

She stood up. Squared her shoulders. 'I've said I'm sorry, and you know me well enough to believe that the weight of this will stay with me for the rest of my life. I cannot undo what has passed, or make the dead walk, but this is a rare mistake on my part, and whilst it is unforgivable, we all make mistakes, Jocasta. Whether you like it or not.'

The physician stopped pacing and turned. In the rays of the sun, dust motes floated like fairies, and the silence was worse than the clomp of her clogs.

'If this was simply an isolated incident, I wouldn't be bending your ear,' she said. 'Yes, of course you're mortified, and obviously it was unintentioned, but look at the holes and channels being dug in the precinct.'

She opened the door, and whether it was her olive skin causing an optical illusion, or her country background insisting that her tunics always smelled lavender fresh, her

clothes never showed the least sign of wilting. To suggest
that would suggest weakness, as well.

'You say what happened with Tibios was unforgivable, but
this is completely the wrong time of year to undertake building
works. The ground's harder than stone, yet those *helots* are
out there, wielding their pickaxes as soon as the sun rises
and they can see to start digging.'

Helots . . . Iliona's conversation with Lysander drifted back.

*Eurotas has no need of further statuary or gold. Not when
food and medicine go much further.*

*Medicine has a tendency to be rather dangerous around
here.*

Simply because my physician is a helot *doesn't make her
guilty of plotting rebellion.*

Every helot *plots rebellion,* he'd said. *It's only a question
of how far they will take it.*

'Works started during the harvest, that the portico might
be finished in time to shelter petitioners from the winter rains,'
Iliona replied. 'The watercourse will channel Eurotas right
inside the temple grounds, thus sparing people the necessity
of trekking even further than they already have, with the
advantage of keeping them snug and dry while they worship.'

'Really? And in what way do two new treasuries benefit
the poor? Will they be admitted to the gymnasium? Can they
peruse the libraries, do you think? Discuss the fine works of
art with the representatives of the new embassies? You've
sold these people out, Iliona. There's no other way to put it,
and *that* is what is unforgivable.'

'Do not ever accuse me of betraying my principles. I have
only done what I have had to do—'

'What you've done is a deal with the King for the sake of
this cushy little job of yours, and you're all the same you
aristocrats. When push comes to shove, you're only in it for
yourselves—'

The slap cut her short. 'You will not speak to the High
Priestess in this manner,' Iliona said. 'I have tolerated your
bad temper, because you're a damn fine physician and
because, until now, I would even have called you a friend.'

But enough was enough.

'This is my temple. These are my decisions. If you don't
like them, I will find a physician who does.'

Raven black hair shone in the sun streaming in through the doorway. It was almost as dark as her eyes. 'You'll regret this.' Jocasta rubbed at her cheek. 'Believe me, My Fine and Mighty High Priestess, you'll be sorry you crossed me.' She jabbed an accusing finger. 'Don't say I didn't warn you.'

The plane trees sacred to the river god were mirrored to perfection in the still, deep waters of the pool that was the haunt of Lacedaemon. Lacedaemon was the demon whose wrath could only be appeased with gold, and once a year, a solemn procession made its way to the Temple of Eurotas. Here the King consigned chalices and candelabra to its depths, for not so long ago it was the bodies of dead kings that went into the water.

And before that, kings who were not dead.

But Lacedaemon seemed happy with royal gold, rather than royal blood, and these days only traitors were thrown to him, trussed up like wildfowl, to be devoured alive.

Beside the pool, herons stalked in search of frogs and snails. From time to time, a river rat plopped into the reed beds, and hoopoes called to one another across the terraced vines.

The agents of the *Krypteia* watched. No one had yet visited the willows, even though three weeks of baking heat and scavengers had taken a heavy toll. The bones – or what was left of them – had long since fallen through the canopy, and lay scattered across the ground. The only thing that came to claim them were the foxes.

Every autumn, the trunks of the plane trees peeled and shed their bark. A slow and graceful process, symbolizing rebirth and expectation, the very properties that made them sacred. That, and the fact that it was an inexorable and measured process, carried out in silence.

Like the *Krypteia*. Keeping observation on the bones.

'There you are, my lady.'

'Yes, Lichas. Here I am.'

Nowhere for the High Priestess to hide, not even in her own temple complex, though the courtyard, with its gentle fountain and luscious figs, had seemed as good as any. Luckily, she'd had just sufficient time from hearing the gate open and seeing her scribe shuffle through to stuffing the puppy inside her chamber. She must find a home for the little mite soon. Before the temptation to keep him was too strong . . .

'I thought maybe you'd gone to the palace, my lady.'

She brushed dog hairs off her robe. 'I suspect your uncle has seen enough of my ugly face lately.'

'Not at all.' He bowed. 'I hear he is most impressed with the spirit with which you have embraced his enhancements to Eurotas, not to mention the suggestions you yourself put forward.'

He'd *heard*, he said. Not the King *told him*, because just like the puppy, he must be kept out of sight. Proof that disability overrides blue blood any day, for in a world of warriors, only battle wounds were acceptable disfigurements.

'Superficial amendments only, I'm afraid.'

'But key ones, my lady, and more importantly you agreed to every one of my uncle's changes, which surprised him. Pleasantly, of course,' he added swiftly.

My lord, I am happy to have all the treasuries built that you desire. Such splendours would please the river god no end, and his blessing would surely bring peace and prosperity to Sparta.

Behind her in the meeting, Iliona had felt Ariadne shuffle.

I am, however, concerned that too much disruption at one time might anger him.

The King had frowned, wanting to know in what way this might be so.

It is not only the poor who come to Eurotas, she had reminded him. *They are simply the most numerous.*

Adding that His Highness would surely not wish to alienate the very people he was hoping to attract in greater numbers and, if she could be so bold, in greater generosity.

Eurotas is venerated for bringing tranquillity as much as fertility to this land. She had wrapped her voice in honey. *A temple littered with cranes, stone blocks, scaffolding and ramps, in which the air is permanently thick of dust, would not be an attractive place to worship.*

It is your view that the current patrons would turn elsewhere?

Ask any shopkeeper and he will tell you. Once custom is lost, it is five times harder to win it back.

'I can't imagine for one moment why your uncle should

be surprised.' Iliona forced a smile. 'However, in his wisdom, the King has decided that works should proceed slowly.'

For the moment, only the new watercourse and portico would be built. The official position being that these would bring the river god closer to the shrine where he resided, and only once they were finished, a testament to Eurotas's power and strength, would His Majesty sanction the addition of the gymnasium, library, treasuries and embassies. One step at a time so as not to disturb the river's flow.

'But since your mother is the King's sister—' though not Ariadne, thank Zeus '—none of this will be news to you, so what was it that brought you to dig the vixen out of her earth?'

'Vixen, my lady! No, no, never a vixen! And in any case, that is the emblem of the *helots* and I would never dream of—'

'I know, Lichas.'

Never tease a man who lacks a sense of humour, and she wondered how differently things would have turned out, had his limbs not been crushed beneath that cart. His royal rank would have thrust him to the forefront of the cavalry, and she pictured him, proud and brave astride his horse. But would he still have been so solemn, so serious? Or would the comradeship of barrack life have brought out a different side to him? And this incessant fawning. Was it part of his nature, that would have made him grovel to his superior officers in time? Or was it something that had been knocked into him through years of being ostracized, not just by any old family, but royalty to boot? For Spartans to remain the greatest fighting force the world had ever known, sacrifices must be made. But how bitter a pill would it have been for Lichas to swallow, knowing his disability was such a source of shame that it reduced him to working out of sight, as a scribe?

And what of women, she wondered? Once he joined the army, his pale skin would have bronzed from training in the sun, and though his hair would still be thinning and his eyes still set too close together, the character that would have been built into him would have had women dropping at his feet. Myles, for instance, would have no problem attracting them. Arrogance is a magnet, reflecting confidence and strength, and there was probably a queue from here to Athens for his attentions. But pushed-in-the-cupboard Lichas? She pursed her lips. In a society that was top-heavy with women, why could a royal nephew still not find a wife?

As much as she'd like to blame it on her mountain of other problems, the sad truth was, Iliona didn't know the answers to any of her questions.

And cared even less.

'The reason I disturbed you, my lady, and I apologize profusely if the moment is inconvenient, but— What's that noise?'

'Noise?'

'It seems to be coming from your quarters and sounds as though . . . well, as though something is scratching on the inside of your door.'

'I expect it is my conscience trying to get out.' She smiled. 'After all, I have somewhat neglected Eurotas lately, in the rush to organize the building works.' Blasted puppy. First her blue sandal, then a perfectly good girdle, and now he's determined to scrabble his way out through the woodwork. She would call him Chip, she thought. Or rather would have done, had she been keeping him. 'You were saying?'

'Ah, yes. There is a young nobleman outside, who wishes to consult the Oracle concerning his—'

'No.'

'No?' The young scribe seemed confused. 'But I haven't yet explained what it is that he wishes to enquire about.'

'It doesn't matter. I haven't countermanded the order regarding preferential treatment for the aristocracy, and the same rules still apply.'

'Unlike the young lady who wanted her wedding blessed, I'm sure this would not take long.'

'Not *as* long, no.' You still can't rush people who donate heavily to the temple. 'But Callipedes' widow is convinced her husband will return with the New Year' – and, heaven help her, Iliona was almost wishing he would – 'and there are dozens of other petitioners to attend to, as well.'

Lichas rippled his long fingers against the whitewashed wall. 'This is family, my lady.'

'And this is urgent,' she said gently.

'He . . . is the best friend of my brother.'

Ah. 'Then you should know better than to have given him hope that I might change the rules, Lichas.' Change them for one, and you change them for everyone. 'The Oracle is the mouthpiece of the river god, and Eurotas does not pick and choose.'

'But you are choosing,' he snapped. 'You're rating a murderess over a nobleman, and ranking the wife of a thresher, whose fever makes him think she's Aphrodite, above a question of love.'

'Love, is it? Well, dear me, I would hate to think the young nobleman might be biting his nails to the elbow worrying does-she-love me, does-she-not.'

'Thank you, thank you so much—'

'Tell him to make an appointment for a month from now.'

Lichas's jaw dropped. 'You aren't serious?'

'Never more so, now please fetch your inkwell and quill.'

'But—'

'And step lively, because we have riddles to set, a banquet to plan and the New Year is only one week away. In addition, we need to organize how best to see the Old Year out, the harvest will need blessing, and for pity's sake people are still griping about Hecate and what might happen on the next full moon, there's that to be sorted as well.'

She clapped her hands, since he seemed as deeply rooted as the fig tree in the courtyard.

'Now, please, Lichas.'

'Yes. Yes, of course, my lady. I understand.' He bowed low. 'Right away.'

But just before he dipped his head, she caught a glimpse of the same expression that she'd seen the other day. The day she refused to meet his request to bless the young bride's wedding.

The day she got wine spilled down her robe.

EIGHTEEN

The Scythians differed from the Greek federation in that the tribes were vastly dissimilar in character. Where the land-locked Arcadians had a tendency to be clannish, perhaps, or the islanders a tad too carefree, their fundamental personalities remained the same. Centuries of colonization had moulded Hellas into a tough, resilient, but principally sophisticated culture, in which philosophy, arts and music played an important and binding role.

Any parallels between the nomads of the barren steppes, the huntsmen of the Sarmatian forests and the fisher families of the Danube delta, however, were few. To draw these disparate elements together, fresh laws had to be agreed, and fresh oaths sworn.

In Aeërtes's chamber in the palace, it was time to swear another.

'During our last pact, gentlemen, there were seven of us, as I recall.'

'Double-crossing bastards.' Karas spat on the floor. 'Got better than they deserved, if you ask me.'

'Seeing one of your own countrymen spitted like a trout and the other left for vulture meat not enough for you?' Tzan enquired mildly.

'No, it bloody isn't,' Karas snapped back. 'They died quickly and cleanly, and that's not my idea of justice, not by a long way.'

'Oh, and what would you have done?'

'Ripped their fucking guts out, strangled them with their own intestines, then left their dirty double-crossing bodies for the jackals.'

Aeërtes stared at the spittle on his stonework. 'Our associates turned greedy and tried to cut us out of the deal, and none of us is happy about that, Karas. But by smothering them in their sleep, we left no trail for the authorities to follow. Which means no accusations of murder can be aired.'

'I still say it was bloody risky, going to all that trouble to give them their tribal death rites—'

'What trouble?' Tzan said. 'The whole of Sparta was busy warding off witchcraft – or has sneaking in and out of the palace become a bit too hazardous for you these days?'

'You watch your mouth—'

'I don't know why they did it,' Barak said, stepping between them. 'After all, it's not as though there isn't enough money to go seven ways.'

'At least Sebastos caught them before they buggered off and left us in the lurch.' Tzan turned to the bodyguard. 'What made you suspicious of them, anyway?'

Sebastos let the wall take his weight. 'I don't trust anyone.'

'The past is the past, gentlemen.' Aeërtes set a large earthenware bowl in the centre of the table. The wine inside swished and swirled. 'It is the future that concerns us, so instead of worrying about whether our associates got what they deserved, let's celebrate the fact that their beliefs have perplexed the authorities beyond measure, and thrown the focus of attention on Athens, rather than us.'

'I'll drink to that,' Karas said.

'We all will,' Aeërtes said. 'Barak. The Pact Maker, if you please.'

Barak reached for the small gold box behind him and handed it across. Inside, on a bed of the softest linen, nestled the claw of a lion brought down in its prime. The five men each held their thumbs over the bowl. Aeërtes pricked each in turn, and watched the blood drip into the wine.

'The pact is made, the oath is sealed. To what shall we drink, gentlemen?'

'To swindlers who get their comeuppance,' proposed Karas.

'To suspicious henchmen,' said Tzan.

Barak shook his head. 'I suggest we drink to the gods, who are blessing our venture.'

'The best so far,' Aeërtes murmured. 'Sebastos?'

The bodyguard leaned forward and dipped his drinking cup in the bowl. 'I say we drink to mathematics, my friends. Because the whole divided by five is much better than when it's divided by seven.'

To a roar of agreement, five cups were raised. The lion

claw was wiped clean and returned to its box. Aeërtes and
Sebastos exchanged glances.

The Servant knelt in the cave, stroking the tresses of the
priestesses he had chosen to serve his mistress, the moon. So
many shades, so many textures. But none, *none*, blacker than
a raven's wing, that shone like polished porphyry in the sun.

Women should not be employed as physicians. That was
a man's job, and she should never have been appointed to
the role. It flew in the face of human morality, disrupting the
natural order of the universe and threatening to turn it back
into Chaos.

No matter. Order would be restored with the Blood Moon.
And what pleasure making that bitch humble then.

'Oh, my!' Iliona swept out of the stables to greet her guests.
The day marking the last quarter of the moon had dawned
with a soft, purple mist shimmering over the valley, that had
burned off to another hot, sunny day. Puffs of clouds skit-
tered overhead, reflecting like dandelion clocks in the river.
'I am quite overwhelmed at such splendour!'

Like the dead rider, all five wore thick, padded kaftans
appliquéd with dragons and wolves, in colours ranging from
scarlet to yellow to blue. Underneath, they wore skilfully
stitched shirts, their customary pantaloons and high, red
leather boots, but if that wasn't a heavy enough burden, their
headgear, torques and girdles were solid gold, too. Each
Scythian also carried a short-sword that hung from a belt
held in place by a strap that passed under his crotch, and a
gem-encrusted dagger thrust into that belt. Karas also carried
his felt saddle over his shoulder.

Aeërtes stepped forward from the group and performed his
characteristic one-two-three gesture. 'For the High Priestess
of one of the most important shrines in Sparta, it would
discredit us to honour you less.'

'Your high opinion is both valued and welcome.' Diplomat?
Spy? Or killer, she wondered? 'But if you wish to take off
your kaftans, Eurotas would not be insulted.' The Aegean
climate was not the climate of the Black Sea. 'You must be
roasting,' she said, with a smile.

'We must be respectful,' Aeërtes corrected, without one.

. . . and since he only kills on the full moon, it's safe to say he's highly disciplined . . .

'Then Eurotas is flattered,' she replied. 'Hopefully, you will allow his Oracle to answer any questions before you set sail in five weeks, but in the meantime, let me show you my herd.'

There were eight breeds of horse within the boundaries of the Greek confederation, and all were revered. Partly this was because only the extremely wealthy could afford to feed, stable and physic them. Mainly, though, it was for the importance horses played in the exploits of gods and heroes, their status in sport, and obviously they were valued for their role in warfare. Due to poor grazing grounds, however, most breeds tended to be stocky, though sturdy, little buggers. But when the floods of your river god bestow an abundance of rich, alluvial soil, perfect for pasture, a different strain begins to evolve.

'Your cousin raises horses for chariot racing, you say?'

'I'm not sure he could really do anything less,' she said lightly, as they strolled round the paddocks. 'It *is* the sport of kings, after all.'

Indeed, he intended to sponsor such a race for the New Year celebrations, and she wondered what the Scythians would make of forty four-horse chariots hurtling round the hippodrome, dust flying, as they converged on the tight turns round the pillars.

'But yours do not race?'

'If I could be in two places at once, then they might,' she replied. 'Unfortunately, Eurotas is so demanding that I spend very little time at the stud these days.' A situation that looked set to change, given Ariadne's rapid rise in her brother's estimation. 'Mine are primarily cavalry horses.'

Fast, nimble and willing to learn, such mounts would be ideally suited to Aeërtes's son.

'They are very different from the creatures we are accustomed to.' The hawk cast an appraising eye over the herd. 'But then our horses are exposed to extreme weather conditions, and are bred for endurance rather than speed.'

Their skins were much thicker, he explained, with dense fur to protect them from the blizzards in winter, and were also quite capable of going for long periods without grazing.

'If they cannot find food under the snow, they will eat bark.' He added that it was not unknown for them to be fed boiled pine needles when times got tough and the weather closed in.

'Dear me.' Iliona grimaced. 'You must spend half your time mixing remedies for colic.'

'Now that, my lady, is something these tough upland ponies have never experienced.'

'Never?'

'Never.' Aeërtes spread his hands. 'Flatulence, on the other hand . . .'

They both laughed, as Iliona signalled for a groom to lead over her most promising yearling.

'This is a very fine horse,' Aeërtes said, examining the animal's hoof.

'You're welcome to choose another, but I think you will find he is the best in the herd.'

'Are you sure I cannot reimburse you?'

'Positive.'

'Then I am in your debt.' He bowed in gratitude. 'Especially since I would otherwise have been reduced to swapping him for one of our long-bodied, fat-storing, squat trekking mounts, and hoping you wouldn't notice the difference.'

'I am not absent *that* long,' she laughed.

'Probably not, but even within a few days, I suspect the impostor would have dominated the herd. They are aggressive little monsters, our horses,' he said. 'A stallion is more than capable of defending his mares against wolves, with the added advantage that they can gallop downhill, if so required.' He patted the yearling's flanks. 'I fear you are in for a shock, young man,' he told it. 'There are no sophisticated fillies where you'll be going, so it's the gelding knife for you, I'm afraid.'

Iliona looked to where the others stood in a small, silent group a little way off. The pack, she thought. The pack that had spitted a rider from neck to coccyx and tied a corpse not once, but twice, in the willows.

'Karas.' Aeërtes's call made her jump.

'Sir?' The young man with the wide-set eyes and toothsome grin bounded over.

'Would you mind if Karas borrowed one of your horses for a moment?'

'Not at all.' The others were advancing at a more leisurely pace. The pack closing in, she thought. The pack closing in . . . 'Be my guest.'

With a theatrical bow, Karas flung off his kaftan and leapt into the saddle, kicking his roan into a gallop. Hooves thundered over the prairie like drumbeats, and in the sun, his oiled curls glinted and his gilded beads gleamed, yet none of it eclipsed the shine of his teeth. On the second lap, he lifted his knees to stand upright in the saddle, gripping the reins first with one hand, then with the other, and, at one point, with his teeth. Then he was galloping at full speed once again, hair and mane flying behind them as rider and mount became one. The roan relished the challenge. Iliona could see it in its eyes and its ears, but as they rounded the shade pine, Karas was suddenly flying through the air. She gasped, fearing broken legs, broken arms, paralysis, even death. But he had merely slid under the roan's belly, flinging himself back in the saddle to twist back to front, front to back, the grin still fixed like glue.

'I am truly breathless,' she said.

'That is how it should be,' Aeërtes whispered, and she wondered why, on such a warm day, her arms should feel cold. 'If life is not lived at—'

'Good afternoon, gentlemen.' A shadow fell over the group. 'My lady.' He saluted, and in the wide open paddocks, his eyes seemed bluer than the sea in midsummer, his hair fairer than overripe wheat.

'My—' She couldn't speak.

'Your what?' he murmured, raising one eyebrow, but before she had a chance to recover, he had turned to Aeërtes. 'I am *Eta*, my lord.' He dipped his head in greeting. 'Pleased to meet you.'

'*Eta?*' The Scythian frowned. 'Doesn't that mean the sun?'

'Myles,' she warned.

'Indeed it does.' His grin was almost as broad as Karas's. 'It is the High Priestess Iliona's nickname for me, my liege. Me being such a little ray of sunshine as a child.' He clucked his tongue. 'She has known me all my life, after all. And before that even!'

The others laughed at the joke. Iliona did not. Neither, she noticed, did Sebastos.

'I was watching from the road,' Myles continued easily. 'That was a very impressive display of riding, if I might say so.'

'Horses are sacred to all Scythian cultures,' Tzan explained. 'In fact, riding's one of the few things the tribes have in common.

'Though not all of us care to show off like Karas,' Barak laughed, slapping his colleague on the back.

'You're a fine one to talk about showing off, when I find you pinned and pawed by Liasa.' Karas turned to Myles with a wink. 'And on my bed, if you please, not even his own.'

'That's not how it happened,' Barak growled, and his face was red, though with anger, Iliona noticed, not shame.

'Gentlemen.' Aeërtes held up his hands. 'This is hardly fit talk in front of a lady. Tell me, *Eta*. Do you ride?'

'It had always been my dream to join the cavalry, sir, but unfortunately only the sons of aristocrats qualify.' Iliona found herself stiffening under the guilelessness of his smile. 'Is that not so, my lady?'

'The cavalryman is responsible for his own horses,' she explained to Aeërtes. 'And the upkeep is expensive in the extreme.'

Not simply the purchase of the animals, but their armour, the grooms' salaries, the fodder, the stables, the smithing, the training. The cost of these things alone exceeded what many artisans earned in a year.

'If the High Priestess doesn't object,' Myles was saying, 'could I perhaps race you, Karas? I don't expect to win, of course, I'm not in your league. But since only the aristocracy race chariots and horses, this may well be my only opportunity to pit myself against another rider.'

'Of course, I have no objection, Myles.' Having been boxed into a corner, she might as well give in graciously. 'Feel free to choose any horse you wish.'

'He's a handsome young man,' Aeërtes observed, watching him strut off towards the stables.

'He's cocky and arrogant,' she snapped back.

'Confidence makes a good warrior, Iliona. He will acquit himself well, I imagine.'

She watched while the groom fitted the saddle. While Myles mounted the sorrel. While Myles cantered off as though he'd known horses all his life, which, in a sense, she supposed, he had. Like blue eyes and fair hair, it was handed down from mother to son, and she had to fight herself not to throw up.

'The lad rides well,' Aeërtes said.

Iliona couldn't speak, and did not even try.

'That was most pleasurable,' Myles said, dismounting. 'Most pleasurable indeed.'

Like he said, he was no match for a professional, but had still given Karas a run for his money.

'What a difference an accident of birth makes,' Aeërtes said, squeezing his shoulder in sympathy. 'You would have made a fine cavalryman, *Eta*.'

'Oh, there's time yet, isn't there, my lady? I am not yet initiated into warriorhood, and – well, who knows what the future might hold?'

He sauntered off, whistling, thumbs looped into his belt. At the edge of the paddock, he turned.

'Almost forgot,' he said, strolling back to Iliona. 'The reason I dropped by this afternoon was to bring you a present.' He reached inside his tunic and brought out a small wooden puppet. 'Cute, isn't it?'

'Adorable.'

'I wish I had time to give you a demonstration of how it works.' He jerked the doll, sending its jointed limbs flicking forwards and back in a dance. 'But then, I'm sure you already know how to pull strings. Don't you?'

NINETEEN

Planting agents, spies and informants inside the palace was child's play for the *Krypteia*. Some did it for the money, others out of patriotism, the majority out of fear, and consequently the files of who was on the take, who was bedding someone else's wife, who was dipping their sticky fingers in the royal treasury grew and grew and grew. The Secret Police didn't always act on criminal activities. Blackmail was a far more useful tool, and so the list of agents grew in tandem. Like the *helots* in the fields, you never knew who might be watching, listening, reporting back on every little thing. Even kindnesses were logged. Character profiles were essential when it came to twisting arms, and the file stores in the dungeons weren't simply extensive. They were also closely guarded.

The slave pushed his heather broom along the stone corridors of the palace, tickling it in the corners and sweeping the residue into his dust cloth when the piles grew large enough to warrant it. All around him, on the walls, Aphrodite sported with her lovers, Hercules battled with his Labours and Poseidon's anger stirred up the violent seas. The slave brushed on. Past Perseus using guile to slay the Gorgon and Jason using charm to win the Golden Fleece. He whistled tunelessly under his breath, while administrators and scribes scurried past, and guards marched one-two one-two at the double. Fellow servants buffed the marble, polished the bronze, topped up the fragrant resins in the braziers and replenished the oil in the lamps. They brought in armfuls of fresh flowers and strewed petals on the floor, and between the fetching of clean linens and the carrying of jugs of water, no one noticed that the slave with a heather broom and a knotted dust cloth had disappeared.

Lysander dropped the latch behind him. His agent, a young maidservant with a deep distrust of foreigners, had found nothing resembling a knife in the shape he had described. Her search, however, had uncovered a number of strange, curved items that sounded as though they might inflict the type of wounds found on the bodies of the dead women. With the Scythians away at Iliona's stud, there was no better opportunity to make a personal investigation.

'Why are you here?' he whispered, turning over counter-panes and shirts without leaving so much as a crease, and rifling their chests without disorder. 'What are you little bastards up to, eh?'

All five gave his men the slip with irritating regularity, and that was no easy feat. Only a fellow professional could lose a shadow they could not see, could not hear, and hell, who might not even be there for all they knew.

Scythia undoubtedly operated its own form of the *Krypteia*, and it could be they were no more than spies. Cautious. Wary. Naturally suspicious.

Oh, yes, and hogs could fly.

It didn't take him long to find the tools the maidservant had described.

'They're in a roll of leather, sir. All five men own a set, and as far as I can see, the only difference is in the engravings on the handles.'

One by one, Lysander untied the bows that held the rolls together and unfurled them on the bed. Inside, nestled into slots, was a series of thin, tapered metal shafts that fitted into a single wooden handgrip. He examined the handles in turn, and whilst the engravings were detailed, minute and exquisite, he was looking for blood in the etchings, not art. Outside, he heard a scraping sound and stopped. But the scratch was of a heavy urn being moved along the corridor, followed by much swearing as it collided with a toe. He turned his attention back to the shafts. Each had an eye in the point, suggesting the tools were stitching awls, and whilst most were either straight or slightly bent, some of them boasted an interesting and distinctive curve.

The maidservant had done well. And because she had also relayed the story of the cat that had hung around Tzan for a while, and which suddenly disappeared, he paid closer attention to Tzan's possessions than the others'. No need. They were every bit as neat and tidy as his colleagues, and if the awls had ever been used on human flesh, they'd been washed clean of any trace.

Thoroughness and attention to detail were the hallmarks of this killer.

Thoroughness and attention to detail was why Lysander headed the *Krypteia*.

The slave returned to shuffling his broom along the palace floors, but Aeërtes's quarters yielded no better fruit. And by the time the slave had shaken off his yoke and become a soldier once again, he had unearthed a gilded lion's claw and many other objects that were hooked and curved and bent and bowed, though none quite as promising as the sewing awls.

What he had not found, however, was a stash of human scalps.

The bastard had a hiding place.

*   *   *

Tibios's wife knelt beside her husband, propped up on his pallet. Seven days on and, to her mind, Tibios weren't no better and if anything, he was worse. A lot worse, looking at them legs. She sucked her teeth. She'd given him the powder, like that lass of a physician said, and she'd burned that sticky resin as instructed. But still he weren't making progress, and it was making her stomach bad for worrying about him.

She dipped a cloth in the clay basin beside the bed, wrung it out and blotted his burning forehead. Odd stuff, that resin. Kind of sweet-smelling, and she had to say its fumes were not unpleasant. They calmed her man, aye, that they did, and put him in a deep sleep, too. And it weren't no lie to say that, when it were alight, she didn't have a care in the world herself. As though the Smoke of the Gods wiped the pain from her mind, and she could sleep, too, that was the odd thing.

'Oh, Tibsy, what are we gonna do, love?'

The straw was sodden, from where she kept dousing him, and his bloated body had become too heavy to turn by herself.

'It's wearing me out, this worrying, and if I fall sick, who's gonna look after you, eh? Answer me that.'

He didn't, of course. In fact, she wasn't sure he recognized her any more, as either his wife or Aphrodite. But while he was so ill, she supposed it didn't matter.

'That physician means well,' she said, patting his cheek. 'And I know she calls in every other day, but her remedies ain't doing you no good, love.'

Sleep itself is healing, Jocasta insisted. Well, maybe so, but you just can't sit around watching your man get worse, can you? Even if he does sleep twenty hours a day without the thrashing.

'It isn't right,' she said. 'It isn't right that your lungs rattle and you don't pass no water.'

His mother wouldn't recognize this red, fat blob as her beloved son, may the gods rest her weary soul. Not when he used to be such a big, strong, strapping jack-me-lad, and how Tibios could dance! Dusk till dawn he drank and danced and sang at every blooming festival, and never missed a day's work after in his life. Now look at him, poor lamb. Helpless as a baby.

'We can't go on like this.' A heavy tear plopped into the bowl. 'We'll have to make atonement to the gods, because it was them who inflicted this burden on you, love, and only them who can make it go away.'

But which god had he offended? Was it Ares, cross that he'd chopped down that laurel tree outside the house, even though it was old and was damaging the thatch? Had Tibios forgot to say the Felling Prayer before taking his axe to its sacred trunk? That would curse his luck and no mistake. Oh, lord, it wasn't Hera, was it? He'd dropped her sacred pomegranate, bruising it a bit on one side when he went to lay it on the altar. Surely she wouldn't hold that against him, though. Would she ...? There weren't telling, that's the trouble, and the thing with being poor is that poor folk don't have the wherewithal to placate every divinity, like the rich. There had to be a way ...

'Got it!'

The Oracle. The Oracle would know *exactly* who'd laid this curse on Tibios. Then she could put it right by appeasing whichever god or goddess he'd offended. It was settled!

'Thank you, thank you so much, my liege.' She poured a libation of fresh water to Eurotas. 'I know you'll have the answer and the means to make my Tibsy well again.'

Look at him, she thought. Bless him, he was getting better already.

Iliona was also praying to Eurotas. For four years, she had served the river god, blessing the fish, dogs and children that swam in his depths, the birds that bathed in his shallows, and the deer and other creatures that drank from his margins. She had consigned prayers engraved on terracotta plaques into the surge of his waters, foaming and white, during the snowmelts. With corn dolls and honey, she had sanctified the floods that enriched the fields with his silt. She had led prayers when he returned to his usual leisurely flow, and praised his generosity and commitment throughout the rest of the year.

But it wasn't enough.

When she took on the role of High Priestess, she'd been determined to bring the god and his people closer together. Not purely the upper classes, who endowed his temple with riches, but everyone who depended on him. The Oracle had

seemed the ideal bridge. Through riddles and illusion – smoke
and mirrors, if you like – she believed she'd found a way to
unite everybody who lived in Sparta, whether rich or poor,
soldier or merchant, male or female, free or enslaved. After
all, she had argued, if all Citizens are deemed equal (at least,
that was the theory), then surely we are all tenants on Eurotas's
land?

There was nothing wrong with this logic. The difficulty
lay in the yawning chasm that separated her vision and the
King's, so it was not for guidance that the High Priestess
prayed to her god, but for forgiveness.

For four years, she'd acted as doctor, confidante, counsellor
and seer. The link between mortal and divine, guidance and
faith, in the hope that people would slowly come to grasp
that, though the Immortals listened to their prayers, the ultimate responsibility for their lives lay in actions of their own
making. That Hermes would help them get their wagon wheel
out of the rut. But only if they gave it a push.

'Fair-flowing Eurotas, son of Gaia, the great mother earth,
I am sorry.'

Ariadne would sweep out the poor like cobwebs in spring,
and that was the tragedy of it.

'I have tried to be all things to all men, and by doing so
I have spread myself too sparsely, and Jocasta is right.'

Iliona had been measured, weighed, and found wanting,
and she prayed for strength that, when the time came, she
could hand the keys to Ariadne without her fingers shaking,
and explain the rituals with lips that did not tremble. She
closed her eyes, wondering how it would feel. How it would
feel to never stand again beside these banks, stony on the
one side, the other lined with oleanders and rushes, willows
and poplars, where storks and other birds made their homes.

No matter. She would travel. Travel to the furthest corners
of the earth, where Myles's shadow could not reach her, nor
Tibios's ghost call out. A place where the smell of leather
and woodsmoke would not recall treachery and deception.
Much less death—

'You did not wish to escort the Scythians round the temple
yourself, my lady?'

Lichas, Lichas, Lichas. Always so bloody conscientious.

'The Keeper of the Eternal Flame is more than capable of

giving them a tour,' she said, dispatching the last handful of hyssop flowers into the river and wondering why she always felt obliged to lie to him. And did he feel snubbed, that she'd entrusted the task to a man of lower social standing? Or was the King's nephew well used to being overlooked? Truth be told, his was another shadow she'd be glad to see gone, and not because of his withered arm and dragging leg.

Perhaps Ariadne was the right candidate for the job, after all.

'The riddle you set for the stonemason's wife, my lady.' Lichas stared at a point just below her kneecap. 'I couldn't help noticing that you directed her to *gather alkanet from a hillside beneath the wandering moon* when—'

'Sorry to interrupt, but . . . my drinking goblet. The very fine one, etched with the Three Graces, do you know it?'

'I know it well, my lady. It is your favourite, I believe.'

'Not is. Was. I found it lying in the middle of the courtyard, in a thousand tiny shards.'

'Good heavens! Have the slaves not cleared it up?'

'No, and that's why I mention it. The girls are usually meticulous.'

'Too busy lifting their skirts for the construction crew,' he sneered. 'Be sure I will send someone over at once—'

'This happened two days ago. I swept the pieces up myself.'

'The Festival of the Heroines!' The young scribe lifted his head, and it made a change to see his pale eyes for once, and not his thinning crown. 'I should have known they'd use it as an excuse for dereliction of their duties, and if you don't mind my saying so, someone ought to teach these hussies a lesson.'

Iliona watched him for a moment. 'Do you perhaps think that someone should be you?'

A light flashed behind his eyes. 'If it pleases the High Priestess, I would be happy to instigate the necessary disciplinary procedures.'

'Laziness must be thrashed out of them, I suppose?'

Now it was his turn to study her. 'Are you teasing me again?'

Actually, she thought, the word was goading.

'Yes, Lichas, I am and I apologize.' What on earth was she thinking of! 'Now about the stonemason's wife. What's the problem?'

The problem, apparently, was that alkanet wasn't in flower this time of year, though surely Lichas knew enough about how the riddles worked to know he could substitute cranesbills, marigolds or vervain in its place? Behind her, the fiery chariot of the sun set its course towards the horizon.

'Let's send her to gather storksbills by the waysides, shall we? Then by the time she returns home, hey presto, the remedy for her cystitis will be . . . well, wherever I said we'd leave it. Beside her husband's bow drill, wasn't it?'

'Chisel, my lady.'

Ah, yes. *Find claw that doth both gouge and pare, the linctus shall be waiting there.* 'Anything else?'

'No, my lady. Nothing further.' All the same, he seemed to be in no hurry to leave. 'I thought you'd have known about the alkanet, that's all.'

Well, yes, of course she knew it wasn't the right season, and had she stopped to think, she wouldn't have made such a stupid blunder. But regardless of her normal workload, there was still a backlog to catch up on, not to mention the portico and watercourse to oversee. And how could she possibly explain about her role with the *Krypteia* and the fact that the full moon was just one week away, much less the strain of Tibios, Jocasta, the puppy, and Myles?

'None of us is perfect, Lichas,' Iliona managed to breeze. 'Not even the gods, which is why they wreak such havoc in our lives.'

'Do you really believe they control our destiny from start to finish?'

'*Don't tell me you believe in that ghoulie-ghostie-witchcraft crap!* Myles's voice echoed so loudly inside her head, he might have been standing at her shoulder. *I can just see the mathematicians who designed these temples having sleepless nights worrying about banshees, can't you?*

He'd been referring to Hecate, and what he called *that hocus pocus in the hills.* And no. Whilst there were no such things as vampyres that came hurtling through the Gates of Hell to suck the souls from newborn babies, Iliona did believe in evil. Very much, in fact. And its shadow was being cast inside this precinct at this very moment . . .

'Sorry,' she said, pinching the bridge of her nose. Behind the high stone wall, the ripe tones of the Keeper of the Keys was explaining to five Scythians in kaftans how Apollo was once so taken with a young Spartan man, that he would serenade him on his lyre beside the banks of the Eurotas. 'Sorry, Lichas. What did you say?'

'I was asking whether you truly believe the gods are responsible for everything that happens, while mortal man has control of nothing?'

Control. Of course. That was why the killer prolonged the pain and the humiliation – and oh, how he must hate women, she thought sadly. To need to dominate them so, then keep their scalps as trophies of his prowess.

'No.' Iliona forced her mind back to the question. 'No, I don't believe that.' Her voice betrayed none of the sickness that had welled up inside. 'The gods may place obstacles in our path, Lichas, but it is up to us how we react. Success or failure is in our hands, I fear, not theirs, and now, if you will excuse me, I really must change into my ceremonial robes.'

She paused. It was still not too late to invite him to the banquet. He was the King's nephew after all, and had organized most of it, anyway—

Mrrroww.

A pair of temple cats, squaring off behind a column, broke the spell, and by the time feline differences had been sorted out, both claiming victory, the opportunity had passed. And maybe her theory about the gods putting obstacles in people's paths should be amended to include removing them, as well.

Iliona did not head straight to her quarters to change. First, she needed to look up Tibios's file. See what guidance the Oracle might have given the poor thresher in the past, with a view to perhaps lessening the bad news that had to be imparted to his wife.

And who was she fooling, she thought bitterly. This had nothing to do with Tibios. May the gods forgive her, she was nothing but a coward, looking for a way to minimize her own guilt, when there was no escaping the bitter truth. It was her arrogance that had condemned Tibios to a slow, unpleasant death, and in the stillness of the night, she knew she would always hear his lungs bubbling and his wife sobbing by his bedside. She stared at the puppet, dangling in her hands. If plunging a knife into her heart would make him whole again, Iliona would have done it. But Zeus, Divine Dispenser of

Justice, had seen what she had done, and his sentence was
to make her pay by living with the guilt.

At least with Tibios on the one side and Myles on the
other, the load was balanced evenly.

TWENTY

J ocasta watched the Keeper of the Keys, as he guided the
five-man deputation round the temple. Like she told Iliona
that morning in the market, she didn't trust men who curled
their hair and plastered so much oil on the resulting ringlets
that you could fry a quail's egg on them in the sun.

'Eurotas is the son of Gaia, our great mother earth, herself
a daughter of Chaos.' The Keymaster's rich, ripe timbre echoed
round the precinct. 'This explains why his brother is the
demon that inhabits the deep, dark pool that I will now take
you to.'

Equally, she mistrusted tribes like Karas's, that practised
shamanism. A process in which the soul was supposed to
leave the body and travel to the realm of spirits, where it was
bestowed with miraculous powers with which the shaman
could then banish plagues, cure the sick and foretell the
future. No one person could do all that, she thought. Much
less in a trance.

Jocasta had no time for Tzan's people, either. What
nonsense, tattooing themselves from head to foot with winged
cats, griffins, snow leopards, eagles, and the like. Why tell
your children that they would only ever have the strength and
characteristics of these creatures, provided they took their
images upon their skin? Nor did it imply that, without the
tattoos, they'd grow up weak, naïve and stupid, but it imbued
in them a sense of superiority that made them look down on
other tribes, and you only had to see the way Tzan looked
at Karas to understand.

She watched the little group troop through the archway,
down towards the river. Aeërtes and Barak hailed from
Colchis, land of the legendary Amazon priestesses, who
covered themselves in snakeskin and bore arms to conduct

worship. The snakeskin was appropriate, she thought. The city of Colchis was rich in culture as well as wealth, but beyond its walls lay a barren landscape beset with poverty. Religion would need all the trickery and artifice that it could think of, to fool the people and keep them under their control, and Barak's mother was one of the priestesses who had helped Aeërtes to power. No wonder he could swallow swords and fire. He would have drunk deception at his mother's breast – and, as for Sebastos, there was something about his piercing stare that unsettled her, not helped by the fact that Jocasta hadn't been able to determine one damned thing about his tribal origins. Here was a man who kept things closer than most to his chest, she thought, but from the way he and Aeërtes were so close, she suspected he was Colchian, too.

As the Keymaster's voice faded, the Song of the Threshing Floor filled its place. She closed her eyes, picturing the circular paved surface with its low, raised rim where asses hitched to a central pole trampled the grain from the husks. Here, the *helots* did not need tunes to give them a rhythm, as they would, for instance, in the fields as they reaped and stacked the wheat. They sang out of joy. The harmony of working together, as a team. Just as they did when they separated the grain from the chaff with the Winnowing Songs, tossing a shovelful in the air at a time, catching the grains as they fell down again.

When she was certain the group would not be returning for a while, she scurried to the Cenotaph.

'This is madness,' she hissed. 'What on earth were you thinking of?'

'Relax.' The schoolmaster stepped out of the shadows. 'The Scythians have already been given a tour of this wondrous monument. They won't come back.'

'Don't sneer at the dead.' Outnumbered forty to one, their spears broken and their swords blunt from combat, three hundred exhausted warriors had defended Thermopylae to their very last breath, hurling rocks, biting, kicking, gouging, punching. Anything to buy time for the army to catch up. 'If it wasn't for them, we'd be breaking our backs for the Persians.'

'Hasn't anyone told you, the only good Spartan is a dead

one?' He turned and spat on the marble. 'At least, that's three hundred less.'

Fewer, she wanted to say. The word is fewer, and what kind of teacher are you, that you don't know that?

'What about the three hundred *helots* who died alongside them?' she retorted instead. No one ever remembered the squires and skirmishers, who'd stayed behind and sacrificed their own lives at the Pass, but without the benefit of decent armour or proper weapons. 'Wipe it up.'

'Pardon?'

'I said, wipe up that spittle.'

The schoolmaster grabbed a handful of her hair and twisted. 'Don't,' he said, jerking her to her knees. 'Don't you *ever* tell me what to do.'

'Let me go.'

'Not until you apologize.'

'Go to . . . ouch!'

'Say it.'

'All right, all right, I'm sorry.' She swallowed. 'I really am,' she said. 'Sometimes I forget that I am a woman and that my place is to be secondary to a man's. To yours,' she added humbly.

'That's better.' He released his grip. 'Now to business.'

She refused to rub where he'd pulled at her hair, even though the pain had made her eyes water. The skin on her knees had grazed, too.

'Firstly,' he said, 'I want to make sure you understand the schedule for taking the hostages at New Year. Co-ordination is vital, so once the beacon on top of Mount Parnon is lit, you will immediately start burning the resin to sedate what few people remain at the shrine.'

It went without saying that, like the ceremony to appease Hecate, only a skeleton staff would be operating that night.

'Boats will be on standby to take the King, the Council of Elders and all other key hostages down to the harbour, where a ship will be waiting. You will therefore need to ensure the High Priestess is as close to river access as you can possibly get her. My men will need to be in and out in the wink of an eye.'

Jocasta considered the logistics of such a finely-tuned operation. Iliona would probably be their first part of call as

Eurotas was some considerable distance upstream from the city.

'How am I supposed to lure her away from the festivities?'

'You're a clever girl. Use your initiative.'

She considered the number of times she and Iliona had dealt with deserters and runaways, and decided it would not be much of a challenge. 'She won't go into the boat without a fight,' she said.

'I'm not expecting any of the hostages to wake up until that ship's under sail, and yours is no exception. Drug her, knock her out with a blow, I don't care. Just make sure she's out cold and close to the river. Oh, and have as many of your medicines packed as you can carry, because you won't be coming back.'

No. No, she wouldn't. Jocasta felt something leap inside. She'd be going home . . .

'In the meantime,' he said, 'it has come to my ears that you've been using the hemp in places you shouldn't, you naughty girl.'

Oh, for heaven's sake, was no secret safe around here? 'I assume you mean Tibios?'

The schoolmaster nodded. 'Very unwise of you, Jocasta.'

'Really? I thought you'd have been pleased.'

'How so, might I ask?'

'Because by experimenting with what I told them was the Smoke of the Gods, I have been able to judge its effects with considerable accuracy.'

He blinked. 'I see.' He blinked again. 'That, um – that shows great foresight. I approve.'

'Thanks to my research, Oh Great Head of Vixen Squadron, you're in a position to tell people the precise quantities of resin that must be burned, and for how long, according to the number of citizens to be subdued.'

'Then you must write down the formula, and I will collect it tomorrow.' He reached out and smoothed the hair that he had yanked. 'You have some wild ways, Jocasta. But come the New Year, all that will change.'

As he disappeared into the blackness, she thought she heard him add something under his breath. 'What was that?' she asked.

The schoolteacher turned, and she felt her cheeks burning

as his eyes assessed the curves beneath her tunic. 'Nothing.'
He smiled. 'I didn't say anything,' he said softly.

'My mistake, then.'

Must be an echo in the colonnade, but it sounded for all
the world as though he said that she would serve him well.
Very well indeed, she thought he'd said.

Raven black hair, oh raven black hair. Pretty, pretty, raven
black hair.

On the top floor of the palace, Ariadne shooed her hand-
maidens out of one door and ushered Lysander in through
the other. He was looking particularly scrumptious tonight,
she thought, noting how he had fastened his tunic at the
shoulder with the gold pins she had given him, the ones in
the shape of her own emblem, the cicada.

'I have just received news,' she said, pinching colour into
her cheeks and reddening her lips with a quick smear of
ochre. 'Apparently, my poor husband will be delayed in
Thebes.' She poured them both wine and lifted one
immaculately plucked eyebrow. 'Nothing to do with you, I
suppose?'

'When a man proves himself in diplomatic skills, I feel it
only my duty to encourage him to remain in the post for as
long as possible.'

'Thebes is a vibrant city,' she said. 'I'm sure he will find
plenty of diversions to keep him amused, but none . . .' She
pulled Lysander towards her by the gold belt she had also
given him. 'None quite as exciting as the diversion I have
found myself falling for.'

'Love is a dangerous game, Ariadne.' He kissed off the
ochre. 'The stakes are higher than either of us might think.'

'I don't care. Once I am appointed to Eurotas, it will be
easy to divorce my husband without scandal, and with you
a widower, there will be no shame attached to our marriage.'

He chinked the rim of his goblet against the rim of hers.
'To no shame and no scandal.'

'I have a better toast,' she countered. 'Come spring, Eurotas
will be well on its way to becoming the most important shrine
in the Peloponnese. Therefore, with you commanding the
Krypteia and me wrapping my brother round my little finger,

like I used to in the old days, I propose we drink to ruling
Sparta between us.'

'To stealth, then.'

'And love.' She reached into a small maplewood chest and
brought out a ring shaped like a cicada.

Grey eyes considered it for several minutes. 'This is not
like wearing your cloak pin,' he rumbled. 'This is a blatant
declaration of loyalty.'

'But will you wear it?'

A smile played at the side of his mouth. 'I think I can find
room on my finger.'

'For a moment there, I thought you were going to say no.'

'For a moment there, so did I.' He held out his hand. It
fitted his middle finger perfectly. 'I have a gift for you, too,'
he murmured. 'Though it is nowhere near so personal, I
regret.'

She unwrapped the cloth from a hand mirror, whose ivory
handle was carved in the shape of a woman. 'Oh, but it's
beautiful, Lysander.'

'As is the picture in it,' he said, bowing. 'And the maiden,
I'm told, is Andromeda. If you look carefully, you can see
the chains that bind her to the rock.'

Ariadne tossed her hair over her shoulder. 'Don't remind
me of heroines,' she tutted. 'What a fiasco, that competition
in the odeon the other day! Did you see those dancers? I tell
you, those girls wouldn't have clumped about like heifers,
had I been in charge. No, sir, I'd have drilled those clumsy
chits until their feet bled to make sure that prize was brought
back to Eurotas – and oh dear lord, as for the choir!'

'Don't know their dithyrambs from their dactylic hexam-
eters, huh?'

She looked at him sideways, unsure whether this was a
joke or not. 'Quite.' She unrolled the plans and spread them
out over the desk with a contented sigh. 'Embassies, treasuries, libraries, shrines. I tell you, Eurotas will be THE hub
for political congress, at least outside Athens, and who better
to be the eyes and ears of these foreigners than the King's
own sister?'

'Who indeed.' He refilled their goblets. 'How do you
propose to put an end to the Oracle?'

'I haven't decided, but Hermes is the messenger between

gods and mortals, not Iliona. Time and again, she has proved herself incapable of running the place, don't you agree?'

A chuckle rumbled in the base of his throat. 'Since when have I ever disagreed with you, my sweet?'

She walked over to where he was standing and wound her arms round his neck. 'I want to thank you. You've worked so hard to help me achieve this post, and I am grateful, Lysander, I really am. My brother is influenced by me, he always has been, but somehow that little bitch managed to sway him when it came to Eurotas. Without you backing my cause, I would still be in the wilderness when it came to that role.'

'We all get what we deserve, Ariadne.'

'Don't we.' With one tug, her gown fell to the floor in a pool of saffron and green. Beneath, she was splendidly naked. 'And this, my darling, is your reward.'

'Hm.' He studied the water clock in the corner. 'It's Iliona's banquet tonight. I need to be at the shrine before that jug tips back down to restart.'

'No wonder you're so well turned out.' She felt the quality of his tunic between her fingers. Egyptian linen, no less, in an exquisite, and very expensive, shade of mauve. 'For her, though. Not for me.'

'For five Scythian men, if you wish to be pedantic.'

'Well, that's a first for both of us. At least, I hope it is.' Laughing, she lifted her arms over her head, thrusting her breasts towards him. 'Darling, darling, darling. I know you're rushed for time, but I'm pretty sure that, if you put your mind to it, you can manage one teensy little fuck before you leave.'

'You misunderstand me, Ariadne.' He unbuckled his belt and pushed her on to the couch. 'I was checking the time, because I'm pretty sure I can manage two.'

Darkness settled over the landscape like death mist. Bats squeaked in search of flies over the river, moths danced round the flambeaux high on the walls, and the temple cats prowled the shadows for mice. In the Great Hall, hung with wreaths of white clematis and decked with holly and bay, servants scurried to lay platters of cheese bread and bowls of dark, shiny olives on the banqueting tables, while a flautist tapped out his beat with his thick, wooden soles. Iliona could hear the murmur of conversation, a deep guttural language with words that would have been too indistinct to pick up, had they even been Greek. She checked her appearance in the shine of a pillar, where her diadem gleamed under a thousand flickering lamps and the gems round her neck glittered like fireflies.

But it was not into the Great Hall that the High Priestess made her entrance.

The office was in darkness, and though it smelled of parchment and ink, another faint odour hung in the air. A light, almost floral fragrance, and for heaven's sake, why shouldn't her scribe use luxurious unguents on his body? She tended to forget, but he was still the King's nephew, even if he was a pariah.

Iliona lit an oil lamp and held it high above her head, casting light over the room. Outside, the three-quarter moon was swelling inexorably, and though she should be out there, meeting, greeting and pressing the flesh, she could not get this out of her mind. She had to know. She had to track down the woman who had taken her son, and ask her why she had broken her promise—

I swear by the River Styx that I will never reveal the name of his real mother. You have my oath.

So help her, Iliona had believed her . . .

'Your guests are assembled and ready, my lady.'

She jumped. 'I thought you'd gone home.'

'Having organized the banquet, I did not wish to leave it unsupervised,' Lichas said. 'Then I noticed a light burning and came to investigate.'

'Did you really.' Was it the surprise of seeing him in the doorway, or being caught out, that put the edge in her voice? 'How very conscientious.'

He was waiting, she thought. Waiting for what?

'Please don't let me detain you, Lichas. I'm sure you have plans for this evening.'

'No, no, not at all, my lady. In fact' – he swallowed – 'in fact, I was hoping to accompany you to the banquet.'

For a moment, she thought he meant lead her across to the Hall. Then she noticed the fine quality of his tunic, the embroidered hem, the belt studded with silver, and the unguent clicked into place.

'Royalty would not be a drawback,' he said.

'Indeed it would not, but there are matters I wish to discuss with the Scythians.'

'If you do not want me as your guest, I could take notes?'

'Personal matters.'

'Oh.' His head dipped even lower, but she sensed a change in his mood. 'I see.'

'If it's an introduction you're after, I can—'

'Please don't trouble yourself on my account.' From under lowered lashes, he shot her a glance that on anyone else would have been vindictive. 'I was merely concerned about you being alone with those savages, that was all.'

He was hurt. He was hurt, because after all these years of being relegated to the sidelines, being slighted did still rankle. But she had made her decision earlier, and had no intention of reneging now.

'Savages I can cope with, Lichas. Real danger lies in a room full of women.' She grinned. 'Now that really *is* a reason to worry.'

'It's indecent, grown men wearing pantaloons! Their boots must stink to high heaven, and did you know they tenderize meat by stuffing it under their saddle? Disgusting! Disgusting and unnatural, all that gold on their fingers, all that grease in their hair, and they drug themselves up with hemp, to put themselves into a stupor, so why would I want to dine with savages?'

'Then you can consider this a lucky escape.'

The lightness of tone didn't lighten his mood, nor did the hint send him away.

'Can I at least help you in whatever brings you to the office at this hour, my lady?'

'No.' Was it his presumption to join in, his hurt at being denied, or his very presence that made her short with him all the time? 'Nothing that can't wait until morning. Thank you.'

'Since I am here, you may as well make use of my services.'

'Oh . . .' She waved a dismissive hand. 'I'd left my seal ring on the desk, so I thought I'd take the opportunity to look up the file on some woman who wanted advice about her investment. Not important—'

'Citizen, *perioikoi* or *helot*?' he asked, lighting another lamp.

She picked an imaginary hair off her sleeve. 'Citizen.'

Not one of the aristocracy, true. But the decent, respectable wife of a soldier, who had desperately craved kids of her own – and wasn't that always the case with barren women? Those who wanted a family the most were those whom Fate had denied? While others, at just fifteen years of age, were able to conceive at once . . .?

'Citizens' files are stored here.' Lichas shuffled over to the niche in the north wall. 'Her name?'

In for a *chalkoi*, in for a *drachm*, 'Coronis.' A plump and pretty woman, with brilliant red curls and broad, dimpled smile. And oh, how those big green eyes had filled with tears, when Iliona handed the baby boy over.

'Coronis?' The scribe's long fingers stopped rifling. 'Not the redhead with the smallholding down near the delta?'

Iliona didn't know about the smallholding. Coronis must have bought it with the money she'd given her. 'You know her?'

'Her husband used to serve in my uncle's bodyguard.'

Once again, she'd forgotten his extraordinary talent for recall.

'He fell at Marathon, and his bones were carried home on his shield,' Lichas said.

Myles, Myles. Why can't you accept that being the son of a dead hero is better than an unwanted noble-born bastard?

'Though I fear there has been a mistake concerning the woman who consulted you about her investments,' Lichas was saying. 'Her name cannot be Coronis.'

'I assure you it is.' You don't forget the name of the woman who takes the newborn child from your breast.

'Then the redhead has lied to you, my lady.' His pale eyes fixed on the floor. 'Coronis died last winter, and lies buried next to her husband.'

TWENTY-ONE

B anquets always started the same way. First there was the ritual washing of hands and, since the feast was always in honour of one god or another, the guests were then garlanded accordingly. The natural choice would have been Apollo, god of music, poetry, healing and prophecy, who rode his fiery chariot across the sky and brought light and heat to the day. Alternatively, Iliona could have honoured the corn goddess, Demeter, an appropriate choice, given the harvest that was being brought in. Or Gaia, mother of the river god whom she served. Even the three Charities, Beauty, Mirth and Good Cheer, would have exploited the occasion, not to mention Dionysus, god of wine and feasting himself.

Instead, she chose Shining Selene, Guardian of the Night, Bestower of Dew, goddess of mystery and enchantment. Hence the garlands of pure white wild clematis that hung in the Hall, and chaplets of daisies and silver-leaved cerastrium flowers.

'To the moon,' Aeërtes intoned. 'To the moon who sleeps on the ocean that encircles the earth, and the stars that harness the steeds of her chariot.'

'To the moon,' everyone chorused, and drank.

Light snacks were served by slaves dressed in light grey, almost silver, tunics, while Iliona's own vestments were of white linen shot with silver, that rustled, and glistened under the lamplight.

'Sorry I'm late, everyone.' Lysander breezed in as though he owned the place. 'Pressing affairs at the palace.'

It obviously didn't occur to you to invite me as an honoured guest, he'd said. No, so he'd invited himself, though it would have been nice if he'd had the grace to inform her. But then surprise was a favoured tactic of the *Krypteia*, and she looked at the ring on his finger. A cicada. The emblem of Aphrodite, goddess of love, and the personal insignia of the King's sister.

Silly, silly, silly Iliona. She'd naïvely thought the battle was with her cousin.

'My kinsman, Lysander,' she said, since at least one of them ought to explain why a regally dressed stranger had joined them for dinner. 'A somewhat distant connection on my mother's side.'

'I do hope you weren't pressed too hard,' she murmured under her breath. 'Palace affairs can be terribly draining, once embarked on.'

'Twice, actually,' he rumbled back, and the song of the cicadas was clear. *Ariadne will be taking your place very shortly*, they chirruped. *Go gracefully.*

Usually, only men reclined, two to a couch, but High Priestesses qualified for an equal role. Out of consideration, they afforded her a couch to herself.

'I'm sure you are more than familiar with our Greek practices by now,' she told her guests. 'Where it is customary at such functions to elect a Leader of Revels by the drawing of lots.'

A slave stepped up to Aeërtes with a bag containing six black beans and one white. The last time anyone had reached into a sack, she thought, three runes had come out that meant watching, parting, death . . .

'Ladies, first,' the guest of honour demurred, waving it away. 'I insist.'

'Draw for me,' she told the slave. It wouldn't do to see the hand of the High Priestess shake.

'It is the white bean, my lady.' The slave held it up, and everyone cheered, except, of course, Iliona. How the gods must be laughing at her.

'Very well, then, the agenda is this. We will start with a course of fish, game and wild fowl, over which we will each tell a story. Afterwards, we will drink wine while the dancing girls perform, and then – well, I'm afraid you'll just have to wait to find out what comes next.'

For all his faults, Lichas had done her proud with the meal. Dishes of pigeons baked in mustard and wine were laid on the table, served alongside octopus, lobster and prawns tossed in garlic, with side stews of herbed lentils, onions and leeks. To round off the main course, slaves brought in silver platters piled high with smoked duck on beds of spiced cabbage, deep bowls steaming with venison braised with cinnamon and honey, a casserole of suckling pig, and tartlets containing smoked ham and sausage.

'Not one morsel of it cooked over fire,' Aeërtes noted, with a nod of approval. 'You indeed honour us tonight, Iliona.'

If there was a common denominator among the killer's victims, the *Krypteia* had not been able to find it, she reflected. True, much of this was because only one of the girls had been identified, yet the bastard must be choosing them somehow. Surely Aeërtes, though, was above reproach?

'Don't be too grateful,' she tossed back. 'It's your turn to start, and since this feast is dedicated to Silver Selene, why don't you tell us a story about your own moon goddess?'

Preferably the one about killing women every full moon.

Aeërtes cracked open a lobster claw and sucked out the meat. 'I will tell you a story about fire,' he said slowly. 'About how, once upon a time, and long before they ever tried to take Greece, the Persian Empire set their sights on what was then a very new Scythian nation.'

Iliona glanced across to Lysander and saw that he, too, had noticed how Aeërtes had sidestepped the issue. In the braziers, frankincense burned.

'The attack was unexpected. The speed of invasion hard to believe.'

'If it's anything like the techniques they used to bridge the Bosporus, lashing boats together, hull against hull, then yes, we have some idea,' Lysander said. 'The army, its baggage train and all its supplies had crossed in a week.'

'Only because they had learned from us, my friend. Only because they'd learned from us.' Aeërtes pulled a prawn out of its shell and waved it at him like a baton. 'When they swooped, they came with nothing. Just a mighty militia force, who planned to live off the land as they advanced through the provinces, but here they were in for a shock.'

'We do not worship the sun without reason,' Sebastos said through a mouthful of pigeon. 'His fire is holy, and sometimes holiness is a weapon itself.'

'We had no time to build defences,' Aeërtes explained. 'No time to gather our warriors, no time to protect our women and children, so we retreated, firing the earth as we left.'

'We lost our livestock, our crops, everything,' Barak said.

'But no army can survive on scorched soil and ash. We defeated the invaders through starvation.'

'Ah, but Scythia is not the only nation to take drastic personal measures.' Sebastos turned to his hostess. 'With your permission, ma'am?'

'The floor is yours, sir.'

The whole point of this banquet was to expose a killer's character through actions and words. Maybe the dour body-guard would let something slip?

'My story begins at an end,' he said. 'The end of the Persian Wars, when Sparta and Athens prove their joint invincibility by taking Byzantium. A brilliant young general is put in charge.' He speared a sliver of duck on his knife, but did not eat. 'A Spartan, by the name of Pausanias.'

He'd done his homework, she thought.

'But within three short years, what happens? The young general is adopting Persian garb and surrounding himself with Persian bodyguards. He even places himself above the law, when he kills a girl and is not held to account, and very soon Byzantium, and every other city state under his command, are crippled by high taxes, poor management and a heavy-handed approach in their government.'

On the opposite couch, Lysander was nonchalantly tucking into the venison. Iliona knew he was hanging on Sebastos's every word.

'With Spartan administration under fire, the mandate passes to Athens, and a worse blow to Sparta could not be imagined.'

The shame of having to hand over the reins to the arch-enemy had been almost too much to bear, and most Spartans still winced at the memory of it.

'Pausanias is brought home, where he stands trial and where, to everyone's surprise and delight, he is found inno-cent of all charges against him.' Sebastos paused. 'Until certain correspondence between him and the Persians comes to light.'

True, Iliona thought, letters did come to light. But were they genuine proof of his treachery? Or skilful fabrications of the *Krypteia*, now that an illustrious hero had become a liability?

'Pausanias hastens to the Temple of Athene.' Sebastos

drummed his fingers on the table to imitate the sound of running. 'He begs sanctuary from the priests, but! Instead of finding refuge, the general who saved the day at Plataea, the definitive victory of the whole Greek alliance, was bricked up inside by his very own people, and condemned to die of starvation and thirst.'

He failed to mention that, in his final moments, Pausanias was dragged out, so that his death would not contaminate sacred ground, but that, she supposed, was beside the point. Between them, Aeërtes and Sebastos were making sure that they understood the kind of people the Spartans were dealing with – and that the Scythians understood them just as much.

And how interesting, she mused. When *know your enemy* was the first rule of warfare . . .

Poppy seed and sesame rolls were brought in, steaming in their linen-lined baskets. Huge loaves of cheese bread were pulled apart in chunks, as well as the famous Taygetus bread, made from fermented flour and water, then left to rise for nine or ten hours to develop its strong and unique taste.

But the conspiracy didn't end with Sebastos. Justifying his story by reminding the assembly that his mother was an Amazon priestess, Barak recounted the ninth Labour of Hercules, the one where he was tasked with capturing the girdle that belonged to the Amazon Queen. The Scythian equivalent of her crown.

'Whether it was his way with words or his celebrated muscles that won her over, we'll never know,' Barak said, juggling five rolls in the air. 'But so enamoured was our queen with your hero, that she handed him her precious girdle as a gift, and yet . . .' One by one he caught the rolls and laid them gently back in their baskets. 'He murdered her anyway.'

Bloody Hera again, Iliona thought. She'd muddied the waters by inciting the other Amazons to attack Hercules' ship – but how do you explain that to people who don't believe in the gods?

'Some men just hate women,' she said.

Aeërtes's knife clattered on to the floor. 'Many people believe the name derives from the word *amazos*, meaning without breast,' he said, bending down to retrieve it. 'That Scythia is populated by tribes of warrior women who burn off their right breasts, the better to pull a bow and throw spears.'

'It's more fun to imagine a race of women raiding neighbouring tribes for sex, raising only the girl babies and killing the boys,' she replied.

'Then it must come as quite a disappointment to discover it comes from *maza*, which is our word for the moon.'

'Under the moon that hangs in the sky, the mountains sleep,' sang Tzan, strumming the three strings of his *komuz* with a plectrum. *'The ravines, the headlands and torrent-beds are asleep. All the creeping tribes that the black earth doth nourish, And the wild creatures of the hills, and the monsters of the deep. The clans of long-winged birds, they, too are sleeping.'*

'A Spartan poem set to Scythian music, played on an instrument we've never seen. I'm impressed,' Iliona said, and she meant it. What Tzan had produced was magical, mischievous, thrilling and cunning, all wrapped up in one.

'As are we impressed in return,' Aeërtes replied, stroking his beard. 'You cannot imagine how stimulating it is, to acquire personal insight into the Hellenic world as it really is, and not as certain self-serving states would wish us to believe.'

'Don't be deceived,' Lysander warned, with a playful wag of his finger, and to look at him you'd never think he dispensed duplicity and death for a living. 'Hellenic banquets have a tendency to start out as deep philosophical debates, only to end up as drunken carousing.'

'I should damn well hope so,' Aeërtes laughed back. 'We did not sail half way round the world to stay sober.'

'Temperance does not lend itself to picking the nits out of trade treaties,' Tzan agreed, still strumming his *komuz*. 'But what of you, my lady? Do you not have a tale to tell us concerning our lady, the moon?'

Bluff and double-bluff, she wondered?

'A romance, as it happens,' she said, relating the story of the handsome youth so beloved by Selene, that one still night the Silver Goddess kissed his eyes as he lay sleeping, casting a spell on him so that he remained asleep, never ageing but with the bloom of eternal youth upon his cheeks. 'Every night, she shines on him with her heart full of love.'

'Moon, moon, moon, what is it with the bloody moon all the time,' Karas snarled. 'Thirteen female cycles and suddenly every woman is empowered by this celestial mother—'

'Karas.' Aeërtes's rebuke carried the full weight of command. 'I'm sorry to interrupt, Iliona, but Karas appears to have forgotten his obligations.' He turned a cold smile on the scowling showman. 'You neglected to bring in the gifts for our hostess. Perhaps now might be an opportune moment, since we all appear to have finished eating?'

The diplomat was earning his pay, she reflected. Which was a pity, because she would have very much liked to have heard the rest of Karas's diatribe.

'*The Moon is my celestial mother,*' sang Tzan.

'You shut your damn mouth or I'll shut it for you,' Karas warned under his breath.

'*—my bow is the crescent moon—*'

'You'd better hurry,' Aeërtes urged. 'There was some mention of dancing girls, as I recall, and it would be a shame to miss out on their lightly clad gyrations, Karas.'

In an instant, the broad smile was back, teeth flashing brighter than lamplight. 'Speed is my middle name,' he said, somersaulting over the table. 'I shall return before you feel the draught of my leaving.'

With that, he cartwheeled across the Great Hall, performed a running jump up the wall, a spin as he landed, and back-flipped through the archway in a spellbinding sequence that had been as carefully choreographed as the rest of the Scythians' performance.

They know we're on to them, Iliona thought with a sigh. The question was, on to what?

Among the roots of the willows and the alders, the agent of the *Krypteia* lay motionless. His face was blackened by soot. A dark cloak covered his head. Flat on his stomach, he was invisible under the three-quarter moon. In the undergrowth, mice and voles scurried about. Owls hooted their territories across the river. From time to time, he would hear the plop of a frog, the slurp of a stag as it drank, and crickets rasping in the long grass. Moths flittered, mosquitoes whined, and, above the smell of leaf litter, the agent could taste wild mushrooms on the air.

He shifted position to avoid cramp in his muscles. For three weeks, he and other agents, either retired veterans or recruits like himself, had been working the surveillance rota without interruption. Unfortunately, boredom was as much an enemy as the Persians and *helots*, and one of the true tests of being in the *Krypteia* was knowing how to combat its deadly embrace.

'Like the Sirens on the rocks, it will lure you towards it,' they'd been warned. 'You must learn to fight it with cunning.'

So apart from weapons-training, fitness, co-ordination and tactics, they became skilled at remaining alert, yet at the same time not so taut that they risked stretching themselves beyond the point of rigidity.

'Focus on the enemy. Keep thinking how they think, and you can't go far wrong.'

For this reason, Scythian customs and practices had been drummed into them, like it or not.

'The willow, in particular, is sacred to them,' they'd been taught, which was why High Command was so sure the bastards would return to the scene of the ritual.

The agent was by no means as certain. Three weeks was a long time to leave bones hanging about, but, then again, it was a long time to be lying on your belly like a bloody snake, too.

He did not trust the Scythians. What kind of justice relies on the fall of a bundle of willow rods? No, no, he didn't like this at all. Say a man's suspected of murder, for instance, but there's no direct proof. Is there a court, a trial, interrogation, torture even to determine the truth? Nope. It's all down to three soothsayers throwing a bunch of willow wands, and it gets worse! Should they pronounce the defendant guilty and he denies it, three more are brought in for a second opinion, even a third lot, in the case of a hung verdict. Talk about justice being blind, and if the rods found him guilty, then the accused's property was shared out among his prosecutors. How fair was that? It was a rotten system, corrupt to the core, and even execution was erratic.

'Let the fire decide,' was the Scythians' motto.

They'd hitch a cart with oxen, fill it with firewood and tie the condemned man on top. The sticks were then set alight and the oxen scared off at a run, and sometimes it went according to plan, sometimes the oxen burned to death with the cart, and sometimes the condemned got away with only a scorching. It all depended on what mood the fire was in, and—

The agent's train snapped with the sound of footsteps. The approach was quiet, but this had more to do with someone picking their way through the undergrowth than any attempt to muffle the sound. The agent hunkered deeper into the soil. Well, well, well. High Command were right, they did come back. Red boots came into sight, and he recognized the one with the slanted eyes. His name was Karas, and the agent had been tasked with following him on a couple of occasions, but Karas was no fool. He'd given him the slip both times, though High Command hadn't punished him for sloppiness, as he'd expected. Four other Scythians had apparently done the same, which meant they were professionals – and exceedingly good ones at that. The agent watched, as he had been instructed to do, invisible under the camouflage.

Karas circled the area, peering closely at the bones gleaming white in the moonlight. Eventually, he picked up what appeared to be a hand. Yes, it was a hand. The agent could see, when he held it up to the light. He watched the Scythian remove the ring from its middle finger and tuck it into his boot. When he walked away, Karas was whistling.

'Well?'

The dancers had finished. The Leader of Revels called for a break. She did not get it from the *Krypteia*, who steered her outside, to a quiet corner of the colonnade, where they could not be seen or overheard. High above, the Dragon coiled itself round the Bear, while Andromeda twinkled in gratitude for being rescued from the sea monster. A soft breeze from the south ruffled their tunics, the fountain babbled and splashed, and the oiled rags that burned in the sconces cast dancing shadows over the frescoes.

'If you're going to tell me Aeërtes's gifts belong to the State, then the State's out of luck,' Iliona said. Rich tapestries, saddlecloths, brightly woven rugs and thick cushions all lay spread across the floor of the Great Hall in a kaleidoscope of reds, golds and blues, along with low padded stools, and piles of blankets embroidered with birds and other, considerably more exotic, creatures. 'These stay with Eurotas.'

Mind you, if that fur cloak made its way into her private quarters, she would not be remotely surprised.

'Surely you wouldn't deny your country the privilege of dipping into that vat of fermented mare's milk?' Lysander murmured.

'I suppose I could make an exception,' she quipped back, because even with a sealed stopper, the vat was liberating a distinctive aroma. 'But as to our guests.' Her mood sobered. 'I'm none the wiser, are you?'

They'd already established the killer was vain, intelligent, crafty and, above all, possessed a deep-rooted hatred of women. Nothing tonight suggested one stood out above his companions, other than perhaps Aeërtes dropping a knife and Karas's sulk. Which in itself might have been no more than an egotist's response to not getting enough attention. It was a very different animal that bounded out of that Hall.

'My search of their quarters revealed a variety of awls with curved blades,' Lysander said, adding that sewing saddles was men's work and no doubt explained the rather neat lock-stitch that held the rider's embalmed innards in place. 'Leather, canvas, skin, it's all the same to a sharp stitching awl, but it's not the weapon that bothers me. It's the scalps.'

He proceeded to outline his conclusion about the killer's hiding place.

'Which could be anywhere,' he said. 'In the palace, the hills, the mountains, the paddocks, and I can't comb every mulberry orchard and trawl through every vine without arousing suspicion.'

'They're already suspicious.'

'As a group, yes, but the bastard who enjoys hurting these women has to be even more careful.' He chewed his lip. 'We've had the whole delegation under surveillance from the moment their ship dropped anchor, but these five are good. Really good.'

'You don't mean to tell me they've actually given the *Krypteia* the slip?'

If he noticed the sarcasm, he didn't react. 'My men most certainly, but I have a feeling these are evasion tactics against their own people.' He paused. 'They're up to something,

something the rest of the delegation know nothing about, and given that Aeërtes is head of this commission, I'm betting he staged the entire trip.'

Iliona looked up at the moon. It seemed to have swelled even as the night had progressed, but perhaps that was just panic. The knowledge that another poor bitch had been earmarked for an appointment with terror – and had no idea what lay in store.

'What do you know about Aeërtes?' she asked.

'The information's sketchy, since the Scythians tend to close ranks, and he's also an expert at deflecting attention from himself in the name of false modesty. But basically he seems to have spent the best part of six years putting together an army to overthrow the government of Colchis, a coup which could not have been achieved without the patronage of the Amazon priestesses, who, as you know, still wield enormous power.'

Built on some very clever propaganda, she suspected. By wearing snakeskin and chain mail, and carrying battle-axes in worship, they were portraying themselves as a force to be reckoned with. It seemed to her that religion gave them authority in what was very much a man's world, and given that there was rarely smoke without fire, Iliona wouldn't mind betting that, at some point in their history, at least one of the priestesses had burned off her right breast to kick the ball of legend rolling – and that Aeërtes knew it. How it must stick in his craw, then. Being beholden not only to women, who he held inferior to men anyway, but women who sailed under false colours.

'He's held Colchis for almost three years,' Lysander was saying. 'During that time he's proved himself a firm, but fair law-maker by all accounts, progressive in his outlook, as well as being respected and admired by the other tribes. Hence his heading this trade delegation.'

'But?' She could sense his suspicions.

Grey eyes fixed on a point in the distance. 'The fact that he continues to enlarge his army is not entirely surprising. A man who takes over by force always watches his back, and a strong defence equals a strong deterrent. It's his cosying up to the nomadic element of the Scythian nation that makes the hairs on the back of my neck rise.'

Iliona considered the implications. 'Tribes who are constantly on the move and carry their possessions in wagons makes them an extremely difficult target for attack,' she said slowly. 'On the other hand, it facilitates any offensive measures they might wish to instigate themselves.'

'Exactly. So why would Aeërtes, riding to power on the premise of restoring Colchis to its former glory, take time out to snuggle up with the nomads?'

For a moment, her mind was distracted by a young man crossing the far side of the precinct. He walked in the shadows, and even though the flickering sconces lent staccato to his movements, his features seemed vaguely familiar. It took a few seconds before she finally placed him. The man who'd waved to the small girl she'd been helping to feed the pigeons. The day Jocasta's scowl made her belittle Tibios's symptoms.

'If Aeërtes is genuinely looking to make Colchis more prosperous, won't he be wanting the nomads to increase their output of furs, felt and hides for the export market?' she said.

The stranger kept checking over his shoulder, and she realized that, because she and Lysander were in shadow themselves, he did not know they were there.

'Not to mention their slave raids on the interior,' she added, as the young man made his way towards Jocasta's *pharmakion*. 'With the rising success of the Greek alliance, slaves are in short supply.'

Mounted raiders could be in and out before the alarm had been raised.

'Maybe.' Lysander dabbled his fingers in the fountain in thought. 'But hemp grows wild and it grows plentiful on Scythian soil. Moreover, it's a key component in shipbuilding, since no boat can sail without ropes, and hemp ropes are proving more durable than parchment.' He paused. 'A point that will not have slipped the minds of Athenian warship builders.'

'So why come to Sparta?' His argument made no sense. 'Why not deal with Athens direct?'

'Why indeed.' He flicked the water from his fingers up in the air and caught the drops on his tongue. 'Why spend months thrashing out a treaty that could have been agreed in a fortnight? Why kill two of your fellow countrymen, then advertise what you've done by placing them where they won't fail to be noticed? Why kill only when the moon is at its full? And why can't we trim five down to one?'

Aeërtes's patience, discipline and dislike of women made him a good contender, she supposed. As did Tzan's passion, Sebastos's attention to detail and Barak's Amazonian connections. But Karas hailed from the Caucasus, so did that rule him out? Or was this a classic attempt by an outsider to 'fit in' with the others through some twisted logic of rituals and sacrifice?

'The night is still young,' she said, 'and who knows? Maybe inhibitions might slacken, once the wine starts to loosen them up.'

'I wouldn't bet on it. The seal on our killer's emotions is tight, and in any case, Scythians drink their wine neat, didn't you know?'

'Barbarians,' she quipped. 'Are there no lengths these scoundrels won't stoop to?'

'Probably not. Shall we rejoin them?'

'There are a couple of things that need my attention.'

'Of course. You need to check on the puppy.'

'Temple business,' she lied.

'That dog's got to go.' It was not a suggestion. 'If word gets out that Hecate's sacrifice ended up as your personal pet – well, let's just say the river god's reputation for impartiality would go up in smoke.'

Back to square one, in other words. Where she'd be stripped of her lands, not just her post, charged with sabotaging a ritual and perverting spiritual justice, and sentenced to three, possibly five years in exile.

'I have no intention of keeping him,' she sniffed. All the same, you couldn't hand Chip over before he'd been taught how to sit, lie and stay. And in between, he needed to be fed, taken for walks, given cuddles and plays with his toys. 'The brat's in my way.'

Mainly at night, when he slept on her bed, his little warm body pressed against hers.

'Just make sure you don't give him a name,' Lysander warned. 'It's much harder to part with them, then.'

'You make it sound as though I'm getting attached to him.'

'So that's not venison wrapped up in that bundle you have tucked up your sleeve?'

'Only fat and gristle.'

'Then you must have been desperately unlucky. They all looked choice cuts to me, but while you're at it.' He handed her a cloth containing what smelled like suckling pig. 'This dropped out of your other sleeve.'

TWENTY-TWO

J ocasta stirred the little clay pot bubbling over the brazier, reflecting that a river whose tributaries flowed right through the seasons was all very well. But for the poor souls who actually lived in those damp valleys, plenitude took a hefty toll on their health.

Give me a copper chalkoi for every hour I've spent mixing agrimony gargles for their sore throats and brewing up thick syrups of horseradish for their chesty coughs, she thought, *and I'd be richer than Midas.*

She tilted her spoon to test the consistency. Still too thin. Lungs and throats she could treat, though. If only it was as easy to relieve the rheumatics in their bones, and in the four years she'd been in practice here, she'd tried everything: oil of bay, garlic, decoctions of germander, tinctures of baneberry, everything her books suggested, and more. Unfortunately, her remedies barely made an impact on their stiff, swollen joints – which didn't stop her from trying. Maybe this latest concoction, though, given to her by a physician from Gaul—

'What the hell is that stink?'

The spoon clattered to the floor as she spun round. 'What are you doing here?' The last person she expected to see again tonight was the schoolmaster, and she wondered if he actually had a home to go back to. It was probably as grim as the expression on his face. 'Did anybody see you?' She glanced into the blackness behind him, even though she knew it was pointless.

'Of course not,' he sneered. 'Do you take me for a fool?'

She presumed that was a rhetorical question. 'What brings you back?' He must know the risks he was running. 'Is something wrong? Has the schedule changed?' She picked the

sticky spoon off the floor and wished her night-robe was
made of thicker material. 'Because if so, it'll be difficult to
bring it forward by more than a—'

'You mentioned a formula for burning the hemp.' When
he closed the door, she felt a sense of suffocation. 'It makes
sense to take it away with me now, don't you think? The
quicker I can distribute it.'

'It's midnight.'

'You weren't in bed.'

'Very well.' With a sigh, Jocasta reached for a small scrap
of parchment and as she scribbled, she could feel his eyes
boring through her diaphanous tunic. 'Anything else?'

'Yes.' Behind him, the lock on the door clicked into place.
'As a matter of fact, there is.'

The truth was, Chip's big, floppy ears and even bigger brown
eyes had wormed their way into Iliona's heart, and she was
damned if she'd give him up. It was irresistible the way he
followed her around, tangling round her feet when she walked
and nipping at the hem of her robe. Many's the time she'd
laughed till she cried, throwing walnuts for him to chase and
seeing his little fat legs go all over the place as he went skid-
ding over the tiles. And quite frankly, the way he'd run around
for an hour, then drop to sleep like a stone, made something
lurch under her ribcage.

She wasn't stupid. She knew the puppy filled a big black
hole in her life, and that his comical antics and unconditional
love was just what she needed right now. What better anti-
dote to the pain of Myles thrusting himself back into her life,
or the guilt she carried for Tibios? But it wasn't why she
hung on to him. True, a warm heart beating next to her own
gave her comfort in nights filled with emptiness and pain,
and the very nature of her job meant it was a path she travelled alone. But it wasn't companionship, either.

'Love at first sight, eh, Chip?'

She tossed his little felt rabbit up in the air. After several
clumsy attempts, he finally ran it to ground, tugging on it
with growls that would not have disturbed the most nervy of
mice.

'All we have to do is keep you under wraps until this other
business dies down.'

Vicious killer notwithstanding, these five were plotting something, though it may well be that it had nothing to do with Sparta. Quite likely there were more personal motives driving them to take such precautions, one possibility being that the two dead men had been sent to kill them, and they got in first. According to the *Krypteia*'s physicians, there were no signs of violence on the bodies, but whilst poisoning could not be ruled out, it usually left some physical trace. The most obvious, of course, being a death rictus, and these two had looked calm, as though they'd died in their sleep. Even so, it was hard to imagine death came from natural causes.

'The thing is . . .'

The venison and suckling pig had been wolfed down so fast that the puppy belched when he rolled over at her feet.

'Can we actually keep you hidden for the six weeks until the Scythians set sail for home?'

He squirmed in delight as her fingers raked his little fat belly.

'How do you feel about being fostered out for a month, eh?'

More accurately, how would she? And would he recognize her, when she came to reclaim him? Would he even want to come back . . .?

'You, young man, are a timewaster, you know that?'

She really ought to return to the banquet, except he was so full of energy after the titbits, that she couldn't just leave him so full of beans.

'How about this, then?' She reached into her coffer, the one inlaid with abalone, and pulled out the puppet Myles had given her.

'Like that?' she said, taunting him with its twitching dance.

He did. He kept jumping up, trying to grab it, his eyes shining with concentration as the legs jerked out of his reach. But with every attempt, his co-ordination skills slowly improved.

'Good boy,' she laughed, as he ran off under the bed with his trophy. 'You chew on that, for a while. It'll strengthen those little razor-sharp teeth.'

She left him, snarling and gnawing on his freshly caught kill, and thanked Zeus that Chip wasn't a barker, or the whimpering kind. Mind you, how she was going to explain those scuff marks on her door to the carpenter was anyone's guess! An exhausted lover, trying to claw his way out? That should get a few tongues wagging.

Still smiling as she closed the gate to the courtyard, she noticed the light was still on in her office. Inside, she could see Lichas hobbling back and forth, probably making copious notes on the Scythians' gifts, where no detail, no matter how small, would be omitted. He'd probably logged tonight's banqueting in all its minutiae, too. Right down to the very last quail's egg. Adjusting her diadem, she thought she really must stop wanting to reward his efforts by giving him that vat of fermented milk.

'Marm?' The voice was heavily accented and crackly with age, but also with something else besides. 'Are you the one what is in charge here?'

Few people mistook the High Priestess in full ceremonial regalia for a dancing girl, Iliona thought. But the woman was wearing a white stole embroidered with red and blue stripes that wrapped tightly around her shoulders. The tunic underneath was equally garish, and no Greek woman would be seen dead in brown leather mules.

'I am the High Priestess of the river god Eurotas, yes.'

'They say you help desperate folk, is that be right?'

The something-else-besides Iliona recognized as fear. It was not unfamiliar to her. 'What is the problem?'

'I is innocent,' the old woman quailed. 'I swear on the eyes of my mother, that I had no intention of stealing. I want only to go home.'

'I'm sure you do,' Iliona said, leading her into the courtyard. High walls were very effective when it came to muffling sound. 'Now take a deep breath, that's better, and tell me your name.'

'Nori.'

'Very well, Nori. Now what is so desperate about your situation that you hide in the shadows and seek help from a temple whose god you do not believe in?'

Rheumy eyes blinked, unsure whether to feign a sudden conversion. Blue eyes stared steadily back. In them, Nori recognized kindness and compassion. She also understood that the blue eyes would not be fooled. She swallowed.

'I was employed by the frankincense merchant, Lokman.' It took her a moment to realize that, just by her presence, the High Priestess had calmed Nori's nerves. My, my, she could actually feel the weight lifting. 'They arrested me as I tried to board big ship home to Arabia,' she explained. 'They bundled us off to dungeons, but there is so many of us that I escaped when guard wasn't looking.' She shot Iliona a crafty glance. 'I can run a lot faster than you might think.'

'Exactly what heinous crime are you wanted for, Nori?' Her stole and those mules might be an offence to the eye, but few people are thrown into jail for poor taste.

'It was not just me! They arrested the very lot of us – all of master's household, that is – and accused us of stealing his treasure.'

'I see. And what did the master have to say about this?'

'Master is dead, marm, that is trouble. Killed himself by locking himself in then slashing his veins, and oh, it was terrible. Terrible! All that *blood*.' She shuddered. 'Up the walls, on the—'

'Yes, yes, I can imagine, thank you.'

'We just wanted to go home, don't you see?'

Iliona did see, though not necessarily the picture the old woman was painting. She saw a house full of poorly paid slaves left high and dry, and a long way from home. The situation that evolved was most likely born of expediency, rather than premeditated theft, but, like most thieves, they didn't expect to be caught.

'I will be frank with you, Nori.' She thrust a goblet of wine into her age-spotted hand. 'This is not my jurisdiction.'

It was a criminal case, nothing to do with the temple, and Eurotas was not a refuge for folk on the run. The right course of action was to hand her back to the authorities, but – she tapped her finger against her lips. The woman was old, she was destitute and in a foreign land to boot. She would certainly not survive two years down the mines.

'On this occasion, however, I am prepared to guarantee you safe passage on the *Nightingale* which sails at daybreak for Egypt.' As it happened, Iliona was sending a gift to the Temple of Aphrodite in Alexandria on that particular boat. Two amphorae of fine olive oil. 'After that, you'll have to make your own way, it's the best I can do.'

'Oh, that is wonderful, marm, wonderful. They said you would help.' The old woman dropped to her knees and kissed the hem of her robe. 'Just like my beautiful mistress, so kind, so—'

'*Mistress?*' If there was a mistress, the whole deal was off.

'Such a sweet girl,' Nori gushed. 'Noble born, too, and that is why Master Lokman killed himself, see? His lovely wife left him, and he could not live with shame of – well, not to put too fine a point on it, marm. Of her having it off with a foreigner.'

'Yes, well, I don't need to know those details, either—'

'I tried to tell him. The day he died, he asks me *was she unfaithful*, and I try to tell him Ay-Mari had been, how you say, fooling around but that she have finished the affair. Leastways I thought she had. Only master, he would not listen.'

'You mustn't blame yourself, Nori. If he was contemplating suicide, his mind would—'

'It could have been yesterday, not three weeks back, I remember it so clear. When Master Lokman told mistress he had one big deal to conclude with them foreigners then he'd retire home richer than Croesus, Ay-Mari was so, so *excited!* The pleasures of the flesh were merely distractions, don't you see. She very young, Ay-Mari. Much younger than him, and she get terribly easily bored, does mistress. Master worked such long hours and she felt neglected. It happens among nobility. All that being fussed over, they are not used to own company, see? So if handsome young lover happen along, she think to herself, well, why not?'

Across in the Great Hall, the music had already started up again. A drinking song, full of cheer and goodwill. But the old woman was sobbing, and Iliona knew how it felt to be alone.

'So your mistress took a lover?' she asked, for the sake of something to say.

'Many, marm, if truth be told, but she was good girl underneath. Never forgot Arab ways, so you could have, what is word, blown me down with feather when she ran off with that last one.'

'I'm sure.'

'I thought she would have *told* me, that is all.' The hurt in her voice came straight from the heart. 'Them affairs did not mean nothing to her. She young and she need young people round her, is natural, but with the baby on the way—'

'Obviously the lover's child.'

'Aye, but I still thought she would have mentioned, that is all. Instead of running off and leaving everything behind, and without so much as a word.' She laid the cup down and tilted her head on one side like a robin's. 'Do you think they let me have mistress's rings, marm? You know. Keepsakes . . .?'

'Don't push it, Nori.'

Shame replaced greed. She returned to kissing Iliona's hem.

'Take this to my scribe, he is still in my office.' She handed the old woman her official seal ring. 'He'll draw up a document giving you safe passage from the authorities, and if you feel tempted to add anything else to the account, be sure you will be handed over to the authorities to stand trial for theft.'

'No. No, no, of course not, I have learned lesson, marm. Thank you.'

The rest of her fawning was lost as Iliona swept out of the courtyard. With a killer on a countdown and five Scythians plotting heaven-knows-what, she really didn't have time for a greedy old woman's tale of hard luck, much less a young bride's adulterous liaison.

Didn't these people have anything better to do, than think of themselves all the time?

You can't, you can't, you can't kill her yet. But I want to. I need to. *You can't. You mustn't. You must wait.* I can't wait. *The moon is swelling.* I am swelling. *Be strong.* I am strong. *Then hold on to your goal. Remember what it is that you want. What you've planned for.* I haven't forgotten, but I need it. I need it now. *I know.* I need to feel her squirm. I need to feel blood trickling through my clenched fists, and I need, I need so badly, to see death in her eyes. *You will. I promise. Be patient.*

It's seeing death before she sees it herself. When I'm telling her, ssh, it'll be fine, just fine. Let me do what I want, then I'll let you go – that's the beauty of it *If it's beauty you want, then what is more pleasing than the Moon bathing her ever-changing form in the Ocean? When she rises, refreshed, to shine her majesty upon the dark earth again, all creatures are subject to her.* I am subject to her. *Not for long.* No. Not for long. *Just six more days.* Yes, that's right! In six days, the Harvest Moon will turn night into day, and as she greets the New Year, so this will be a new beginning for me. *Nine priestesses.* Nine. *Thrice the sacred number three.* New, full and waning. Birth, growth, and decay. Virgin, mother and crone. *Your destiny waits.* I only have eight. *The ninth will not disappoint.*

On the contrary, the ninth will be the best! The ninth signals completion, and, in her suffering and torment, she will learn how I shall dominate her for eternity.

You will cut the arrogance out of the bitch.

Her screams will unchain the haughtiness in her. She won't be so proud, when she's begging.

You will show her humility.

I will show her supremacy.

You will catch her dying breath.

I shall! I shall catch it in the phial, the same as I have captured all the others. A silver phial, that befits my mistress, the moon. A phial that contains the souls of the priestesses that I have personally chosen to serve her.

And with the ninth?

With the ninth, I will wait until the Blood Moon that rises to follow the Harvest. Then, and only then, will I stand naked in her silver light and drink their souls.

Servant will become Master.

Servant will become Master for ever, but in the meantime, right now, I have needs. Desperate needs, I'm at the end of my tether . . .

You must not weaken. You must not take the ninth priestess before her time, or you will never master the moon.

I know, I know, but it's been so long. So long since I've tasted terror on my tongue and dangled death before their eyes.

So long. Too long. Please don't make me wait . . .

Gradually, the music of the drinking songs floated back in to the Servant's consciousness. The sound seemed to come from the other side of the mountains, as though funnelled through a pipe or from the end of a long, lonely tunnel. Ethereal, super-natural and strange.

Then the rhythm kicked in. His mind cleared.

Little by little, he pulled on the mask of normality and returned to a world that was quite unsuspecting.

TWENTY-THREE

By the time Iliona approached the Great Hall, the round of lively drinking songs was drawing to a close. Deciding it would only disconcert the musicians and singers if she strolled in at end of their performance, she felt it better to wait until they had finished. And as she stood, half-hidden and dwarfed by the pillars, images fluttered through her mind like butterflies. Of this atrium decked with gorse during the spring equinox. Of the colourful processions that passed through the precinct. Garlanded children chasing the scapegoat of winter to the sound of drumbeats and flutes. Eurotas brought riches and plenty to Sparta, so it was only right that his reward should be in the form of laughter, music and song. And if it wasn't pan-pipes whistling out a jig, it was *kitharas*, trumpets, triangles and horns, or the rumbustious bellow of a bull-roarer shaking the rafters.

She inhaled deeply of the flower-filled vases, and the frank-incense that burned in braziers set high on the wall. No blood was spilled in the name of the river god. It was the demon, his brother, who needed appeasing, so for the past four years Iliona had organized foot races to be run from the gates, insti-gated drinking contests on public holidays and presided over choir competitions between the local villages. She'd had little ones scampering around for the annual nut hunt, torchlit toasts for the adults, and it was from here that she'd decided a burning wheel should be rolled down to the river every midsummer solstice to music and chanting and dance.

And that stupid prick of a King wanted to turn it into a showcase for silver and gold!

Or did he? She remembered the gold cicadas pinning Lysander's tunic in place. Far more likely that someone planted the idea in her cousin's head, and she wondered how long Lysander and Ariadne had been plotting this conspiracy. The very fact that he wore her ring meant it was no casual liaison, hinting at darker motives still behind this sudden rash of embassies and treasuries. Motives revolving round power, rather than wealth . . .

The Leader of Revels returned to the banquet with her usual professional smile.

'I know you don't believe in our gods, gentlemen, so next on tonight's agenda is a dance depicting the hero Theseus's clash with the Minotaur. A ferocious beast, half-man half-bull, who lived in the depths of the labyrinth, feasting on human flesh.'

At her clap, the musicians struck up. A string of dancing girls in dark, flowing robes skipped into the room, hands joined in a line. At first, their movements seemed random, but as the line swayed back and forth, it became clear they had formed as a serpentine pattern. The girls themselves became the Minotaur's maze. In bounded the monster, naked except for a tiny loin cloth, his oiled skin glistening under the lamplight. Yet it was not his splendid bronzed form that attracted the eye. It was the bull mask and horns on his head. As he danced, the maze moved, too. Ever changing. Ever fluid. And it was into this that the hero was thrust.

'Amazing,' Aeërtes enthused, once the finely choreographed duel had culminated with the Minotaur's head being carried in a triumphal dance round the Hall. 'Absolutely breathtaking, my dear.'

Yes, and if only those girls had kept in step in the odeon the way they had tonight, the prize would be on Eurotas's altar, not Aphrodite's.

'And you're right,' he said. 'We are indeed baffled by the concept of gods and goddesses who, if you don't mind my saying so, seem to spend their entire time whoring and warring.' He indicated the frescoes on the wall with a nod of his head. 'The sun brings us fire, light and growth, the moon brings calmness, peace and rain. You tell me which has the greater power.'

Either side of him, Barak, Karas and Tzan rumbled agreement. As usual, Sebastos said nothing, but held her gaze with the hardness of stone.

'Ah, yes, power.' Iliona turned her smile on Lysander. 'Something every man craves, wouldn't you agree?'

'Hm,' was all he replied.

'And it's perfectly true, Aeërtes. Our gods love, they hate, they bicker and squabble, and dear me, they lust an awful lot after other people's wives. Is that not also the case, Lysander?'

This time the growl in his throat was much deeper.

'But in doing so,' she continued, 'the gods bestow on us something far greater than power. They give us ethics.'

'Ethics?' Aeërtes turned his gaze on Aphrodite over there in the corner, petulantly turning a young husband into a lion, because she didn't feel he'd thanked her enough for her help in winning his wife. 'You call a nymph being transformed into a tree for rebuffing a god's advances moral?' he goggled, pointing to another painting by the arch.

'As a matter of fact, yes, I do. Through their exploits, whether petty or great, the gods set themselves up to be judged. Frankly, it's only by pondering their deeds – was what they did right? Was it fair? What would we have done in their place? – that we determine our own set of values.'

Servants set down a dessert of nuts, figs, grapes and cheeses accompanied by sweet honey cake, scattering rose petals across the floor to scent and freshen the air.

'By their very frailties and strengths,' Iliona told Aeërtes, 'the gods demonstrate the significance of choice, for without choice, no man is free.' She paused. 'In short, our gods give us freedom, and isn't that the most powerful concept of all?'

His face darkened. Something flashed behind his eyes. Anger, she thought, and something else. Whatever it was, he had a fight on his hands to control it.

'Too often,' she pressed on, 'people misunderstand the meaning of the word power. Especially, I'm sad to say, men, where it tends to be synonymous with the word domination.'

'You have a low opinion of our sex,' the bodyguard growled.

'I have a low opinion of bullies, Sebastos. They use fists to oppress and knives to control, because without them, they are nothing but pathetic, insignificant little worms – are you all right, Barak?'

'Bad oyster.' The sweat was pouring down his face,

soaking his headband and dripping on to his shirt. 'If you'll excuse me?'

While her attention was diverted, she had a feeling an exchange had been made between Aeërtes and Tzan, who had suddenly reached under the couch to bring out a stringed instrument that was at least the length of his arm, if not longer.

'I have composed a tune in your honour, my lady. May I?'

'Be my guest.' The moment had gone, the tension was lost. No one was rising to her bait about domination and power, anyway.

Holding his fiddle outstretched, with its neck level with his waistband, Tzan balanced the base of the instrument against the outside of his left knee. Plucking the strings a few times to check the tuning, he then drew out an implement not unlike a bow, scratching it back and forth at an astonishing rate to produce music like nothing she'd heard. And as he played, man became one with his fiddle. Lost to everything, except his art.

'That was extraordinary,' she said, once he'd wound to a close.

While he'd played, Myles, psychopaths, Tibios and conspiracies had been washed away with the music. The jig was uplifting, exhilarating, lively and gay, and surely no man who could coax such tunes out of catgut was capable of butchering women? Yet his clan were imbued with the notion that they were not responsible for their own characters. That they adopted the qualities of whatever creatures were tattooed on their bodies, and Tzan had birds, he had lynx, he had wolves. Viewed through those eyes, there was no contradiction between music and murder.

'Our oriental instruments have many advantages over your own,' he was saying. 'Your *aulos*, for instance, delivers a pretty tune, but does a strap which ties round the musician's head to keep it in place make for spontaneity or comfort?'

Certainly, the dye in his hair testified to vanity, she thought, his music to dedication and discipline. But as the discussion turned to harps versus fiddles, kettle drums versus musical stones, Iliona saw that the tables had also been turned. There would be no more deep talk that night, no further conversational probing, in fact nothing contentious at all. And by the time the choir rounded off the banquet with the traditional hymn of thanks to the gods, her head was spinning from so much small talk. What a relief to wave her guests off, tell the slaves that *will be all*, and not have to smile and pretend any more, at least not for another few hours.

One by one, she extinguished the lamps in the Great Hall, drinking in the silence. This was the first moment she'd had to gather her thoughts after the shock announcement that Coronis was dead. Being in no fit state after that to set a formal banquet in motion, she'd fled to the plane grove to compose herself, only to be confronted by Tibios's wife, blundering in by mistake. The poor woman's agony thwarted any attempt to rally her own feelings, but now that everyone had gone, Iliona's thoughts returned, as they always did, to Myles.

Obviously, grief had triggered this mission to root out his real mother, and although Coronis had broken her promise, it wasn't hard to sympathize with a dying widow's desperation at not wanting to abandon her son, and having him think he was alone in the world.

You know how to pull strings, don't you?

Despite his assertion to the contrary, Iliona suspected that that was actually the first Myles had learned of his adoption. On Coronis's deathbed. What else would explain his anger and bitterness, and he was bound to be confused, lashing out in his grief and craving love from his natural mother in a bid to fill the gap Coronis left behind. Also, by immersing himself in the cavalry, he hoped to have status, recognition and more importantly, a name, so he wouldn't feel deserted and alone. Unfortunately, life wasn't that simple. Iliona unclipped the diadem from her hair and laid it on the table. Coronis had longed for a child, and for that reason she'd loved Myles with all her heart. There could never be any substitution for—

'That must be a weight off your mind.'

How long had he been standing there, arms folded, leaning against the pillar? In the last remaining lamps, she could see the cicadas glittering on his shoulder. As sharp as the glint in his eye.

'What must?'

'The diadem. You know, heavy? Weight off your mind? Excruciatingly funny?' One shoulder shrugged. 'Or not.'

He strolled across to the table and strained wine into two
drinking cups. 'You look like you need this.'

That bad, eh? She drank, but what she needed wasn't wine.
She needed strong arms around her, muscles harder than iron,
crushing the pain and the heartache to dust.

'A woman came to me tonight,' she said, upending the
goblet. 'Her name was Nori, she's Arabian and well past her
prime. But do you know what's even more remarkable than
an old Arab woman trekking all this way, purely on the off
chance that I might be able to help her? It's that by some
miracle she escaped from the dungeons. Quite a feat, wouldn't
you say?'

'Did you?' Lysander took another half pace towards her.
'Help her, I mean.'

'You fixed for her to escape.'

Who else would tell her to go to the Temple of Eurotas?
How else would she, a servant, an Arab, living twenty-five
miles away in the port, know where to come?

'I suppose it's not impossible that one of the guards may
have left the street door open by accident.' With his little
finger, he looped up a blonde curl that had fallen loose of its
moorings. When he slipped it back into her hairpin, she shivered. 'I must remember to reprimand them.'

'Why—' She couldn't stop watching the pulse that beat at
the side of his throat. 'Why did you send her to me?'

He laid down his cup and picked up the diadem, running
his finger over it, as though it was skin. 'The *Krypteia*
keeps tabs on all foreign businesses, and the frankincense
merchant was no exception. His file showed that he was
competent, law-abiding, comfortably off, so when reports
reached me of Lokman's suicide, my first thought was
murder.'

'But it wasn't?'

'I couldn't be sure.' He didn't take his eyes off the tiara.
'But when his entire household tried to decamp with their
late master's treasure chests and not a single travel document
between them, I became even more suspicious.'

'That must have been quite an achievement.'

A muscle twitched at the side of his mouth. 'I prefer to
think of it as professional insurance, but the very fact that
Lokman's servants blustered and blubbered, then came up

with twenty differing accounts, made me determined to get
to the truth.'

'And what would you know about truth? Like the new
portico, the watercourse and the King's fancy new treasuries,
the *Krypteia* construct it to order.'

The hand hesitated in its caress of the diadem. But only
for a fraction. 'Would you mind telling me exactly how we
accomplish such miracles?'

'I'm too tired to play games with you, Lysander. Or is a
slave's testimony under torture not considered the truth any
more?'

Every time she crossed the agora, she couldn't help thinking
of the poor bastards screaming in agony under her feet.

Lysander laid down the tiara. 'I suppose much depends on
where you live,' he said equably. 'The Athenians believe a
slave has no allegiance to anyone except himself, and therefore by default must be a liar. It is my view, however, that
if you put a man to the torture, he will only tell you what
you want to hear. I therefore find it expedient to use other
methods to get to the truth.'

'Of which I am one?'

When he smiled, it was colder than ice. 'You measure
the drops in the ocean and count the grains of sand in the
desert. Surely an old woman's ramblings weren't much of
a challenge?'

The hour was too late to engage in battle, and her head
was pounding from too many monsters. Iliona repeated word
for word what Nori had told her, and while he digested the
information he had been given, something niggled at the back
of her mind . . .

'Tell me again what Lokman told Nori?' he asked.

'You mean one big deal and he'd be made for life?'

'One big deal with *foreigners*, you said.' Grey eyes
narrowed, like a wolf's might, when it picked up a scent.
'Think about it. Here we have a man who's lived here for
four years, trading in frankincense and similar commodities,
and it's made him prosperous, sure, but not wealthy. Suddenly,
though, he's bragging to his bride about going home rich
enough to retire, and when a man like Lokman talks about
foreigners, I doubt he's referring to Spartans.'

'Aeërtes.'

Of course. Lokman's circumstances changed once the Scythians arrived, suggesting his big deal was with them.

'No wonder he was leaving at the end of the summer.' Lysander ran his hands through his hair. 'The bastard was running before he got caught.'

The question was, what on earth could an Arabian frankincense merchant offer that was so attractive, so vital, that Aeërtes and his band of brothers would pay so handsomely for? Slaves? Scythia was well renowned for its regular forays into the interior to hawk human flesh in the slave markets on Delos. But a man who kills himself because his wife shamed him by abandoning her Arab traditions didn't sound like a man who had no qualms in trading in misery. And in any case, if the Scythians were running slaves, they could do it quite openly.

'What was so dangerous that they needed a middleman?' he mused. 'And why the frankincense merchant?'

The niggle fell into place. 'Three weeks.'

'Huh?'

'Nori said Ay-Mari left her husband three weeks ago.' Iliona chafed arms that were suddenly cold. 'She went, leaving everything behind, and three weeks ago the moon was full.'

Dark, springy hair. Slightly hooked nose. Plump body, and very full lips. The victim found by Abas the kitchen slave on the night of Hecate's festival was Nori's mistress, she'd bet money on it.

'Then Lokman sliced his veins for nothing,' Lysander said, through a mouth full of gravel.

And that was the real tragedy of it. Ay-Mari didn't leave her husband for a handsome young buck. Ay-Mari was already dead.

Fine. Now a second victim had been given a name, but it didn't bring them any closer to unmasking the killer. And in the near darkness of the Great Hall, soldier and priestess stood close, almost touching, and an owl hooted more softly than a lover's caress.

'It would help if we knew what connected the victims,' she said.

Physical similarities had already been ruled out. The killer was targeting women for their vulnerability, not their looks, which made him ten times more dangerous than any hot-blooded chancer.

'In the same way a huntsman will follow a stag,' Lysander said, 'tracking its hoof prints, its dung and its habits until he is certain that his quarry will be at a certain watering place at a certain hour, so our murderer knows exactly where to be to make his kill.'

Yes, but for any normal person, antlers on the wall were adequate reminders of patience and skill, and of Artemis's help in securing the hunter's victory. This brute took scalps. Did he, she wonder, thank the moon for blessing his torture . . .?

'We've established he's a loner, who has learned to hide his inadequacies under a veneer of good social skills,' Iliona said slowly. 'We know he's vain, we know he's clever, and we also know that he's crafty, which means he's more than capable of flirting with women to mask his intense hatred of them if needs be.'

In the stillness, the only sound was the rise and fall of Lysander's chest. 'Suppose he got close to the victims, because they trusted him?' he suggested.

'Or at least didn't feel threatened,' she said. There's a difference.

For a while he stood motionless, absorbing the adjustments, weighing the change, evaluating what impact this new theory might have on the investigation. And with every exhalation, his breath brushed a loose strand of her hair on her forehead.

'Nori said Ay-Mari was having an affair with a foreigner,' he said eventually. 'Could he have been sleeping with his victims?'

The ultimate humiliation. Make them fall in love with you, so crave the touch of his hand . . .

'If he was,' she said, 'Nori will know.'

When he stretched, sinews stood out on his bronzed skin. 'Assuming you trust me to get answers without hanging anvils off her ankles,' he said, 'I think I might go and ask the old dame one or two questions.'

'Then you'd better hurry. I've assured her safe passage to Egypt, and since the shipping season is short and this is the calmest month for the oceans, the *Nightingale* weighs anchor at dawn.'

He grimaced. 'Dawn?'

'Dawn.'

'Then the proverb is true, there is no rest for the wicked.' His mouth twisted. 'Mind if I borrow your horse?'

'Why ask? The *Krypteia* always takes what it wants.'

Grey eyes locked with hers, measureless as fog on a heath. 'Not always,' he rasped. 'Not always it doesn't.'

For one ridiculous moment, she thought he was going to lean down and kiss her. But of course not. He wore Ariadne's ring, and she knew in that moment the two planned to rule Sparta together. With the King's sister installed here at Eurotas and the head of the *Krypteia* her lover, or more, their combined influence on government policy would be formidable. No wonder they wanted her out of the way.

It was with heavy limbs and a head pounding with hammers that Iliona finally returned to her chamber. Chip was so fast asleep on her bed, the little felt rabbit next to his head, that he didn't even stir when she let herself in. Her heart ached with loneliness, love and despair.

What she needed right now, more than anything else, was the warmth and reassurance of another body against hers, and he'd soon go back to sleep.

'Come here, you.' She leaned over to scoop him into her arms and froze.

The lolling head told her. The cold skin confirmed it. But she couldn't stop shaking his limp, motionless form, trying to coax him back to life.

'Chip, wake up! Walkies! Look, here's your rabbit!'

Too exhausted to vomit, too shocked to howl, she slid to the floor and curled into a ball.

The dog's got to go.

Surely not. He couldn't. He wouldn't. Would he . . .?

But somebody had. While Iliona was clapping the Minotaur dancers and applauding Tzan's love songs and epics, someone had crept in to her room, and calmly wrung the puppy's neck.

The thresher's wife stirred. She'd trekked to the Oracle yesterday evening to seek guidance on which of the gods her man had offended, and for reassurance that he'd be all right. She had never consulted the Oracle before. For one thing, she'd been scared – he was a god, after all, and it's one thing saying prayers at a shrine, another actually talking to Him in person. And for another thing, well, really, she wasn't sure her problems had been big enough to bother Him with in the past. He was that busy, was Eurotas, always crowds of people milling around, and she wouldn't want Him to think she was wasting his time. But this wasn't too small an issue to bother about, though nothing was as she'd expected.

On previous visits, in other words on feast days and festivals, the High Priestess had led the rites in crisply pleated vestments, flanked by acolytes shading her with parasols made out of big, fancy feathers. Sometimes, she'd walk through the crowds, hands outstretched at waist level in ceremonial posture, carrying the Horn of Consecration. Other times, she'd wait stiller than a statue on the temple steps for worshippers to gather. But what struck her every time was the priestess's serenity.

The Oracle was no less richly robed. She'd even worn a diadem, that sparkled like pond-water in the sun. But her skin was drawn, her eyes hollow and red, like she'd been crying, and Tibios's wife supposed she should not have been surprised. The Oracle was not the High Priestess. The Oracle was the river god himself, the Lady Iliona simply his vessel, and when this humble mortal stumbled upon Him in the plane grove yesterday, He had been pacing and wringing his hands.

What was it he'd kept repeating under his breath? Sounded like Coronis, but was probably coronets, because Oracles foretell the future for kings, but whatever it was, the thresher's wife sensed this was a bad time to interrupt. The river god looked so utterly miserable, and in any case, she suspected she'd come in the wrong entrance. The reason she'd done that, of course, was so as not to be seen by that young female physician. Meant well, bless her, but frankly the poor girl wasn't up to the job, though for the life of her Tibios's wife wouldn't want her to know she'd been sneaking around here behind her back. Instead, she'd done worse, barging in on the Oracle while it was predicting. She'd made to creep away quietly.

'Don't go.'

Tibios's wife flung herself prostrate on the ground in embarrassment. 'Forgive me, my liege—'

'Please. There's no need for abasement.' The Oracle's hand

was trembling as it helped her to her feet. 'I know why you have come.'

This was something else she should have realized. That Eurotas knew everything, and he would, of course, because He was a god.

'As the moon waxes then wanes and the corn ripens and is cut, so all things have their season, faithful and loving wife of Tibios.' The Oracle's voice was cracked – not like the High Priestess's, and high priestesses don't weep like waterfalls, neither. 'The blame lies entirely at my feet. I am sorry, I truly am.'

The Oracle spoke in riddles, so what did it mean, blame, and the Oracle's feet? With a gasp of horror, she suddenly realized that it was *her* fault, not the gods! Eurotas was telling her that it was her fault Tibios had come down sick, and that if she didn't do something about it, he'd die. Her knees buckled.

'Oh, my liege, my liege,' she sobbed, 'what am I to do?'

She'd been born during the winter, in the month protected by Hera, and that was the month she and Tibsy got married, as well. Therefore it must be to Hera the sacrifice must be made – only Hera was Queen of Heaven, wife of Zeus, and you don't surrender cooking pots and drinking horns to a queen! Hera wouldn't overturn this kind of decision with a few honey cakes and a libation of wine on the side! She'd need silver. Copper. Gold, even.

'Where am I going to find the money I need?'

The Oracle seemed taken aback by her request, but she knew it was probably just the High Priestess coming out of her trance. After all, what else could it be?

'Wealth will not be a problem,' the Oracle replied gently. 'That I can assure you. When you hear the cockerel crow for the second time, look for two silver swans. Riches will be waiting for you.'

'Silver swans . . .?' Hadn't she passed something like that on her way in? On the pediment of that tiny countryside shrine to Aphrodite, on the road that led to Eurotas?

'Where the quince doth flourish next to the apple,' the Oracle had said. 'Love brought you here, and love is where you must seek.'

It was! It was that little shrine where she must go after

cock crow! The quince and the apple were Aphrodite's emblems, and Aphrodite was goddess of love. Another riddle solved. No, wait! Aphrodite!

'Does this mean the Golden Goddess has forgiven me for impersonating her divine self?'

'Aphrodite is flattered that she was able to help.'

Thank the great gods for that – but what about the Queen of Heaven, Hera herself? 'Do you think it will make Hera happy, my liege?'

Was gold enough to overturn the curse?

The Oracle had considered the question for several moments. 'I do not think Hera is going to smile on your husband, if that's what you mean. But I will return in the morning, we . . . we will discuss the issue further.' She'd laid a soft hand on the woman's shoulder. 'I will be better prepared to talk to you, then.'

And so the thresher's wife passed the night wrapped in her cloak, neither asleep nor awake, but drifting in and out between the two. Often she heard sounds. Splashes, as though someone was crossing the river, but who would cross in the dark? Then come back? She'd heard talk, soft and low, not lovers' talk though. One sounded like the priestess, the other deep and more gravelly, as though they were trying to sort out a puzzle. She'd seen shadows flit back and forth, heard owls and all sorts of other night noises, even sobbing, she thought, but who cared about any of that?

In her mind was one picture, and one picture only. The Fates, huddled together in their black robes, measuring out the thread of Tibios's life. All she asked was that she be spared the sound of that snip for many more years.

When the cock crowed the second time, she didn't even realize she'd been crying.

TWENTY-FOUR

'Lichas.'

'My lady?'

Outside in the precinct, purifiers and sacristans were rushing hither and thither, heralds announced the news, slaves called out the hour, and dust from the workmen turned the air white.

'Look me in the eye, please.' Strange, pale things, his eyes. Another reason her cousin relegated him to obscurity within the palace, she imagined. 'Thank you.' She smiled. 'It is my pleasure, Lichas, actually it's my enormous pleasure, to inform you that your services are no longer required.'

Pale or not, they could certainly bulge. 'Is . . . this another of your teasings, my lady?'

'No need to pack your quills and things now. I will arrange for them to be sent to the palace.'

'B-but are my files not in immaculate order?'

'Flawless.'

'My notes not detailed and neat?'

'Without compare.'

'Have I not been a help with the flood of petitioners, then?'

'Invaluable. Are you still here?'

'My lady, please!' He grabbed at her sleeve. 'Please, I beg you! You can't dismiss me like this!'

She prised away his hand with distaste. 'How strange, I thought I already had.'

'H-have I not seved you well?' He hopped round in front of her, two red spots shining like camp fires on his lily-white cheeks. 'Iliona, please. I don't understand.'

'Yes, you do, you vile little worm. You understand exactly why you're going.' He'd believed his disability, his fawning, indeed his very vulnerability would give him a free hand and elicit compassion. Until, that is, he was crossed. 'You spilled wine down my robe.'

'An unfortunate accident.'

'One which occurred after I'd overridden a decision you had no right to take, and then you smashed my goblet. Again, this was immediately after I'd denied you a personal favour, and you left the pieces lying in the courtyard where I could not fail to see them. Something you wouldn't have done had it been an accident, but then why would you have been in my personal quarters, carrying my favourite drinking cup into the courtyard in the first place?'

'I can explain.'

'Save your breath, I know why you did it. You wanted to make yourself important, and there's nothing like a young girl wanting her marriage blessed to bump up your value. You promised you'd get the Oracle to pronounce the auspices, and when the Oracle refused, you ruined her robe.'

Tell her it's all or nothing. You can wrap it up in whatever diplomacy you like, but fundamentally the girl has a choice. Either she waits until the panic's died down or she can join in one of the mass propitiation services that I shall be holding.

'How galling it must have been, to have to crawl back with the news that she wouldn't be getting special treatment after all. Just like you had to explain to your brother's best friend, with whom you hoped to curry favour and, dear me, win his respect.'

'These were the nobility,' Lichas hissed. 'Yet you ranked them lower than lepers and whores.'

The right provocation gets the right results every time. His true character was showing at last. 'Wrong. I ranked them lower than panic and despair, and if you had any sense of duty, even an inkling of leadership in your pathetic little bones, you would have seen this. But the puppy. The puppy, Lichas, that's inexcusable—'

The scribe stiffened. 'You are making a big mistake dismissing me—'

'—and purely so you could feel important in front of a group of strangers who will be sailing in a matter of weeks anyway.' Or not, if the *Krypteia* had their way. 'Get out. Get out of my sight before I am sick, and if you ever set foot in Eurotas again, so help me, I will have you whipped.'

Pique. He'd spoiled her dress, smashed her goblet and strangled her dog out of pique. Was Lichas like this because of childhood catastrophe? Had he been whole, would he still have carried a grudge far too far? Iliona neither knew nor cared, she just hoped his wrecked arm ached every night and his dragging leg sent pains into his spine. Those things she wished on him with all her heart, and yet Tibios, who she'd met only briefly, had worse inflicted on him, and it wasn't his fault, the poor bastard.

But his wife proved the biggest surprise in that sorry interlude. Last night, in the plane grove, even though she'd come all this way in the hope of good news, her reaction to her husband's prognosis was scandalous.

Where am I going to find the money I need?

Iliona suspected it was shock, rather than greed, that brought on this unexpected bout of self-preservation.

Do you think it will make Hera happy, my liege?

Hardly the normal response from a woman who'd just been told that her husband was dying, but—

'Phew.' Myles ducked inside the office, pulling a face. 'That was quite an emotional moment, back there. Not that I was eavesdropping on purpose, you understand. I just bumbled along, heard what was going on and waited outside until it was over. Aren't you proud of my tact?'

'What do you want?'

'You're upset. Do you want to talk about it?'

'No.'

'But he killed your puppy. You must be heartbroken. So lonely. So empty inside . . .'

Iliona stared at the calendar nailed to the wall. Five days before the Harvest Moon. 'I know Coronis is dead, Myles, and I understand what you're going through. You're angry, you're bitter, but I'm not rising to the bait. Grief is crushing and, despite what you might think, I'm not unsympathetic. But I am not the answer to your problem. Really, I'm not.'

'I've shaved off my beard. Looks better, don't you think?'

'Myles—'

'Shows off my strong, manly chin.' He perched on the edge of the table, swinging his strong, manly leg. 'Have you spoken to anyone? About the cavalry, I mean?'

'Stop it. You and I both know it's too late to switch disciplines. You're a warrior, and you should be proud.'

'I am proud. Most definitely. But I'm not actually a warrior yet, remember? Or maybe you'd forgotten there's still that little matter of the initiation test?'

The reason he'd approached her in the first place, of course. With Coronis in her grave beside his adopted father, the swagger was hiding a whole host of insecurities. *Eta, Tau, Omega.* If Iliona owed him one thing, at least, it was not to dismiss his future lightly.

'No, I hadn't forgotten.'

He picked a small leather bag off the desk, the sack containing the beans to elect the Leader of Revels, and tossed it slowly from hand to hand. Chink-chink. Chink-chink. Chink-chink.

'I've chosen a bad time to talk,' he said, clucking his tongue. 'You're feeling wretched, there's a lot of work to catch up on, and you'll be busy with the Ceremony of the Cypress Trees, as well. So how about you and me spending New Year together? Get to know one another a bit better?'

You know how to pull strings, don't you?

'Let me spell it out for you, Myles. We are not going to spend New Year or any other time together, and it has nothing to do with temple commitments or whatever frame of mind I might, or might not, be in. You are Coronis's son, not mine, and the sooner you come to terms with it, the better.'

'Aah. You're grieving for your teensy-weensy liddle puppy. That's *so* much more important than a long-lost son turning up—'

'What I am doing is none of your business, and once again, I am not your bloody mother.' Why did it always have to end in anger? Why couldn't she just be nice to him for once? 'But . . .' She smoothed the pleats of her robe. 'Before you set off for your initiation test, I will be glad to interpret the runes in detail for you.'

Another lie. She could no more read stones than make the sun rise in the west, but, like everyone else who came to her, she could give him reassurance and support. The world was a huge, dark, empty place when you were young and completely on your own – and she should know. He was the living proof of that.

'Very well.' Chink-chink. Chink-chink. Chink-chink. 'A starving dog is grateful for any crumbs it's thrown, and I'm

not really worried. You'll come to love me in the end.' He
shot her a broad wink and even broader smile. 'I'm just so
damned irresistible, that's the thing.'

He tossed the leather sack across the room and stood up.
Iliona made no attempt to catch it. This was his game, not
hers, and she refused to be drawn in.

But somehow another hour had been called before she
finally stopped shaking, and when she looked down, the beans
had spilled across her office floor. With a sigh, she bent down
to pick them up.

Every one was white.

The island of Chios, close to the coast of Asia Minor, was
one of the largest islands in the Greek Federation. Rich in
grain, famous for its figs and producing the finest wine in
the whole Hellenic world, its greatest claim to fame was
mastic gum. Strangely, only trees growing on the southern
part of the island produced this distinctive, aromatic spice,
which was used in liquors, cakes and pastries, as well as by
physicians to heal internal ulcers and calm a gastric upset.
Evergreen, and not unlike the olive in its size and shape and
colour, it produced red, brush-like flowers, and the gum was
collected in the summer months by making cuts along the
branches and letting the sap ooze out. The drips were known
as Chios Tears. Translucent in liquid form, the tears dried to
a brittle resin which, when chewed, turned into a thick, white,
mouth-refreshing gum. It was the export of this mastic that
made the island rich. But wealthy states need protection. The
Athenian navy was without equal.

During the day, their triremes patrolled the straits that
separated the island from the mainland, since Persia had
already claimed Chios once, in a reign that had lasted a
hundred years. At night, the fleet returned to harbour, so that
the sailors could do what sailors enjoyed doing most.
Drinking, eating and carousing.

The men weren't drunk. But having rammed a pirate ship
with their bronze prow after a chase that lasted half the afternoon, cheering as the waves engulfed her deck, their spirits
were high and their perception blunted by success. The sun
was sinking. As though sliced in half by the promontory of
the bay, one part lit the sky like a beacon's flare that gilded

the granulated clouds that clustered over the horizon. The other half reflected the flames in waters that were darkening to the colour of the rocks.

The girl had just been swimming. They watched her emerge from the sea like Aphrodite from the foam, her long, blonde hair dripping round her shoulders, her skirts slit high up to the hip.

A prostitute.

The four young oarsmen slithered down the rocky slope, their shadows lengthening before them. They asked, *how much?* She shook her head and said, *for what? Anything*, one of them replied. *Everything*, laughed another. The girl said, *she didn't understand*. They said, *like hell*, and unbuckled the belts of their rough rowing shirts. The girl shrieked and ran. *A chase*, they said, *whoopee*, and whatever she was charging it was worth it, they shouted, bounding after her. They liked a bit of sport.

The girl's foot was wet, the rock was sharp. In the fading light, she slipped.

When the sailors caught up, she was lying on her back, arms spread wide and moaning.

All four took her. When the dizziness passed and she finally managed to focus, the girl found they'd left her with a silver coin stamped with the Chion sphinx.

And a monster growing inside her womb.

Where Iliona came from, all the women wore slit skirts and showed their thighs. Where the sailors came from, such conduct was unheard of.

Women – respectable women, anyway – stayed hidden behind doors, and their skin was supple, soft and white. They wouldn't dream of putting suntanned limbs on public display, or go swimming in the sea like fishes and youths. In any case, by the age of thirteen, Athenian girls were married off, as were girls from Chios, Corinth, Thebes and indeed everywhere else in the Greek world, other than Sparta. As dutiful wives, the only time they strayed from the house was to attend religious rituals and family gatherings. So how could four sailors who'd never been beyond this stretch of water know that Spartan girls competed with the boys in everything from wrestling to running, discus to javelin, poetry, oratory and music?

Emancipation was something even Iliona had taken for granted.

Until the day the sun set over a little promontory in the Aegean.

The tears of Chios dripped on.

TWENTY-FIVE

'I have bad news.'

Iliona lifted her head at the sound of his deep, gravel voice, but didn't rise from her knees. 'How bad?'

Worse than a puppy having its neck snapped out of spite? Worse than reliving the night four men raped you and left you with child? Worse than condemning Tibios to die through your negligence? Or worse than the expression on Jocasta's face this morning, as though a weight was crushing her bones?

Are you all right? she'd enquired gently.

Blank eyes turned on her, their flame of passion extinguished. *I will be.* Her voice was filled with unspeakable sadness. *In time, I will.*

The man who called on you last night? Did he—?

No visitors came. I was alone all night long.

But I saw—

Then you were mistaken. This is just a bad headache.

Jocasta could be a gruff, abrasive bitch at times, but she was also a poor liar . . .

'Very bad,' Lysander was saying. He knelt down to face her, and the scent of woodsmoke and leather mingled with the floral oils that burned in the braziers. 'The *Nightingale* may well have weighed anchor at dawn, but Nori wasn't aboard.'

Stupid old woman. 'She probably got the name wrong and is wandering round the docks—'

'She didn't make it as far as the docks,' he cut in. 'I found her body as I was leaving last night, very close to the gate.' He paused. 'She'd been strangled.'

Iliona closed her eyes. It was here, in this soaring, silent, windowless sanctuary, that people believed Eurotas made his home. So it was here, beneath his colossal bronze statue, that the High Priestess laid the offerings his devotees had left. These gifts remained at his feet for a full turn of the moon, after which the likes of armour, cauldrons, chalices and jewellery were taken away, to be stored in the temple depository. Terracotta artefacts such as vases, lamps and figurines were ritually broken, and it was this task – long overdue – that she was now undertaking. Yet even here, in this sanctuary, death stalked the shadows.

'By the time I found her, her cheek muscles had barely started to stiffen,' he said, 'putting the time of death around two hours before.'

'While the Scythians were here.'

'Or shortly after the party broke up.'

Wasn't that just perfect, she thought? While she'd been standing in the Great Hall, feeling sorry for Lokman and his wife, an old woman was having the life throttled out of her at the temple gate.

I can run faster than you might think.

Oh? And how fast would she need to run, to outpace the three-headed hound that guarded the gates of Tartarus? Had the Ferryman's oars speeded up, making her journey quicker and therefore easier, because she'd kissed the hem of his tunic . . .?

Didn't these people have anything better to do, than think of themselves all the time?

Iliona smashed a crock-pot to a point well beyond ritual damage.

'It could have been any of them, it could have been all of them,' Lysander said, breaking the handle off a clay oil lamp and tossing it into the basket. 'Right under my nose, too, the bastards.'

Crack-smash. Crack-smash. Pretty vase, she thought. Crack-smash. Crack-smash. Don't think about it. Look at this mug, chipped long before it was given to Eurotas, and what a fine little salt cellar. Excellent detail of the two painted wrestlers, and no wonder they didn't want this oil-jar, the pourer's all wonky, and as for this—

'If there's any consolation,' he growled, 'it can only be that they silenced her because Nori knew something. Even though she might not have realized its significance.'

Iliona blocked out his voice by snapping prayer tablets in half. There's only so much you can take, she thought, before your mind and your heart become numb. You see, but you don't focus. You think, but you don't feel. You live, but you really don't care.

'Imagine what went through their minds, when they saw her in the temple grounds.' He smashed the neck off an inkwell. 'They know we're on to them, and when they saw Lokman's creature in the precinct, I very much doubt they considered this a fluke.'

Iliona laid down a wine cooler and pushed her hair out of her face, because sometimes you can't run and you can't hide, you just have to face things head on. Dust motes danced in the flickering lamplight. 'Suppose she recognized one of them as Ay-Mari's lover?'

'Two birds with one stone and expedience rules the day?' He shrugged. 'Everything's possible, but it seems an untimely coincidence.'

'The concept of wrong time and wrong place might be the archetypal cliché,' she said, 'but it cost an old woman her life.'

She lifted her eyes to the river god, staring into infinity from his throne of ivory and gold. The Olympians had the power to make or break everything from battles to droughts, marriage to harvest, and therefore tributes were paid to them through animal sacrifice. Darker forces such as Hecate needed to be placated, so their evil was also exorcized with the spilling of blood. But the majority of the lesser gods received personal gifts, either in thanks for favours already conferred or in anticipation of help in the future. And even though Eurotas had the power to parch the landscape of Sparta, his, too, was a benign presence.

For how much longer, though?

Three women had been butchered on his soil, an Arab maidservant strangled, a puppy's neck broken, two men murdered and their corpses lodged as exhibits. Such insults would not continue to go unpunished.

'I need to purify the river,' she said dully. His waters had been polluted and his priestess must put that right. 'We cannot afford to make an enemy of Eurotas.'

'Talking of enemies.' Lysander returned to snapping clay

tablets in half, and in the rays of the flickering oil lamps, the silver strands at his temple shimmered and danced. 'I've just returned from the palace.'

'Oh, those pressing affairs. How they must burden your day.'

A muscle twitched in his cheek, and Iliona did not think it was humour. 'I bumped into Lichas in one of the corridors,' he said, 'and you want to be careful. He's still the King's nephew, and whether in spite of being a cripple in a world of perfect male specimens, or simply because of it, mark my word, he'll plot his revenge all the harder.'

'Dear me, I must try not to lie awake at night worrying about it.'

His glance was sharp. 'You're not bothered?'

She let out a breath she didn't know she'd been holding. 'Let's just say there are weightier issues on my mind at the moment.'

'Then let me reduce at least one of them,' he said, rising to his feet and pacing the chamber. 'I've called a number of veteran warriors out of retirement to increase the surveillance on our happy band of savages. There will be no more butchering of innocent women, at least not on Spartan soil. In fact, as of now, it will be impossible for any of them to so much as sneeze without my—'

'Savages.'

'Pardon me?'

'Thinking of Lichas reminded me. He called them savages, and it struck a chord.'

Though for the life of her, she could not put her finger on it. He'd mentioned pantaloons and boots, but no, that wasn't it. Tenderizing meat by tucking it under their saddle? Not that, either. He'd talked about the gold on their fingers and the oil in their hair—

'Hemp.' She clicked her fingers in recollection. 'He was extremely disparaging about their use of the substance. The way they smoke it, to put themselves into a stupor.'

'And hemp resin,' Lysander said, stopping abruptly, 'closely resembles frankincense in terms of appearance and texture.' The wolf returned to his pacing. 'What odds that enquiries among our merchant's imprisoned staff will reveal an early meeting between him and Aeërtes – but only the one?'

After all, he explained, if Aeërtes needed the Arab as a middleman, he wouldn't risk being seen with Lokman more than once.

'But if Aeërtes has been smuggling hemp into Sparta,' she said, 'using Lokman as his agent and paying him so handsomely that he'd retire home rich, what's his motive? He has no need to ship his own merchandise under cover of secrecy.'

'You are assuming,' Lysander said slowly, 'that Aeërtes is the mastermind.'

Of course. If he was the means, not the motivator, it cast a whole new light on the matter. 'Then who's behind it?' she asked.

'Behind *what?*' He blew out his cheeks. 'Regardless of their suspicions, we have no idea what the bastards are actually up to.'

'A problem which won't be solved by curtailing their movements.'

He knelt down on one knee and weighed a clay foot in his hand. A gift to Eurotas from a tile-maker whose chilblains had been miraculously cured by poultices left by the river god.

'Thwarting a potential breach in national security is worth more than assuaging mere curiosity.' He began to knock the toes off, one by one. 'If the Scythians sail home with their reputations intact, who cares, providing Sparta is safe?'

'You do.'

Iliona might not be able to count the drops in the ocean, but she knew what was going on behind those unsmiling grey eyes. Next week, next month, maybe even next year, Aeërtes would find that his wine tasted just that little bit sour, or the fake knife Barak swallowed had been swapped for a real one. The *Krypteia*'s role was to dispense justice on Sparta's behalf. Once, a whole generation had passed before Nemesis struck.

'To gain promotion from head of the Secret Police to the Council of Elders, you'll need that pat on the back for unmasking the villains.'

'Is that how you see me?' One eyebrow kinked. 'A politician?'

'To be honest, Lysander, I prefer not to see you at all.'

A smile played at the corner of his mouth. 'You rarely do,

and that's the beauty of it.' The smile widened. It was as chill as an avalanche in a blizzard. 'A man needs to keep an eye on one's investments, Iliona, and I have a lot invested in you.'

'Blackmailers invariably get out more than they put in.'

He picked up the big toe and fondled it between his fingers. 'You don't like me very much, do you?'

'Does it matter?'

'Probably not,' he said, rising. With great care, he ground the clay toe to dust under his sandal. 'There is one other thing. My agent reported that Karas recovered a ring from the corpse in the willows last night. It was a seal depicting the wryneck bird, but why come back now? Why not remove it when they tied him to the treetops in the first place?'

So much for reverence, and the collecting of bones to inter in their homeland. 'Greed?'

His nose wrinkled. 'Compared to the gold each man carries on his person at any one time, it's nothing.'

'Lokman's death might be a factor.'

They wouldn't have foreseen him committing suicide, that's for sure.

'Could be.' Lysander rubbed a weary hand over his jaw. He hadn't slept either, she noticed. There was a faint rasp of stubble under his hand, and hollows under his eyes. 'It would explain why they left it on his hand when they tied him up.'

'Which you'd assumed was a clue for you to follow?' A wild goose chase deliberately designed to deflect the authorities' attention.

'Exactly. But I'm wondering now whether they'd miscalculated, and then, having made a mistake, decided it had to be rectified. Oh, well.' He stretched. 'If you have any thoughts, let me know. Meanwhile, I'll have men conduct enquiries down in the docks – see if anyone can connect the two dead men to Lokman – while I trawl through his records in the hope of tracing the hemp.'

Smashing pots had left a layer of white dust over his long, warrior's hair. She thought, so that's what he'd look like in thirty years' time. She stared into the lustral bowl at Eurotas's feet. Her father once said that no other adornment made a handsome man more comely, nor an ugly one more terrifying.

The *Krypteia*'s commander was far from ugly. Why, then, did the fear not diminish?

'You switched a bag full of black beans for white ones,' she said. 'In full view of six people.'

'Come, come. Any self-respecting Oracle who walks the winds and sees through the eyes of the blind must surely understand how the quickness of the hand deceives the eye. Why, only last week, a tavern keeper on Pear Street was flogged for gambling with loaded dice.'

'How?'

'He drilled a hole in the knucklebone, filled it with lead, then glued a silver of bone back over the top.'

'No, I meant how did you make the switch, when the sack was on the table in front of me the entire time? And why was it so important that I be elected Leader of Revels?'

He shot her a sharp sideways glance. 'You're slipping,' he said. 'I made the substitution long before the bag entered the Hall.'

'Of course.' With hindsight, it was both obvious and simple. But then that's what made illusion an art.

'Given our killer's deep loathing of women, I was hoping that having to defer to one, even his hostess at her own banquet, might provoke a reaction, but it seems I was out of luck. He's too clever to fall for an old trick like that.'

'I know. I tried the same thing and he outsmarted me, too.' Iliona shook the pleats of her robe and brushed the dust off her hands. 'What worries me is that if he's too clever to be fooled by simply psychology, and bright enough to shake off his tail, he's certainly shrewd enough to have a contingency plan.'

Lysander paused in front of the double oak doors. 'What are you saying? That he'll kill again in five nights' time?'

'I can't see any way to stop him,' she said wearily. 'Can you?'

The Servant combed the tresses of his eight priestesses with loving strokes. Through their service to the Lady of the Light, they could emulate Her chasteness and spend eternity atoning for their wickedness. No more fornicating with men beneath their noble station. No more fears of crossbred mules.

He had saved them from themselves.

He looked at the line of silver phials, turned to face the cave mouth so his Mistress could watch her noble priestesses assembling in her shrine. The Bright Keeper of the Wheel of Stars understood the pains that Her Servant had taken to ensure their immortality, and She knew it wasn't always easy. For instance, judging the precise moment when the soul of that little Arab bitch departed its mortal shell had been particularly challenging. And with that stupid white-haired Nordic cow, he actually feared he'd miscalculated, and that she'd expired before he'd had the chance to place the vessel over her mouth at the moment of death.

But justice had prevailed in the end. Her soul was now firmly contained within the sacred vessel, just as his seed had sealed her ravaged hymen, while his crescent blade enforced purity upon her disgusting, polluted body.

Carefully re-tying the bows on the ribbons, he hung the tresses back inside the shrine and closed the door. As much as he would like to spend time with his memories, reliving their screams and terror as he taught them the power of domination, there were things to do. The memories would have to wait. Of course, the wickedness would never stop. Come the New Year, they would be at it again, the dirty little whores. Wives, fornicating with men who were not their husbands. Widows, soiling the memory of the dead for the sake of baseborn lust. He couldn't put a stop to all the mules, but once he'd brought this ninth, and final priestess, to bow before the Mistress of Enchantment, he could start to put his plan into action.

By drinking their souls from the phials, their last breath into his, the Silver Queen would bestow immortality upon him. From then on, he would be free to put an end to this disgusting contamination.

For it was over life itself that the Servant would have mastery.

The new order was just beginning.

TWENTY-SIX

'**C**olchis seems a long, long way away, don't you think, Sebastos?'

Dark eyes followed Aeërtes's gaze across the foreign landscape as they stood beneath the ancient olive, its fruits slowly ripening from green to black. 'Aye, it's certainly different from the lush, green foothills of the fatherland.'

These harsh, bleak crags couldn't begin to compare to the softly rounded crests, the gentle bays, the pink-red rock and flaming sunsets. And although the throbbing summer heat had peaked and the breeze was no longer sticky, the temperatures were still higher than they were used to at this time of year. Both men were sweating uncontrollably.

'Remember how we used to laugh about men in skirts, who tied thongs around their ankles to keep thin flaps of leather on their feet?' Aeërtes said.

'We said they bathed too much, it was harmful to their skin. Now we're in the water just as often, if not more, and when I take my kaftan, boots, torque and rings off at night, I might've been lugging a dead cow around on my shoulders, I feel that light.'

'Which reminds me. You did remember to send our lovely priestess those items of jewellery?'

The big man nodded. 'Coiled panther bracelet, pair of earrings with chariot, horse and rider dangling from tiny chains, swan brooch and a cloak pin fashioned like an owl, all solid gold.' He paused. 'Why did you give her such wonderful pieces, my lord? The bitch is on to us.'

'The bitch has *suspicions*,' Aeërtes corrected with a laugh. 'Instinct tells her we're up to mischief, but there is no evidence and certainly no proof. And in the meantime, let's not lose sight of the fact that we are diplomats. It would be the height of bad manners not to thank our hostess with gifts. Especially when she has given me such a magnificent horse for my son.'

Sebastos wasn't convinced, and made no efforts to disguise

his scepticism, either. Around them, crickets rasped lazily in the long grass, kites glided overhead on outstretched wings and the smell of freshly scythed hay drifted on the wind. He'd watched the recruits training on the plain, and could see why Sparta's city wasn't walled. The phalanx was a ferocious fighting force, and only a fool would attack this country on a battlefield. It was, he supposed, why Athens resorted to less obvious methods to oust their rivals in a bid for Hellenic domination.

It was, he supposed, why Scythia exploited it.

'I swear she knows this delegation's just a cover,' he said eventually.

'So what?' Aeërtes shrugged. 'Providing we continue to draw up the trade treaty, what can they do? Arrest us for negotiating fair terms? These people want our smoked fish, timber, hides and furs, my dear friend, not to mention our gold. And if we are to consolidate our position as a dominant force and an empire to be reckoned with, we need their porphyry, their pots and their horses in return.'

Porphyry, because it was more expensive even than marble, and the green variety was found nowhere else in the world, other than Sparta. Its matrix of crystals would dazzle all those who passed through the gates of Colchis and send a very powerful message.

Scythia also needed pots, because increased trade meant increased transportation, and they did not have the capacity at home to produce adequate storage vessels for grain, honey, wine and oil.

And horses, because their dumpy, chunky beasts were fine for crossing vast tracts of open steppe and enduring harsh winters, but for speed there was nothing to match a Spartan gelding. Speed was what would make the difference between success and failure in Aeërtes's plans.

He considered the tribes that comprised the Scythian nation. Some were nomads, living in felt tents on the plains. Some eked out their days in wooden houses built on stilts above the marsh. Others preferred life in stone cities, like Colchis. This was not dissimilar to the Hellenic way of life, which ranged from hilltop villages to coastal fishing communities via the marble and stone that was Athens. But there was a major difference between this democratic culture and his own.

Among the emerging Scythian federation, the clever ones had turned themselves into an elite ruling class, leaving the 'natives' to work the grain belts and the mines. Consequently, a division was growing between educated and unschooled, rich and poor, powerful and oppressed. A gap which Aeërtes pledged to make much wider.

'This delegation is the perfect cover to help bring about the *helot* rebellion,' he said. From his own days as a revolutionary, he was more than familiar with their desperate desire for freedom. 'And nothing could suit our own ends more, my friend.'

The plan was simple. While Sparta was thrown into turmoil by the New Year uprising, his armies would be swooping on colonies along the Black Sea, leaving Athens facing a choice. Either defend the Greek outposts, or turn their resources to annexing those city states that currently relied on the archenemy for protection – and which would be left exposed, once Sparta recalled their warriors to fight the insurgency at home.

'You're convinced Athens will exploit Sparta's vulnerability?'

'Everything comes with a risk, Sebastos.' Aeërtes stroked the curls of his beard. 'But given their aggressive expansionist policies, I can't see them passing up an opportunity to enlarge their portfolio, can you?'

They couldn't be in two places at once, and a powerful stronghold in Greece was better than scattered trading posts along the Black Sea. But with the likes of Odessus, Apollonia, Pontica and Olbia, and possibly even Sinope, under Scythian control, Aeëtes would have a monopoly on all goods shipped through the Bosporus.

'The plan to hold key dignitaries hostage is a good one,' Sebastos said. 'Yours, by any chance?'

'Mine,' Aeërtes acknowledged modestly.

The bodyguard clucked his tongue. 'The *helots* don't have a cat's chance of succeeding.'

'No, but they think they do and that's all that matters.' Aeërtes swatted a fly that had landed on his arm. 'You and I will be long gone by the time these streets run red with the blood of the rebels.'

Sebastos grinned. 'The schoolmaster gets his hemp and what he thinks is his chance for freedom. We get all we can carry when the temple treasuries are sprung open on New Year.'

'More than enough to fund a combined land and sea invasion.'

Parts of Mesopotamia and Syria were already under Scythian rule, and whilst their incursions into Judah and Palestine had proved unsuccessful, Aeërtes's motto was never say never. He chewed his lip. 'The others still suspect nothing?'

'Not a thing, my liege. They believe we are aiding the *helots* for personal gain. Greed is every man's downfall.'

'Greed and women, Sebastos.' His voice took on an edge. 'Never underestimate the destructive powers of the gentler sex. They will sap your strength and suck your soul, if you let them.'

'No chance of that happening,' the bodyguard growled. 'What instructions do I give the others for New Year?'

'Tell them to behave like the perfect guests the King believes they are. Tell them to perform, as per rehearsals. Tell them to eat, drink, dance and be merry. Right up to the point where our schoolmaster lights his mountaintop beacon.'

The bonfire on Mount Parnon was the signal for the *helots* to start burning the hemp. Their masters, already fatigued from the festivities, would soon fall into a drugged sleep, along with the rest of the household. Time for Aeërtes and his team to collect payment.

'You will have a cart waiting outside the Temple of Athene. Mine will be at the Temple of Zeus, Tzan's will be at Hera's, Barak will collect from the Sanctuary of Apollo, and Karas from Castor and Pollux.'

'Not Eurotas?'

'My dear Sebastos, the wealth from that shrine wouldn't equip a blind horse, never mind an army of mercenaries, supply train and weapons. Why do you ask?'

'No reason.' The bodyguard ran his hand up and down the sheath of his dagger. Behind them, the sun started to dip. Soon it would be lost behind the mountains, and in the meadows, long-beaked hoopoes darted in black and pink flashes. 'Not long now,' he murmured.

'To the uprising? No.' Aeërtes nodded in satisfaction. 'We have done well, Sebastos.'

Knowing the delegation would be under constant surveillance, he employed the frankincense merchant to smuggle in the hemp resin, having recruited two of his countrymen to act as liaison between Lokman and the schoolmaster. However, once the shipments had arrived safely and been distributed, the Scythians were redundant. With nothing to do, but with money in their purses, Aeërtes couldn't risk loose talk. He had Sebastos plant fake letters between them and the schoolmaster, then convinced Barak, Tzan and Karas that their colleagues had double-crossed them and must be eliminated. It was no disadvantage, either, that the burial rites would serve as a distraction.

'Once the five carts reach the docks, we load as swiftly as we can. By my calculations, our ship will be rounding the headland before the authorities even notice that their treasuries have been sprung.'

'With the government and the entire priesthood in enemy hands, theft'll be the least of their worries.' Sebastos leaned his back against the gnarled bark of the olive. The wood was warm through his shirt. 'Under your sovereignty, Scythia will be greater than Persia, grander than Egypt and wiser than Greece. I am proud to serve under you, my lord.'

'Thank you, Sebastos, but I am not king yet. I need to conquer the Greek colonies and put a stranglehold on the Bosporus before I can make the tribal elders prostrate themselves before me, and for this we need total secrecy.'

'You've done it once, you'll do it again and even better, I am certain,' the bodyguard replied. 'And you know you can rely on me to tidy up the last loose ends.'

'Indeed I can, my friend, which is a shame, in a way.' Aeërtes sighed. 'I have grown quite fond of Tzan's musical abilities, but his people come from the far side of the Black sea, Karas is from the Caucasus, and Barak's mother is one of the Amazon priestesses who helped us to power. If they suspected for an instant I was planning to take charge of the entire Scythian nation, they'd talk.'

This was his invasion, his power and his glory alone.

'And anyway. Why let them fritter three-fifths of the proceeds, when five-fifths will set us on the throne and make Scythia great?'

'Why indeed.' Sebastos drew his dagger out of its hilt and

held it up to the setting sun. 'Their throats will be cut before they have a chance to board ship. Just as you ordered, my lord.'

High in the branches of the olive tree, Liasa thought she would faint. She had only come here because she'd seen Karas come here. He'd sit in the shade most afternoons, either fletching his arrows and pumping them into a target, or practising standing on one hand or performing some other clever gymnastic feat. Until now, Liasa had only watched from a distance, her heart filled with longing as his muscles rippled under such rigid control. Tzan was wrong. Any man who could exert such discipline and at the same time exercise such restraint would make a wonderful lover, she thought. All Karas had to do was get to know her a bit better, and to do that she first needed to get him alone and explain how she'd tripped on her robe and landed on Barak. That it wasn't how it had looked.

Too much time was passing, and she had to tell him how wonderful it had felt, to be engulfed in bedclothes that bore his own personal smell. To feel the actual pillow where he'd laid his handsome, sweet head. And tell him the love that lay in her heart . . .

The priestess had warned her to be careful. She said the more Liasa was rejected, the harder she'd yearn, and that if she didn't watch out, her whole life would pass chasing a shadow. But the priestess didn't know Karas. He was a perfectionist, that's why he hadn't noticed her yet. He was too engrossed in his performance. And surely any man who beaded his hair and oiled his body with such care would make a loving husband and father?

Then it came to her! If she climbed into the olive tree and jumped down to surprise him, he could hardly fail to notice her then! She'd waited all day yesterday, and he hadn't come, but Liasa wouldn't give up. She would have sat in the snow on a bed of thorns, if needs be. She'd walk through fire for Karas.

Instead Aeërtes came! Him and Sebastos, and she'd been so scared, she nearly fell off her branch. They were up to something, them and Karas, Barak and Tzan. Liasa didn't know what, but they had their heads bent together too often

and in places where they could not be overhead for this to
be open and above board. What it was didn't matter. After
all, what could they get up to out here, hundreds of miles
from home? She suspected they were plotting to screw the
Scythians on some trade deal, but the point is, Aeërtes and
the others met under this tree quite often, and if he thought
she was up here, spying on them, he would take a very dim
view of it.

Liasa had seen what happened to spies and traitors in
Colchis. They were flayed alive in the market place, and if
she'd jumped down and pretended it was a joke, he wouldn't
have seen the funny side. The Amazon priestesses mistrusted
and feared him, believing he intended to undermine their
power by doing away with their order. She couldn't risk it.
The only thing she could think of was to pull the coins out
of her hair and throw off her bracelets and anklets. It was
the quickest bit of thinking she had ever done in her life,
because at least she wouldn't jangle when the breeze ruffled
the leaves. She prayed to Txa that they wouldn't look up.
Praise be, her prayers had been answered.

But what she heard made her sick. Not only the shock of
their plans, but the cold-blooded way they'd plotted, right
back in Scythia, to lead the *helots* on for their own ends,
knowing all along they intended to kill Tzan, Barak and her
own true love.

Hurriedly gathering up her jewellery from the hole where
an old branch had fallen away, Liasa marvelled that she could
actually breathe. Well, there was no worry that Karas wouldn't
notice her now! She tied the coins back in her hair. She must
find him at once. Let him warn the others—

She stopped. He *would* believe her, wouldn't he? Yes, of
course he would! Why would she make up something like that?
Suppose, though, he went running to Aeërtes with the tale . . .?
Naturally, Aeërtes was going to deny it, and maybe Karas would
believe him and maybe he would not. The trouble was, Aeërtes
would need to take out insurance – and how could Liasa protect
herself? She'd seen the knife with which Sebastos was planning to cut the others' throats. A vicious-looking curved blade
with a gleaming silver handle. She didn't want to tangle with
that.

She counted to a hundred, even after the two men had

returned inside the palace, before clambering back down to the ground. Unkilting her skirts, she remembered there were still three days to go before the New Year. Rather than rush to tell Karas straight away, she would try to find some other way of saving his life.

And hers.

TWENTY-SEVEN

From the door of her treatment room, Jocasta stared at the peak of Mount Parnon until her vision blurred. Right across Sparta, in fact right across the world, people were preparing to kiss the old year goodbye and see in the new. A time of endings, and new beginnings . . .

Hoes had been hung up on their hooks. Ploughshares cleaned, saws and chisels stashed away. The threshing floors were still, the blacksmith's anvil ceased to clang, the quarries for building stone and porphyry had fallen silent. Down in the river, the oxen had been washed and their horns garlanded with flowers. Ribbons adorned the necks of goats and the plaited tails of horses in the paddocks, but though the kilns and furnaces were cool, there was no sense of calm. The potter's wheel may have ceased to spin and the looms no longer clacked, but the air throbbed with excitement and anticipation.

Tonight there would be a sacrifice to Zeus, thanks for bringing the harvest and the old year to a triumphant close, but what of the year ahead?

The first month fell under Apollo's protection for good reason. Shining Apollo! All-Knowing Apollo! God of Light, who saw everything from his fiery chariot in the sky, and whose arrows were the rays of the sun. Depending on his mood, he could fire shafts of love, insight, healing or death, so appeasing him was vital, especially with the autumn equinox in a fortnight's time. This was the cue for the grapes to be picked, the wheat and barley to be sown, for fruit trees to be staked and manured, and unless folk were to starve, every one of these tasks needed his blessing. So, come midnight, a bull would lay down its life on his altar and people would feast off its flesh. As they ate, they would absorb its power and strength, and through song and dance, poetry and music, Apollo would be worshipped.

Her fingers probed the sticky block of resin. After the schoolmaster first brought it to her, disguised in a loaf, she'd made it her business to research the properties of hemp. Similar to flax, only coarser and much taller, Jocasta discovered that smoking the leaves of the plant produced a sedative effect. While burning the seeds in a metal dish over flames induced a euphoria that led to hallucinations. In the wrong hands, she thought, this would be a very dangerous drug.

But it was not in the wrong hands.

It was in hers.

She continued to stare at the point on the mountain where the beacon was to be lit. Over the past few days, she'd devised various ways and means of treating patients whilst at the same time avoiding Iliona. She could have saved herself the bother. Either by accident or design, Iliona hadn't come anywhere near the *pharmakion*, and did that make things better, she wondered? Or worse?

Are you all right? Iliona had asked her, the morning after the schoolmaster's midnight call.

I will be, she'd replied. *In time I will*, but before the words were even out, she'd regretted them.

This was her secret. Her shame . . .

The man who called on you last night? Did he—?

For one wild, heart-stopping moment she thought Iliona had found her out. Then she realized such things were impossible, and she re-grouped. *No visitors came. I was alone all night long.*

But I saw—

Then you were mistaken. This is just a bad headache.

Maybe it was her imagination, but it seemed Iliona's face had mirrored Jocasta's own apprehension and foreboding. As though the Oracle had looked into the future and seen the treachery that lay coiled inside Jocasta's heart. Again, though, this was nonsense. Iliona's claim to prophetic powers was purely for the benefit of folk who knew no better. She could no more read the future than Jocasta.

The High Priestess will be at the palace at New Year, she'd told the schoolmaster. *Wouldn't it be just as easy to leave her there, rather than lure her back to Eurotas?*

It is never wise to store all one's eggs in the same basket, he'd replied. His eyes undressed her while he spoke. *Are you worried you won't have the stomach to kill her, if the order's given?*

She'd pulled her thin robe closer round her body. *I'm worried about how I'm supposed to lure her away from the royal celebrations without arousing suspicion.*

You're a clever girl, he'd whispered, reaching out. *You'll think of something.*

Which she had. During the last four years, they'd risked their lives many times to help deserters escape the harsh regime of the army. If she sent a message in their special code, Iliona would come straight away.

And if she closed her eyes, Jocasta could still hear the lock of her door clicking into place behind him . . .

Still hugging the block of resin to her breast, she returned inside her treatment room, wrapping herself in the familiar odours of horehound ointment, poppy salves and marjoram infusions.

You'll have to leave all this stuff behind, the schoolmaster had said. *With the hostages, there'll only be room for your instruments and scrolls.*

I know.

Endings and new beginnings.

Freedom for the *helots* at long last . . .

With a heavy sigh, she laid the hemp on her bench and slowly carved it into tiny pieces suitable for burning. Like all Greek festivities, the revels would begin at sundown, with feasting and dancing, acrobatics and juggling, fire-walking, snake-dancing and games.

But not at Eurotas.

Here, there would be a purely nominal guard, the Keeper of the Sacred Flame, of course, and maybe an acolyte or two, no more. Everyone else would have gone to the New Year celebrations, leaving the shrine of Eurotas deserted.

And as silent as the grave.

Pushing all thoughts out of her mind, Jocasta concentrated on weighing heaps of resin on her finely tuned physician's balance. It was imperative the measures were exactly right.

*   *   *

Zeus is the first, the last, he wields the dazzling lightning.
  Zeus is the head, the middle, in him all things have their
end.
  Zeus is the foundation of the earth, and of the starry sky.
He is the breath of every living thing.

The Hymn of Omnipotence rang out beneath a velvet sky lit
by a fat, yellow harvest moon. Masked actors cavorted through
the streets, the glutton with his cheeks puffed out, the buffoon
dressed in motley, the hunchback pretending to lift the girls'
skirts as they passed. On the acropolis, ropewalkers teetered,
using their outstretched poles for balance. Down in the agora,
astrologers offered to tell people's fortunes for a fortune in
return. But as the Old Year was despatched and the New
toasted in with wine and merriment, fear crawled like ants
in Iliona's stomach.
  Between the magicians and the mimics, Apollo's praises
were being sung on every corner and lyres strummed in his
holy name. The smell of sizzling meat and sticky pastries
mingled with rose oil, sweat and incense, but the elation
couldn't last. In a matter of hours – five, maybe six – these
same streets would be littered with nutshells and crab claws,
olive stones and apple cores, not to mention revellers slumped
in heaps in exhaustion.
  She could only pray that the dawn wouldn't rise, rosy and
warm, on another mutilated victim. That a woman's screams
weren't being drowned, right now, by shrieks and drunken
laughter . . .
  'Peppered wine?'
  'Pickled sea urchins?'
  'Honeycombs, lady?'
  The vendors failed to recognize her. In her pale-pink robe
borrowed from her niece and her blonde hair twisted into a
bun, she was just another noblewoman pushing through the
crush. In fact, it was only by discarding her ceremonial robes
that Iliona understood how the Scythians had been able to
give the Secret Police the slip. Apart from Karas, who beaded
his, their oiled curls were probably wigs, just like the one
worn by the spitted rider. If so, then how simple to slip into
a Greek tunic, heft a sack over their shoulder or pick up a
barrow – who on earth looks twice at a slave? Tzan's tattoos

were more challenging, but a priest's long robe and covered head would do the trick, and what a nuisance she hadn't realized it this afternoon.

In her capacity as both High Priestess and second cousin to the King, she'd had no choice other than to attend the races, though her position wasn't lofty enough to earn her a place in the royal box. Nevertheless, three rows from the front was a desirable position, and she'd been so busy watching the delegation that she hadn't noticed the *Krypteia* squeezing in beside her. Not until she smelled that distinctive blend of woodsmoke with just a hint of leather.

'They did it again, the slippery buggers.' Grey eyes concentrated on the sanded surface of the track. 'All five wriggled through my net this morning, and that's with double the surveillance team watching them.'

Iliona continued to study the five, solemnly bowing their heads as the sacrifice was offered at the circular stone altar. Clapping as the charioteers paraded round the hippodrome, whip in one hand, reins in the other, their long, white tunics tightly strapped to stop them tangling in the wheels.

'Perhaps I'll get lucky,' he said, as the chariots lined up in the stalls. 'In full sun and full regalia this afternoon, and under the weight of all that gold, the slimy sods might just poach to death in their own perspiration.'

A white rope was stretched across the starting line.

'Quite frankly,' she said, raising her voice to make herself heard above the trumpets, 'if they fell dead on the spot right now, it'd take the mortician three days to chisel the grin off their faces.' Smug wasn't the word. 'And as exciting as these four-horse chariot races are, I don't think prime seats close to the winning post is the cause.'

'I wish I bloody knew what was,' he rasped.

At the steward's signal, the rope was tugged away and forty riders whipped their horses into action.

'I've been through Lokman's records with a fine flea comb. Two months ago, he received the second of two bulky consignments on ships he'd never used before and which had come via the Bosporus, a route that was also new to him. Both shipments were listed as "oriental frankincense", the only two in his books, and the description of the two dead men is a perfect match to the men who collected these deliveries.'

'Except you've no idea where this "oriental frankincense" went?'

'The only leads I have are bones on the floor of the willow grove and a corpse rotting on a spit. Neither are feeling particularly talkative, even though I've put them to the torture.'

'Very funny.'

'I thought so.'

The horses thundered down the track. Forty chariots. One hundred and sixty horses. Six hundred and forty hooves, kicking up clouds of choking dust, every rider desperate to hug the central spine and gain advantage on the turn. Earlier, Karas had staged his own performance, much to the delight of the crowds, who loved the lavish, decorated harnesses and the bronze breastplates on his horse almost as much as the daring, bareback riding stunts. Last, but not least, he gave a performance of his archery skills, curling three fingers round his bowstring and pulling it right back to his ear before releasing. The King was stunned. Greek archers pinched their bowstring between thumb and forefinger and pulled back to their chest, while Karas could fire in retreat, the parting shot for which his countrymen were famous, and still hit the target every time.

'They're heroes now,' she said. 'Untouchable.'

'True,' he said sagely. 'But like that green chariot whose horses have just shied at the obelisk and turned over, accidents will happen.'

Out on the track, things were hotting up. Chariots were being crowded into the wall. Hubs through the opponents' spokes was another dirty trick. Perhaps this was why it was called the sport of kings.

'One dead delegate might be dismissed as unlucky,' she said, as a rider was knocked out of his basket and nearly trampled. 'Five would be grounds for declaring war.'

'Not,' he rumbled, 'if they happened to be sightseeing on a boat, and the ship hit the rocks with all hands lost.'

She spun round on her cushion. *'You'd sacrifice an entire crew?'*

'If it saved my country, yes. And white skin doesn't suit you. I prefer it when you have colour in your cheeks.'

She'd misjudged him. Until now, she'd thought he was hard, because of the job he had to do. Now she saw he was a bastard to the core.

'You've had no problems with Lichas?' he asked.

It took Iliona a few moments to compose herself. 'Should I?'

'I'd be a liar if I said no, and it's because I've never trusted him that I had my agent keep an eye on him.'

Not that I was eavesdropping on purpose, you understand. I just bumbled along, heard what was going on and waited outside until it was over.

'You don't mean Myles?'

Few things surprised the head of the *Krypteia*, but his eyebrows had risen before he could control them. 'You know him?'

'I . . . knew his mother.'

'Coronis.' He nodded thoughtfully. 'They say the good die young.' He seemed not to notice the excitement on the race track. 'His father and I served in the King's bodyguard together, and since the lad proved himself conscientious on the training field and keen as mustard off it, I decided to bring him into the *Krypteia* for a spell.'

All soldiers served in the Secret Police for two years, whether in one long stretch or several short ones. Until now, Iliona had never thought of it as being an honour in terms of timing.

'Did he . . .' Shit. 'Did Myles acquit himself well?'

'Extremely. I wanted to test his patience by posting him in the willows to keep watch. He waited three weeks before Karas showed, and not a peep about the boredom of it.' He rubbed his jaw. 'We need men like him,' he said. 'He'll go far.'

I won six races here, y'know. I did it by starving myself for three days beforehand, and promising myself a meal if I won. I thought you'd be proud of such a quality.

He'd said that on their very first meeting.

I just bumbled along, heard what was going on and waited outside until it was over. This was what he'd said of Lichas. *Aren't you proud of my tact?*

Her own words echoed back. *You're a warrior, you should be proud.*

I am proud. Most definitely. But I'm not actually a warrior yet, remember?

Pride. He wanted her to be proud of him, but she was not. Not one tiny little bit.

You'll come to love me in the end.

Oh, no she wouldn't. Coronis had loved him. Coronis was his mother, not Iliona.

I'm just so damned irresistible . . .

From somewhere in the distance a gravel voice was speaking. 'I notice the girl with the coins in her hair hasn't joined the delegation.'

Liasa? Yes, she'd thought it odd, as well. Perhaps she was unwell or simply had no time for men strutting their egos on a race track? And yet considering the way she'd banged on to Iliona about her feelings for Karas, you'd think she'd be here this afternoon, cheering him on.

'I notice Ariadne is not in the royal box,' Iliona said instead.

'No?' He pretended it was the first time that he'd been aware of her absence.

'Probably having a fitting for the high priestess's crown,' she said acidly.

'Don't think so.' Lysander paused. 'She's already had it.'

Bastard, she thought now, pushing through the revellers. Couldn't help but rub her nose in it, and they well deserved one another, him and Ariadne. A pair of snakes in the snake pit of the palace.

How, then, shall I sing of you?

Of golden locks and lyre sweet?

The paean to Apollo of the Silver Bow rang across the agora.

The Muses, voices clear, sing with you,

And the music carries down to us from heaven.

Iliona barely heard the harmony. She'd left the temple in full ceremonial robes, borne high upon a litter. But at shortly after midnight, with the revels at full blast, a litter would never cut through the crowd. But there were stables just outside of town where she could hire a horse. Speed was of the essence in returning to Eurotas.

'Jocasta, Jocasta,' she muttered under her breath. 'You should have had something better to do, than hang around the temple at New Year! Whatever am I going to do with you?'

Never turn your back on a helot, Lysander once told her.

Every helot *plots rebellion. It's only a question of how far they're prepared to take it.*

Yes, but in the end, you have to trust someone, Iliona thought, and for four years she and Jocasta had risked their lives to help deserters. If you can't trust someone after that, who can you trust?

Beneath the full, fat harvest moon, the priestess hurried on.

Liasa did not have time to attend the chariot races. She had seen a way to save Karas's life and her own, and though she felt bad that she couldn't do anything about Tzan and Barak, it was the only way.

Which explained why she was crouching beneath a sacred cypress outside the temple of Castor and Pollux, staring up at the point on the mountain where the beacon was to be lit.

If she lived to be a hundred, she'd never understand these strange, Hellenic tribes. Castor and Pollux were Spartan heroes, the one a warrior famed for his horse taming skills; the other, the finest boxer of his time. To this day, they were known as the Heavenly Twins. Yet they were born at the same time as their sister Helen, whose affair with a Trojan sparked a bitter ten-year war! On top of that, both 'twins' rode white horses, yet neither man nor rider were represented at their own temple. Just two gold and silver pillars joined by a crossbar, which the Spartans called iconic but which gave Liasa the creeps. She'd never known anyone worship at a goalpost before.

There were no coins in Liasa's hair tonight. No bracelets that made her jingle when she walked, or earrings that made her jangle when she laughed. The gold was gone. Exchanged for a passage on another ship, for she had everything planned to the last detail.

Once the beacon was lit, *helots* right across the city would start to drug their masters. By dawn, hostages would be taken and the temple treasuries sprung, and from her hiding place she could see the wagon that would accommodate the riches from this shrine. From time to time, the mare in the harness snickered. Liasa saw no point in leaving empty-handed. When Karas came to collect his dues, she would explain Aeërtes's treachery. Together they would load the cart, but instead of joining Aeërtes and the others at the docks, they would proceed

to a different destination. Poor Tzan. Poor Barak. It made
her sick to think of them, but what else could she do? Together
she and Karas would escape.

He would love her then.

The Servant gazed up at his mistress, the moon. Tonight,
She was at her most fruitful in every sense of the word.
Round, low and yellow, She was at the most fertile point
in Her monthly cycle, bridging the cutting of the wheat and
the gathering of the grapes. He loved the Harvest Moon
with all his heart, just as he loved Her other shining faces:
the cold Wolf Moon of winter, the Growing Moon of spring.
He knelt down on one knee and drew a horseshoe in the
dust.

'I have been with Thee from the beginning, Bright Keeper
of the Wheel of Stars. I will serve Thee to the end, Thou hast
my oath.'

But now. Now it was time to capture the ninth and final
soul inside his silver phial. Only then would he be able to
drink the contents and become master of life and death
itself, but this time – oh, this time he would take his time.
Really take his time. He'd make the bitch beg like none of
the others had before her. Do things no paid whore would
ever do.

The Servant sloughed off his skin of normality and smiled.

With every victim, he was learning. Improving his tech-
nique. Prolonging the agony for them, the exquisite pleasure
of it for him. Tonight, though, he would push the boundaries of degradation and humiliation even further. He had
it planned right down to the finest detail, just as he'd
mapped his campaign of terror for the others. With care
and with precision. He'd followed. Noted. Studied.
Listened. The Servant of the moon did not make mistakes,
and that's why no one could ever catch him. He was smarter
than them all.

And tonight? Tonight he would take the scalp while he
was showing the haughty bitch what fornication really was.
While she was writhing underneath him, being shown what
pleasure was, oh yes, oh yes, he would slice his precious
trophy from her stupid, bobbing head.

He couldn't wait.

'Between us, you and I,' he whispered to his knife, 'we will cow this conceited bitch into obedience.'

It was for her own good, anyway, and she knew it.

Jocasta inhaled the sweet hay scent of fenugreek, whose seeds left her hair so glossy. The almondy aroma of meadowsweet, whose buds dulled pain and whose flowers lessened heartburn. The strange exotic perfume of the resin.

Across the hills, the beacon was piled high with tinder, waiting to be lit. Beneath the full moon, she went down to the river bank to pray.

'Broad rivers to their source flow back,' she intoned. 'Magic calm the angry seas and make the clouds withdraw. And from the high mountains that shake and darkest forests quake, bestow on me that strength tonight.'

For a moment, she thought she heard footsteps. She stopped. It was nothing but her imagination.

'Give me the strength of all the winds—'

There it was again. She turned. Peered back towards the temple. Nothing. An animal, probably. Come down to drink, and obviously as nervous as she was. Silly. She lifted her arms to face the full moon.

'Give me the strength of every wild beast—'

The crack of twig, dry and resonant, cut through the night. In the moonlight, she saw a shadow moving towards her. She spun round.

'Oh, it's you.' Jocasta couldn't hide the relief in her voice. 'You know, for a minute there, you had me scared.'

This was it. This was the moment that he lived, worked and breathed for. The exhilarating, triumphant, definitive victory.

The moment he knows that he has them—

—and their last breath will be his.

Across the world, the Old Year was gone and another was beginning. Full of hopes and dreams and promises. Who knows what the future holds?

TWENTY-EIGHT

The Servant opened his eyes. He did not remember falling asleep.

He tasted blood.

He liked blood. In fact, he liked blood very much. He liked to watch it spurt, he liked to watch it run, but most of all he liked to suck it out of the dirty, filthy whores, slurping on its salty, sticky warmth. With blood came pain. He liked pain, too. But only pain that he himself had inflicted . . .

His head hurt.

He tried to move, but couldn't. Through the darkness and the fug, he had a sense of being bound hand and foot and all points in between, but this had to be a dream. He was the Servant. Master of life and death, whose mistress was the moon. He wondered if She'd cast a spell on him. Certainly he was worthy of Her love, he'd proved it time and time again. And maybe, like that other legend, She'd kissed his eyes as he lay sleeping and rendered him immortal. A reward for all the glory he deserved.

And yet . . . if he was paralyzed by love, why was he still able to move? Why, when he wriggled his fingers, did he feel splinters pricking them?

It made no sense. How could he be tied to a wooden board with ropes? He struggled to recall, but his head throbbed with pain behind his eyes and he couldn't focus.

He remembered coming to Eurotas. Seeing the light in the bitch's chamber. Feeling the familiar flutter of excitement when he peered in and saw her, long blonde hair cascading over her harlot's robe of pale pink. Perfect. He'd glanced left and right. No one else about. Just a few lackeys, and *so* easy to avoid being seen by them.

He'd checked again, to make certain, but no.

Just him and Iliona.

He'd gripped the phial. Felt the exhilaration pounding in his chest.

And then—?

*   *   *

'And then you walked into my bedroom.' Her voice was calm. 'You said, *You're mine now, you bitch, you dirty fucking whore*. You said you would teach me humility, show me my proper place, and that I would serve you for eternity and be grateful.'

Her face slowly ground into focus.

'What have you done to me?' he rasped.

'Me? Nothing.' Iliona smiled, and the Servant had never seen such sadness in those big, blue eyes. 'It was my physician who hit you with a spade from behind the door.'

They'd been waiting for him? How? He struggled against his bonds. 'You can't treat me like this. I am a man. Your master—'

'You are nothing.' Her voice was like a slap. 'And tonight you will see just how insignificant you are, when justice is finally served for the women that you butchered.'

'Oh, really?' Wasn't that a laugh. 'And what do you think your precious authorities will say, when they hear your stupid, wild claims? Who will they believe? You, a feeble silly woman, who cries over puppies and simpers over the sick and the poor? Or a man with my reputation, who—'

'Who said anything about the authorities?' She turned to the dark-haired girl in the corner. 'Did you hear me mention anybody else?'

'You can't kill me and get away with it.' He tried to spit in her face, but she stepped aside. 'I will be missed.'

'Vanity has always been your weak point.'

Iliona stared at the knots in the rope. In the end, it wasn't difficult to narrow down the killer. The disciplinarian. The perfectionist. The charmer. All five gave one hundred per cent to every undertaking they embarked on: Tzan, whose face contorted with the emotion of his song, and whose tattooed creatures moved with his music and his pain; Karas, the showman, who trained for hours every day and couldn't live without attention and adulation; Barak, for whom one slip of the arcing knives meant he'd become the fool, and not the juggler in the show; Aeërtes, who gave years of his life to the taking of Colchis, and whose ego would never let him stop expanding his empire; Sebastos, who watched with eyes as hard as seasoned oak, ever ready for attack and for defence.

Which of them was the loner, the inadequate, the crafty outsider?

Which of them hated women so much, that they sliced, raped and humiliated them while they were alive, then discarded their bodies like rubbish when they were no longer of use?

Iliona looked down on her prisoner.

For all our analysis, we're still no closer to identifying which of the five is responsible, she'd told Lysander at the odeon.

Assuming he is one of the five, he had said. *Which is why it would be foolish to jeopardize the trade mission until we have proof.*

I disagree.

Then you would be wrong, and you'll just have to trust me on this.

Ah, yes, trust. Trust was the lynchpin of this nightmare situation, and her mistake – her big, big, big mistake – had been to trust this bastard's word. She was not, of course, the first.

'I should have exposed you at the moment of your birth.'

From the very beginning, she knew she'd been carrying a monster.

Iliona picked up the runes from the side of her bed, the stones invisible beneath the tears.

'You didn't select the runes at random, Myles.' Lysander gave her the clue, when he switched the beans at the banquet. 'You'd already taken them earlier.' The *Krypteia* were trained to sneak in and out without being seen. 'You had them in your hand before you reached into that sack.'

Eta, tau, omega. The sun, parting and death.

'You were taunting me, even back then, and do you know, when Lichas told me that Coronis was dead, it never crossed my mind that she was murdered.'

And who better to cover it up, than her devoted son? Laying out her body by himself. Wrapping the mutilated evidence inside her shroud.

'Dirty whore,' he hissed. 'She was sleeping with a labourer, a *helot*, just like that bitch over there, and you can't have mules clomping round the country, it's not right. Sparta needs thoroughbreds—'

'Oh, but Myles, you're a mule yourself.'

'Don't you think I know that?' He flailed against the ropes, his strong body trying to force the knots apart. 'Why do you think I undertook this mission in the first place, you stupid bitch? To put paid to any more of your pernicious damage.'

'You said I'd come to love you in the end.'

I'm just so damned irresistible.

'They all do, and when I'm free, so help me, you'll both be begging for it, exactly like the other eight. Pleading with me to hurt you harder—'

'Eight?'

Iliona counted back, and then she understood. Lonely, widowed Coronis finally found love again, but with a man who was not a freeborn Spartan. That had been the trigger that set Myles off on his road to carnage, and admittedly if it hadn't been that, something else would have set him off, but that was beside the point. He'd killed Coronis on the full moon back there in the winter. And having got away with it, he'd taken it as a sign from the gods – from the moon – that he could continue.

Iliona felt the vomit rise in her throat.

Coronis's deathbed confession about his adoption and who his real mother was would have been given through agony and torture. *And to think Iliona had doubted her . . .*

'You knew the Scythians were coming, and having heard about their predilection for scalps, you were – what would you call it, Myles? Inspired?'

'Aroused, my darling mother. The word's aroused.'

She saw now why his victims trusted him. Nicodemus's mother wouldn't have thought twice about accompanying her son's young colleague any more than Ay-Mari would refuse the escort of a warrior in uniform. While his training had essentially honed his stalking skills.

In the artisan quarter that day, when she thought she was being followed, that was him. How long had he been stalking her before that, though? Weeks? Months? Watching who she talked to, who she met, keeping a note of her habits and jotting down her likings, her foibles, her routines. And then, when he revealed himself as her long-lost son, what pleasure he must have had, watching her squirm as he kept torturing her with her own guilt.

'I made a mistake eighteen years ago,' she said levelly.
Eight women had died because of her. Eight women who
deserved so very much better. But no more. 'It is time to put
things right.'

'You.' He sneered. 'You can't do one damn thing right,
you silly cow. But it doesn't matter, honestly it doesn't.
When you're serving my mistress, it won't matter that you
killed a poor harmless thresher through your own arrogance.
Or that you lost your job through negligence. Or even that
I'm so much cleverer than you, and you know what?' He
curled his lip in disgust. 'I'm going to do you, too, you *helot*
freak.'

Oh, that raven black hair beside the blonde . . .

'I'm going to slice your tongue out piece by piece and
feed it to you – umph.'

The Servant twisted, but the physician pinched his nose
and when he gasped for air, the gag went in his mouth.

'Now who's the freak?' the black-haired bitch whispered
with a smile.

'You strangled Nori because she recognized you,' the blonde
bitch said. 'Probably even approached you for help.'

Too damn right, stupid old crone. Thin scrawny neck. Easier
than snapping that itsy bitsy puppy's.

'But it's over, Myles. No one else is going to suffer because
of you.'

The wood beneath him moved. The door opened, and he
could see his mistress shining down on him. He tried to call
to Her, but shit, She couldn't hear him through the cloth. He
kicked and strained, but the ropes binding him were tight and
wouldn't give. He squirmed, he thrashed, he writhed, the way
his victims had. But he, like them, was powerless.

For the moment.

The plank began to move. He recognized it now. The trolley
that the staff used, when transferring the heavier donations
from the temple to the depository. Slowly, the little procession rumbled across the courtyard. He heard the latch of the
gate click.

Bitch. Fucking, bloody bitch. When he got free – and by
his Silver Lady of the Stars, he would any second now – he'd
break her fucking jaw and cut her prying stupid nose off.
Then let's see how bloody proud she was.

You'll be sorry you started this, he mumbled through the gag. He was too big, too strong, too clever to stay trussed for long. In any case, no mother has the stomach to cut her own son's throat. Of course, that stinking *helot* might try to poison him, but even if she did, his body would show the torture he'd been put to. Lysander wouldn't fall for that.

You'll never get away with it, he sneered through the gag. *You're not clever enough, you stupid bitches.*

He could hear the sound of water gurgling over rocks as it danced towards the sea. Above him, the stars twinkled in disdain as the trolley halted beside the deep pool that was the haunt of the demon.

Good. Down here no one would ever hear their screams, and now he had them. Any second, these ropes would snap and he'd have not only his final phial, but both of their last breaths would be his. Could he do it? he wondered. Could he do them both together, slicing, biting, scalping them, and fix it so they both expired at the same time? Of course he fucking could! He laughed. He was The Master!

'You seemed concerned that you'd be missed,' his harlot mother said. 'Well, Myles, let me put your mind at rest.' He heard her sigh. 'For many years, Jocasta and I have been helping deserters to escape. Lysander knows of this. He uses the knowledge to blackmail me, and he will see your absence as just one more example of our talents.'

You'll pay for this, he shouted through the gag. *I'll make you hurt so much for even* thinking *of making me out to be a stinking coward, that you'll be begging me to kill you.*

Any moment now and he would show the bitch. The pair of them. They'd see. But then the trolley tipped, and he was sliding. Sliding into a dark, wet, godless place, where the moonlight never shone. Down, down, down to the bottom of the pool, where only the demon heard him scream.

In a cave in the hills, eight candles fluttered out.

TWENTY-NINE

'**A**re you going to be all right?'

They were in her *pharmakion*, where Jocasta had held her head while she vomited, bathed her forehead while she cried, held her until the shaking finally stopped.

'Yes.' Iliona nodded weakly. 'Don't worry, I'll be fine.'

But she knew she'd see his face every time she closed her eyes to sleep. The cocky grin. Eyes just like hers. But if the gods were just, she would see him exactly as she had on that first day in the plaza. Strong of shoulder, broad of back, pulsing with the characteristic arrogance of youth.

Not the twisted killer, whose face was filled with hate and loathing.

Nor the head, the last thing to disappear beneath the waters, with its longer than average warrior's hair somewhere between the colour of ivory and overripe wheat . . .

'Lichas didn't kill the puppy, did he?' Jocasta said, stoppering the jar of basil oil that she'd rubbed on Iliona's temples to allay her fatigue.

Everything had tumbled out tonight: the rape, the murders, Coronis. In fact, no detail, however small, had been omitted after Iliona interrupted Jocasta's prayers down by the river then begged her help to end the slaughter once and for all.

'No.' Iliona sipped the mix of vervain tea and other herbs, without realizing how efficiently it would counteract both exhaustion and the shakes. 'Myles killed him, because he knew I loved that little dog.' She rubbed her swollen eyes. 'I suppose I'll have to apologize to Lichas.'

'Forget it, he's a creep,' Jocasta said.

It might have been weak, but it was still a smile. With just a touch of wickedness behind it. 'He is, isn't he?'

Yes, my lady. No, my lady. I'm so grateful to you for everything, my lady.

Iliona stood up and wondered what her niece would think, if she knew her pale-pink robe had been borrowed with the express intention of committing murder.

'Thank you.' She opened her arms to hug Jocasta. 'You've been a good friend—'

'Don't!' Jocasta pushed her away with both hands, her eyes flashing with anger. 'I am not your friend!'

Over Iliona's shoulder, she looked at the mountaintop where the beacon was still waiting to be lit.

It never would.

In many ways, *helot* life was no less harsh than that of their Spartan overlords. Both sides worked all hours of the day and night for their country, and the same river that fed citizens fed *helots*, too. She looked at the boxes lined up on the shelf that contained the chopped hemp resin. Whether we like it or not, Jocasta thought, we are every bit as Spartan as they are. Worse, ten generations of serfdom would make us strangers in our own homeland, and who is then going to divvy up the land? Those who live there now, and work the soil, would say it's theirs. Why should they hand over ninety per cent of it to strangers? But even if, by some miracle, everyone agreed on a division, how would thousands of displaced *helots* actually live? Poverty would be rife, and right now, they were poor – but they weren't destitute. They owned no marble mansions, no treasure chests, no horses. But their masters never let them starve. They housed them, clothed them, fed them, physicked them, and if we fight, she thought, it must be for freedom proper. The freedom to work under contract, for pay, or any other negotiated term.

But as free men, not slaves.

Are our people really ready to take responsibility for their own actions? she'd asked the schoolmaster the other night. *When they've had masters telling them what to do, how easy do you think it will be for them to start thinking, and fending, for themselves?*

Like she said, she was no friend to Iliona. She would willingly have drugged her and held her hostage if the cause was right, but the plan was doomed to failure from the start. The schoolmaster, of course, arrogant as ever, wouldn't listen. And when he'd closed the door the other evening—

Is there anything else?

As a matter of fact, there is.

—and he confessed he had a rather personal complaint that needed medication, Jocasta had to wrestle with her conscience.

I'm a physician, she'd told Iliona. *I'm supposed to save lives, not take them.*

But when the schoolmaster left the treatment room an hour later, the potion he'd just drunk was deadly hemlock.

With an ache in her heart, she thought of all the *helots* out there, waiting for a signal that would never come. The disappointment, the frustration, the sadness and the anger. Likewise, though, they would see the schoolmaster's death as a sign of Apollo's displeasure. And since Apollo was Sparta's protector, the god citizens worshipped above all others, why wouldn't he punish the man who tried to harm his people *and* on his New Year celebrations? Jocasta snorted. Stupid little prick. Did he honestly think she'd leave all this behind? Years of research? Years of preparation? Years of helping *helots* through everything from jaundice to gout to pleurisy, via coughs and nits and piles?

His pupils would have no trouble finding another schoolmaster, she thought crisply. One who knew when to use 'fewer' instead of 'less'.

At the temple of Castor and Pollux, Liasa shifted position. It would not be long now before the rebellion began. Karas would be surprised to see her, but how pleased he would be, when she told him she was saving his life and that they would still be rich!

She loved him so much.

Karas stared at the ring he had taken from the bones in the willow grove. Right from the start, and despite the bluster he'd put on in front of the others, he'd felt bad about killing one of his own countrymen, even though the bastard tried to double-cross them. He reasoned that, if perhaps he retrieved the ring and returned it to the widow, she would at least have something tangible to grieve over. It didn't seem right, leaving it there.

But now, as the crowds thinned from the New Year celebrations, he saw a different future for the ring. For while he'd been here, Karas found what he'd been waiting for all his life. He'd found love. And once the treasuries were sprung, he had no intention of heading back to Scythia with the others. Sod Aeërtes and his bloody empire-building. Karas was driving that cart straight to Athens/Argos/Delphi, in fact anywhere that wasn't Sparta, where he would set up home with his one true love.

With a sigh of happiness, he kissed the boy who lay sleeping next to him. Then tenderly slipped the ring on to his lover's middle finger.

Tzan watched the kitten curled up inside the shell of his *komuz*. Its left eye was gummed up from infection, it had an abscess on its tail. Holy *Txa*, another little waif that had attached itself to him, just like the mangy tabby that followed him home from the city and then hung around for scraps, looking sleeker and much healthier until one day it spewed up vomit black as jet.

It nearly broke his heart to cut its throat, but the poor thing never saw death coming, and he couldn't let it suffer. Liasa would have to push the issue, wouldn't she? Raking over scabs, but never mind. That was in the past, and any minute now the beacon would be lit, the temple treasuries would be sprung, and he'd be rich.

A noble young villager, honest and brave,
Owned a house, a herd, all things other men craved.
Everything, except the woman he loved.

Maybe then, armed with fine raiment, frankincense and gold, he'd have the courage to tell Liasa how deep his love for her had gone.

And tell her to her face, not in a song.

In the palace, in a chamber on the upper floor that overlooked a courtyard filled with fountains, the King's sister hurled a vase against the wall.

'I thought you loved me,' she spat at the man who'd ducked every missile that she'd thrown.

'How could anybody not, my sweet?'

'Then this isn't your doing?' she screamed, sweeping her hand over the trunks and packing cases that littered her bedroom floor. 'Banishing me to fucking Thebes?'

'My dear Ariadne, is it my fault that your husband is doing such a remarkable job with his diplomatic negotiations, that the King – your brother – feels it only right that you should join him?'

'Why? That's what I don't understand!' The lamplight distorted her striking features into ugliness. 'For gods' sake, Lysander, *why?*'

He shrugged. 'Thebes is second only to Corinth when it comes to Sparta's allies. And with Athens constantly pushing for expansion—'

'I know why he's there, you bastard, and I know all about the bloody links he's building.' His powers of mediation were legendary. 'I meant, why did you send me away to join him? It says here, it's a three-year bloody posting!' She screwed the scroll that brought the message into a ball and hurled it at him. 'Was I not good enough in bed?'

'I doubt the best-paid whore could satisfy a man better.'

When she slapped his face, he barely flinched. 'You've humiliated me in front of everyone.'

'How so? Our romps were conducted with the utmost discretion, and I took great care not to flaunt your cicadas outside these bedroom walls.'

'You wore them to the banquet!'

He ducked a jar full of wine that left red stains on a fresco of Echo and Narcissus. 'I had a need for them that night, but rest assured, as head of the *Krypteia*, I have ensured that your reputation for devotion to your husband remains intact.'

Ariadne didn't want her reputation intact. She wanted power, she wanted fame, but most of all she wanted Lysander – and she thought she had him, too. Except she'd forgotten that the word cryptic came from the organization that he served. The pig had been playing her, the way he played everybody else.

'Get out,' she snapped. 'Get out and pray I never see your face again, or I won't be answerable for my actions.'

She waited, hoping he would apologize and see the error of his ways. That he would admit that he could no more live without her, here in Sparta, than she could in Thebes without him by her side. Instead, he bowed and closed the door oh, so very quietly behind him.

When the maid came in to clear the debris, Ariadne beat her till she bled.

Of the four Athenian sailors, one had his arm broken in a tavern brawl. Unable to row, and unwilling to learn a new trade, he robbed and burgled his way through the following two years, until a house owner, miffed at a thief digging holes in his walls with a view to stealing his life savings, mashed his head to a pulp with a fire dog.

The second married a sweet maid from Athens, and discovered the best way to make her compliant was at the buckle end of his belt. A system that seemed to work equally well on his children.

The third decided marriage was too tedious and required far too much effort on his part, mainly in the provision of income. Abandoning his family, he invested his earnings in harbour side taverns, where dice didn't nag you to put food on the table and the wine didn't expect you to pay for its children's schooling.

While the fourth found that cheating his own brother out of his inheritance didn't quite work out as planned. It culminated with being charged with theft and serving six years in the silver mines, where the backbreaking digging crippled his spine and the dust scoured his lungs. Jobless, penniless, friendless and in poor health, he died trying to strangle a whore who'd just discovered he couldn't pay for his perverted desires. It never occurred to him that a prostitute might actually carry a knife.

None of the sailors ever gave the incident on Chios a second thought.

THIRTY

The Harvest Moon, paler than a corpse, sank into the boat that was waiting for her every morning on the ocean that encircled the earth. With her cold light gone, the creatures of the night retired to their dens: the bat, the badger, the screech owl and the fox. Apollo, glowing from the honours that the world had given him last night, harnessed fresh horses to his shining chariot, while Eos, in her saffron robe, drew open the gates of heaven with her rosy fingers.

'I presume you've heard the news.'

Iliona was standing on the rocks beside the pool in which

the demon made its home when the shadow fell across its deep, dark, swirling waters. The shadow smelled faintly of leather and woodsmoke.

'About Ariadne packing up for Thebes?' She watched a swallowtail butterfly flitter round the plants that lined the rim: dewcup, lemon balm and sage. The butterfly didn't stop to rest or feed, but fluttered on. She wished she was a swallowtail. 'I'd heard.'

Lysander picked up pebbles and began to skim them, skip-skip-skip-skip-skip, across the water. 'I thought you'd have been pleased.'

She'd just killed her own son and put paid to a monster. How much more pleasure can a girl possibly take?

'Why have you been helping me?' she asked.

'Have I?' Something twitched at the side of his mouth and was gone. 'I rather thought I'd been helping my country.'

'In what way? You know I only sanctioned the watercourse and portico because they'll bring people closer to their river god and beautify the temple.' She watched bees buzz round the water mint and explore the rosemary. 'I will never agree to the extra treasuries, much less a clutch of embassies.'

'Precisely the kind of stubbornness I was banking on,' he said, and sometimes she forgot how much gravel he kept down his throat. 'After all, this is Sparta, my lady. Ostentation is hardly the image we austere bastards should be promoting.'

'In your opinion.'

'In the *King's* opinion.'

'So he will have no objection to my continuing with feasts for the poor, dramas for the *perioikoi*, as well as stag hunts and poetry recitals for the rich?'

Measureless eyes looked up at the dawn. 'None whatsoever, I imagine.'

She thought of the way his body had pressed against hers in the plane tree. The smell of fresh mint on his breath. The gold cicadas that pinned his tunic and glinted on the band round his finger.

'You had me fooled,' she said.

'I wouldn't be any good at my job if I hadn't.' Lysander skimmed the last stone across the pool. Eight skips before it disappeared. But the bubbles from the monster would last for ever. 'Just like you, Iliona, fooling people is what I do best.'

She clenched her fists and thought, he'd never know the half of it.

'Well, next time you talk to my cousin, have a word with him about adding on a deal for Scythian horses in that trade agreement.' They were tough, adaptable, sure-footed beasts, and yes, they needed to be shorn like sheep twice a year, but they didn't need shodding and were completely colic free. Such animals would be invaluable in the army's supply trains, but more importantly, 'Any horse that can gallop downhill will give Sparta yet another edge on the battlefield.'

'Hm.' He stroked his lower lip. 'Your knowledge and connections never cease to astound me, but while we're on the subject, I think I'll go and see what those slimy sods are up to.' He rubbed his hands together. 'No good I'll warrant, but at least we're spared another mutilated corpse.'

Indeed.

'Thanks to our increased surveillance measures, none of the five was able to slip away last night. That's one more woman safe, praise be, and the delegation will have sailed before the next full moon, I'll make damn sure of that.'

'I don't doubt it.'

And if he cared to think his sharp surveillance techniques were responsible for putting an end to this butchery, so be it. Hushing it up was what he'd wanted all along. Preventing panic on the streets, with women afraid to venture out at night and every man viewed as a potential predator. After all, better the *Krypteia* take the credit than have him think she had any involvement in the matter. He wouldn't be so keen to enlist her services next time.

'This surveillance has really pissed them off, mind,' he said cheerfully. 'All five have faces darker than thunder clouds this morning. And by the way . . .' He grinned. 'Happy New Year.'

Endings and beginnings, Iliona thought, rubbing the gold panther bracelet that coiled around her wrist. One chapter closes, no matter how painful the process, and life goes on. It had always been the way of it.

In a month's time, the trees would turn and begin to shed their leaves. The Snow Goddess would wake and throw her cloak of blue ice over the mountains. Ponds would freeze.

Wolves would howl. Blizzards would drive in from the north. But come spring, the snows would melt, the buds would burst, and the rivers would flood the land to leave a layer of life-giving silt behind. Then the wheat would sprout, the grapes would swell and foals would drop, as the cycle of life began all over again. Joyous. Plentiful. Warm. But most of all, filled with radiant beauty.

In between, though, in the bitter, empty, windswept months, things would surely die. The shrivelled leaves, uneaten berries, even the graceful swallowtail butterfly. This was also the way of it. But through decay, so the balance was restored to the earth. As it was with plants, so it was with humans. Inevitability was as important a component of life as water, air and blood, and time, after all, was the healer.

Perhaps by spring, the pain of what had happened would have eased. Perhaps by throwing herself into decking the temple with birch for the autumn equinox, celebrating the sowing of the seed, the fermenting of the wine and honouring the gods with feast and sacrifice, Iliona would find the guilt and heartache dulled. That the joy on the faces of worshippers as they dabbled their hands in the new watercourse or sheltered beneath the portico would balance matters out and make everything worthwhile.

It was as she'd told Lysander. Never had it been her intention to allow further construction on the site, or more disruption, and she knew enough about her cousin's peccadilloes to be able to persuade the King to turn his attentions to embellishing a different shrine. Iliona was her father's daughter, after all. Killing, plotting and hiding evidence came naturally. As did resilience.

Endings and new beginnings. Life goes on. And now, on this idyllic sunny morning, the first day of the New Year, that carried just a hint of the first woodland mushrooms on the breeze, the High Priestess of the River God Eurotas knew she must turn her attention to interpreting the wind chimes and the flight of the sacred doves for the scores of hung-over revellers who believed that they were truly dying—

'You humiliated me in front of my uncle and my father,' a familiar voice said.

Lichas? Iliona turned. Always the wrong time, the wrong place. But when was there ever a good one with him? 'Happy New Year, Lichas.'

'I will not be made a fool of, especially an accusation of something I didn't do.'

She sighed.

I suppose I'll have to apologize to Lichas.

Forget it, he's a creep.

Subtlety and tact were not in Jocasta's character, but succinctness was. And though his fawning grated on her nerves, his filing system was second to none and his memory prodigious. The only way to put things right was to apologize and give her scribe his job back. Serves her bloody right.

'I'm sorry, Lichas—'

Too late she saw the flash of metal.

Felt a sharp punch to her stomach.

Fell forward on her knees.

Whether in spite of being a cripple in a world of perfect male specimens, or because of it, mark my word, he'll plot his revenge all the harder.

Lysander's warning echoed from a thousand years away. Iliona stared spellbound at the hilt. Bejewelled, as befitted a dagger belonging to the King's own nephew. She watched the first dribble of blood oozing through her robe. From somewhere she heard screaming. Shouts of the alarm being raised. People were rushing towards her from every direction, crowding round her, clubbing her assailant to the ground. She tried to speak. Couldn't. It didn't matter, anyway.

This was just another monster in her belly.